DIRK VAN DEN BOOM

THE EMPEROR'S MEN

PASSAGE

ISBN 978-3-86402-559-4

Cover © Timo Kümmel
Editor: Rob Bignell

www.atlantis-verlag.de

Dirk van den Boom

Passage

1

Jan Rheinberg was no friend of monuments.

This had certainly to do with the fact that since his childhood every year he had been forced by his father to endure hours in front of the stone images of German glory at different occasions. Victory monuments, statues of heroes, kings, emperors – the old cavalry officer missed no opportunity to teach his son the correct attitude toward remembrance. Rheinberg indeed remembered endless hours spent with garlands, as rain worked through his festive suit and devout calm and respectful attention was expected. He remembered how he took the details of these memorials in and memorized them out of sheer boredom. Each striking lineament, every sword raised, every laurel wreath. Each carefully set plaque. Young maidens holding flowers. Inscriptions that spoke of the heroic death of the fallen, and the victors, and the Empire, and the fatherland. During his career in the Navy, he had have to go through these ordeals again. Here, many hundreds of years earlier in the past, he had to realize that the Roman and the German Empire, despite all other differences, shared a great common interest. The passion for statues, monuments and other forms of stony commemoration bound them through time. At least this curse was one the Captain hadn't been able to escape through his journey.

And so he stood with arms behind his back in front of the newly unveiled statue that towered on a marble base and listened to the speeches. He kept a respectful and attentive expression, practiced in decades of similar experiences. The statue was a product of perfect craftsmanship, at no point worse or less lifelike and elaborate than those he had visited with his father. It showed the idealized representation of Captain Jonas Becker. He wore his German officer's uniform whose idiosyncrasies were reproduced by the artist with great love of detail – for that, one of the infantrymen had stood as a model for hours. Becker looked with angular face into the distance, holding a Roman sword in his right, and behind him was the standard of the Empire with the letters SPQR. In a sense, the statue was a perfect symbol of their situation here in Rome, nevertheless Rheinberg didn't *want* to like this monument. It reminded him of the fact that the cause for the erection of this larger than life memorial was Jonas Becker's death, the death of a friend and companion, who Rheinberg missed painfully.

He suppressed a sigh. Many eyes were on him, those of the Germans and the Romans who gathered for the dedication of the monument; a Roman, military Prefect Renna, held the short but pathetic speech. Rheinberg wasn't listening, he knew the words. The Roman officer had submitted them to him for comment because he wanted to be sure that the right words were said also for the German ears. Rheinberg had been relieved to see that Renna remained brief, which was the right thing in any case. Becker hadn't been too talkative either.

Rheinberg kept his attitude until Renna had ended. Thus, the official part was over. Of all those present were now expected to indulge for a few moments in the sight of the artwork, make appreciative comments, especially in the presence of the artist, who stood with beaming eyes beside his work, and then to withdraw to a nearby marquee in order to share the displayed delicacies.

In one other thing the Romans differed little from the Germans – the buffet. Rheinberg didn't escape the hungry glances, especially from the enlisted personnel who also were represented with a delegation. He didn't reproach them. Once the gathering dissolved, he was just as relieved as those men who made off with subtle restraint, but determination, toward the tent with the food.

Rheinberg had to exchange pleasantries. The first one was Renna, whose arm he took according to Roman tradition.

"A worthy, a moving speech," he said loudly and fervently. In addition to the military prefect, the bishop of Ravenna, two other priests, and General Arbogast were present, emissaries from the imperial court. The praise was intended more for them than for Renna's ears, and the Prefect was well aware of this fact.

"Thank you, my friend," the gaunt Roman said. "He was a great man and deserves every honor." Rheinberg only smiled and spared a reply. In Thessaloniki, a large tomb was built with superb facilities for the fallen Captain, funded at public expense and with donations of grateful notables of city rescued from the Goths. Rheinberg had decided not to transfer the body here, the "German village", the newly created and continuously growing district of Ravenna. They needed symbolic places like that tomb, so sad the occasion might be, to promote the integration of the time travelers into the society of Rome of late antiquity. This required the goodwill of Emperor Gratian, which they had earned before Thessaloniki – but that was only one requirement and in no case sufficient. If the citizens of the Greek metropolis recognized the large memorial as theirs and showed some pride in it, they would also learn to accept the strangers with their supernatural technology, and, with luck, word would get around to other parts of the Empire. Word like the fact that here, in the village of the Germans – a de facto independent, small town right on the coast – each inventive, technically gifted and eloquent Roman citizen could make his fortune if he was willing to learn and ready to throw certain prejudices overboard. And another project to prove the usefulness of the newcomers was nearing completion. Rheinberg was eager to get acquainted with the latest developments in this regard, but until then to complete the dance of necessary courtesies.

He stayed especially long with the bishop of Ravenna, an old, half-blind and half-deaf man. It was Rheinberg's belief that he was an utterly spineless tool of Ambrosius, still one of the greatest critics and opponents of the Germans. The scanty information he received from the court of the Emperor, who currently stayed in Trier, clearly said so. However, it was considered to make Ravenna the capital, as Rheinberg has recently been appointed *Magister Militium*, Commander-in-Chief of the Roman forces. Rheinberg was, for some time at least, indispensable here, although he knew quite well that an immobile commander of the Roman forces ultimately had to be doomed. It was von Geeren, promoted to Captain, who currently stayed as Rheinberg's official deputy with the Emperor and who, so his dispatches said, disliked the intrigues of the court heavily.

The military situation was calm. Since defeating the Goths, the rule of young Gratian seemed strengthened. But ultimately they had fought only a respite before Thessaloniki. The real reason for the onset of mass migration – the onrush of the Huns – was still present, and the internal structure of the Empire, especially because of the reforms Rheinberg had initiated, was fragile and impermanent. It was boiling in many corners of the Empire and for very different reasons. And the cooks, who mixed this soup, belonged to Holy Ambrosius, not yet a saint, but a very clever and inventive church-politician who made no secret of his rejection of Rheinberg and the time travelers. The official cause was the suspicion that the Germans use demonic magic powers to perform their miracles, but actually the young captain was pretty sure that the real problem lied in the creed of religious tolerance he used to preach – tolerance between the various sects of the Christian church, the Arians and Trinitarians, and tolerance with respect to the traditional religions of Rome, which were already in a natural decline and ultimately didn't hope for more than to die in dignity. Senator Symmachus, one of the most vocal advocates of the old Roman beliefs, was one of the supporters of the Germans in the Senate and was therefore an ally. He was one of the few Rheinberg was ready to rely on. Renna also, yes. But then?

Rheinberg was not even sure if he could trust his own crew. The failed mutiny of the former first officer von Klasewitz had left wounds, established a basic mistrust. Rheinberg had the mutineers punished, but not as severly as the law – German and Roman law alike – actually allowed. Instead of condemning them all to death, he had established a kind of "punishment battalion". With the explicit possibility of parole and return to normal service when the delinquent behaved decently and showed active remorse through zeal and discipline. He couldn't just execute a few dozen men with their knowledge and experience that he still could use in this ultimately very strange world. He needed them, probably even more than they needed the company of their contemporaries. The example of men like Köhler and Behrens showed that one could achieve something in the Roman Empire on his own, if necessary. Formally, a state of war was in place on the *Saarbrücken* and purely from a legal viewpoint the crew members had no time limit for their service. But Rheinberg did not give himself to any illusions. He had to allow his men private contact with the population, which ultimately also led to the desire for a different life. He was by no means immune to this yearning. And the example of the young ensign who had disappeared with his bride was a warning.

He had finished greetings and acknowledgments at the end and now could, with the remaining guests, go to the marquee where zealous slaves with trays and pitchers were already running around to provide all visitors with food and wine. Renna had invited and so the assembly was presented with the best delicacies of Roman cuisine. But the cook of the *Saarbrücken* had had his take as well and filled his own table with food. So there was something for everyone and they were all full of praise. Rheinberg accepted a wineglass and sipped politely from the liquid. He still had a lot to do and wanted no alcohol to distract him. When he looked up, he saw Chief Engineer Dahms nodding, and made a path through the crowd. When he reached Dahms, who held a small glass of brandy in his hands – with cordial greetings and good wishes of the distillery of Behrens and Köhler, who also had a very well thriving tavern in Ravenna –, they separated themselves in order to talk reasonably undisturbed. As most of the guests were already busy to fill their stomachs on the expense of others, this wasn't a big challenge.

"What's up?" Rheinberg asked.

The engineer looked extremely happy. "We're right on schedule, Captain," he said. "The *Valentinian* has been completed on time and will go to sea as planned."

Rheinberg was very pleased with this information. Their efforts to build a steam engine on the basis of the best available alloy – bronze – were successful. Added to this was the introduction of a new ship design, an ocean-going vessel of wood with a steam engine, not unlike trade clipper ships from the period at the beginning of the steam power. Unlike most Roman ships, the *Valentinian*, their prototype, wouldn't be creeping along the coasts and fleeing each coarse swell in protective harbors or bays. Equipped with four steam catapults the ship was militarily far superior to every pirate rowers or sail ships. The new pride of the Roman Mediterranean fleet, built in newly constructed dockyards, should be on her maiden voyage in a short time – with a crew that consisted for ninety percent of Roman sailors. They were still not entirely clear about the destination, but yesterday he had a long conversation regarding this topic with the enterprising NCOs Behrens and Köhler, both presenting him with fairly precise ideas. It had only sounded insane at the beginning, but as Rheinberg had slept one night over it, the idea no longer seemed so absurd. He would, of course, discuss it with Joergensen, his new first officer, and the ship's doctor, Neumann, who were among his closest confidants.

"This is excellent. Your people have done an incredible job," Rheinberg said.

"They are good men," Dahms replied proudly. "The Roman shipyard workers and carpenters have absorbed our designs like they were sponges in water. They were excited about the new ideas in regard to sailing ships, but of course, even more about the steam engine. The *Valentinian* is, like her whole class of ships, both a sailor and as well as a machine-powered cruiser. She is large enough to serve as a fast freighter for important or perishable goods and armed to eradicate pirates. I am confident that with a squadron of these ships the Mediterranean will soon become a very safe place. The basic ship design we also will sell to the trading and shipping companies, who can then rebuild it if they can. After some time, the first will be able to construct steam engines – well, it might actually take a while. As planned, we won't keep this technology secret. It wouldn't be possible in the long run anyway."

Rheinberg nodded. Langenhagen, the new second officer, had advocated to treat the steam power as a state secret and equip only the Roman Navy. There had been an intense discussion. Dahms had remained neutral – his interest was the technical challenge, not politics. Ultimately, however, his arguments had made the difference: Even if you distributed the technology freely, it would take at least two years until resourceful Roman craftsmen would be able to build a prototype without German consulting. Until then, the manufacturers in the "German village" should be able to produce steel in sufficient quantities. So far, however, they hadn't been able to, and that was the reason for Rheinberg's next question.

"What about the puddling furnace?"

Dahms made a sour face.

"We have a third trial started but have not yet come to the temperatures necessary for steel production. This is of course only a matter of time. But even then, our experimental furnace won't able to produce significant amounts. We need many furnaces and a lot more resources."

"Gratian has assured us of his full support."

Dahms still looked as if he had bitten into a lemon.

"That's all well and good, but what does it mean if you look at the current economic situation? Intra-Roman trade is down, there is a full-blown crisis. Your reform proposals, as well intended as they are, will only bear fruit in the midterm, but we really need anything right now to make real progress. Iron ore, oil, rubber ... I've got a long list."

"I know your list."

"Then I don't need to add anything."

Dahms wasn't indignant. Maybe a little bit frustrated. The navy engineer wanted to achieve too much at once, Rheinberg thought. He had to be occasionally slowed down in his enthusiasm, so that no greater frustrations arose.

Rheinberg decided therefore to optimistically examine the issue to cheer the man up a bit. "I had a long talk with Köhler and Behrens. After the men have blessed the Roman Empire with brandy, they forge further plans."

"I've heard that both seek, among other things, a much better beer," Dahms said with some nostalgia in his voice. The Roman *cervisia*, like many others of Germans, he found outright distasteful.

"Yes, that too. But that is related to the type of brewing and can ultimately be achieved with local agents. The raw materials are available."

"People will always drink," Dahms said. "So what are they cooking up?"

"Cooking says it quite well," explained Rheinberg. "What many of us miss most – apart from the beer – is another drink, namely ..."

"Coffee!" It came like a shot. Dahms' eyes lit up. "My God, every morning I drink these terrible Roman teas, and every morning I long more for a strong, black coffee!"

"You're not the only one. And it would also make economic sense to introduce the coffee bean sooner than in our own history: Just as the Romans have obviously been thrilled to accept brandy, coffee should be a big seller. We need our own economic base if we don't want to be overly dependent on the Roman intrigues at court. Köhler and Behrens are among the specialists – like you – who we need to spread technical innovation."

"For coffee, I would unhesitatingly give all I have."

"That won't be necessary. Köhler has suggested that we use the maiden voyage of the *Valentinian* not only to demonstrate our new technology, but equally to embark on a small expedition. It should go to Egypt, to Alexandria. There Köhler wants not only to propose the idea of a second shipyard – consider the economic benefits for the poor if we introduce river steamboats – but also to advance to the southeast. He wants to travel with Behrens to Aksum."

"Aksum?"

"In our time, the Empire of Ethiopia."

Understanding loomed on Dahm's face. "I once saw pictures of our embassy there. A great building."

"The Kaiser has always attached great importance to show considerable presence at the court of the Emperor of Ethiopia," Rheinberg said. "But what is much more important is the Ethiopian Highlands are the place where we hope to find the wild coffee bean. If we can persuade the Aksumites to harvest them, planting them to develop the crop, and sell the yield of us, it would be beneficial for everyone involved. One just needs to spread the idea."

Dahms was completely thrilled; it was abundantly clear for everyone to see. He looked downright dreamy when he imagined himself to be able to enjoy real coffee again.

"So you see, Mr. Chief Engineer, we take care of the important commodities!" Rheinberg concluded grinning.

Dahms nodded eagerly. "The *Valentinian* will be ready, Captain. Hell, I'll even immediately rush back to the shipyard and lend a hand! Coffee! We will bless the Roman Empire more than these people can imagine at this time! Proper coffee!"

Rheinberg laughed and shook his head.

But he didn't fail to give the man credit for his feelings. He was also suffering the herbal teas as well as the abundance of wine. A real breakfast was only possible with coffee, and he would send Köhler and Behrens with pleasure on this trip.

His face darkened as he thought that his own path would soon lead him back to the imperial court.

Sighing, he emptied the wineglass in his hand and waved one of the slaves who stood ready with filled jars.

Köhler and Behrens were to be envied.

2

Volkert was hoarse from screaming. He coughed, felt the leaden pressure of something cold on his lungs, hoping that he hadn't caught any inflammation. Wrapped in a thick coat, he trudged through the knee-deep snow and tried to get the most out of his voice. The men assigned to his command did their best and dug a wide swath into the snow, from the fortress to the nearby river. Once the water was free of ice, the Legio II Italica awaited reinforcements. If the riverboats reached here, the men needed free access to the fort, and it was the task of Decurion Thomas Volkert – or Thomasius, as he was known by everyone – to ensure that his men just did that. With big shovels and a lot of muscle, they had already cleared a path from the main gate, a good hundred meters long and ten meters wide. That was quite an achievement for a morning. The critical glances thrown to him from his Centurion standing at the ramparts of the fort, however, spoke a different language. That Volkert had received only fifteen men for his hard work, delinquents who were supposed to be punished for a number of small infractions of discipline, was none of the concern of the young German's direct superior. As always, miracles were expected from those who obeyed. Volkert was used to that; in the armed forces of the German Reich it had not been fundamentally different.

And having been there, it wasn't fun at all.

While the cold crawled up his legs, he thought of how far away his time in the German Empire appeared now – although since his fatal decision to desert, for the love of senator's daughter Julia, only to be pressed into the Roman army, not too much time had passed. He hadn't seen Julia for months, but the mere fact that his love still deeply blazed in his heart, almost painfully burning, he felt as a confirmation that he had ultimately made the right decision. And if it was not the right one, then at least one anyone with a heart could understand.

Not that the pain of separation had subsided. It had become a silent companion, constantly growing, always admonishing, a source of anxiety as well as a reliable friend. It gave Volkert orientation and stability and helped him to endure the rigors of a service in the Roman army as well as the omnipresent fear that someone will discover his true identity and would hand him over to the captain of the *Saarbrücken*.

According to the news which had traveled even to Noricum, Rheinberg was now the commander of the Roman forces and began to rebuild the Empire with the blessings of the Emperor. The official confirmation of the edict of toleration had been only the first step. What happened now was a permanent part of the conversation at the evening campfire and Volkert, despite his origin, felt actually not much smarter than his new comrades. He was very careful in these discussions not to prove too much knowledge of the strange foreigners who now were Roman citizens and held highest offices. Desertion lead to death, and Volkert wanted to live. That he was in a very difficult situation seemed to be quite obvious. In some ways, he was very grateful for assignments such as his present, because they helped him to postpone important decisions. Eventually this would have to end.

"This has to go faster!" Decurion Thomasius cried hoarsely, trying to look grimly. The poor legionaries who laboured under his supervision didn't even try to murmur. Since they were all reassigned to punitive duty, no one would behave unpleasantly in order to get punished worse. In these times, it was very easy to get acquainted with the whip. Although Volkert was no slouch, the idea of having to flog soldiers didn't fill him with anticipation. Many of these men, forced into the service like him, he had become to know as basically decent fellows, victims of a bad fate. Despite his surprising promotion, emotionally he had more in common with them than with the non-commissioned officer corps of the Legion, which he was now formally a part of. He didn't want to flog anyone.

But he did also not want to draw the displeasure of Centurion Levantus toward him, an irascible man who was known to distribute his sentences with silent, grim cruelty. Volkert could deal with an angry screamer who got loud seizures once something wasn't going well. It was much worse to work with someone who was able to issue the deadliest commands with a straight face, as if all this didn't concern him at all. Levantus was a strange man, enigmatic and always very attentive. The man's eyes, which never turned away from Volkert and the other men, were always on the lookout for a flaw.

What Volkert most craved at the moment was his pipe. He had left it, like so much else left from his old life, on the *Saarbrücken*. He didn't know whether the tobacco's low stock was now at least as valuable as the coffee on board of the ship. He came more and more to the conviction that tobacco was probably unknown in the Empire. He had seen enough pipes among the legionaries and met a man whose craftsmanship in carving such devices was known and who produced pipes for a few coins. Volkert had tried to place a commission, but had refrained when he had determined what the legionaries actually smoked – mainly herbs such as lettuce or marjoram. Some of the men praised even dried ox dung as particularly delicious. They didn't puff their pipes, as Volkert was accustomed to, but inhaled the smoke deep into their lungs, usually accompanied by a sip of wine. Volkert had decided not to want to try this, and therefore pretended to have no interest in smoking, which had been generally accepted. If it was true what the young man suspected and the only tobacco could currently be found in unknown America, then it was probably due time to say adieu to this vice. When in doubt, he could still get drunk with the bland wine which was served in the fort.

Stunning perspectives for his life, indeed. Volkert folded his arms around his torso and croaked more encouragement toward his men. It was not yet time for *cena*, Roman lunch, where warmed and spiced wine was served in the winter to relax the cold bones. As decurion, he had not sufficiently risen in the hierarchy of the troop to excuse himself while his men toiled, therefore the former ensign resorted to warm thoughts and stayed where he was.

If it served to make him look better in the eyes of Centurion Levantus, perhaps it was even worth it. He could use every bit of good will he could take hold of.

Through the open portal strolled Septimus Secundus. He was decurion and took it up, motivated more by esprit de corps but genuine sympathy, to introduce the newcomer to his duties, so the *tesserarius* – or company sergeant major – wouldn't have to too much to complain about them, quite apart from Levantus. Secundus was a career soldier, body and soul, but not ambitious enough to ever grow beyond his current rank. He had served for ten years in the legions, four of them in the Legio II Noricum, and no matter what might be said of him he knew his stuff.

And he was a source of news, because his brother was one of the scribes of the commander. If someone wanted to know what the rumors said, he turned to Secundus, who was generally willing to share his wisdom with the world if provided with a jug of wine. Comrades who carried the same burden like him – to be forced to deal with unwilling and incompetent legionaries and to justify their failure upwards – he told everything immediately and without the necessity of bribery. Volkert was surprised that Secundus so casually strolled through the snow, wrapped tightly in his cloak, with a warming leather cap instead of the metal helmet on his head. But then he realized that Levantus had found other things to do than to watch him. The sense of opportunity Secundus had was second to none and spoke volumes about his skills in dealing with superiors. Volkert could still learn much from him.

Secundus joined his comrade, looking around, as if planning to sell something that no one should see, then opened his coat with conspiratorial gesture and took a tightly sealed, small pitcher with a narrow opening out and handed it to Volkert. With greedy hands, the German grabbed. The pitcher was warm, almost hot, and when he untied the small cork, the pleasant smell of spiced wine immediately evaporated toward his nose, which reminded him of the Christmas wine in his elusive homeland. To immediately distract himself from the ascending melancholy, Volkert put the opening at his mouth and drank deeply. The pleasant effect of the warm liquid and the alcohol contained in it was immediately noticeable. With a suspective look at the ramparts of the fort, he swallowed a second time before he put the cork back and returned the flask to Secundus.

"Thanks," he said sincerely, patting the decurion on the shoulder. "Thank you very much!"

"You're welcome," his comrade parried. He ignored the envious glances of simple legionaries just like Volkert did. Rank did in fact has its privileges, however small they might be. "I have news."

"Tell me."

"My brother has noticed that new commands have been received from Treveri. The generals are obviously not very enthusiastic about it, but probably primarily because they simply don't understand what this is about."

"The campaign will start?"

Everyone knew that an attack against the Germanic people of the Sarmatians was imminent. Volkert himself was a victim of a recent attack by those warriors, where he had earned both his promotion as well as lost his friend Simodes. The Sarmatians were living in a land Volkert knew from his time as Switzerland. Like all mountain peoples, they were particularly stubborn when it came to the domination of the Romans, and they probably thought to use the current weakness of the Empire after what happened at Adrianople for an uprising. Theodosius, the new commander of the East, had been busy trying to raise another army to resolve this issue, when he was dismissed a few weeks ago and ordered to Trier. Volkert and his men were then returned to their garrison in Noricum and waited for further instructions.

"No, it has nothing to do with the campaign," Secundus said. "It looks like as they prepare a large-scale Eastern reconnaissance mission. Anyway, all legions lying near Germania were invited to nominate staff for this project."

"An exploration?"

Secundus nodded, acutely aware of his own importance. He enjoyed to divulge information and required the sincere admiration of his comrades for them to draw the interesting pieces out of his nose. In addition, as apparently it was cold, it seemed appropriate to take a deep gulp of hot wine before talking.

"It's probably the Huns. The rumor is that the strange visitors have given the Caesar the idea that all the problems of recent years, up to Adrianople, had a single cause – a people from the Far East, exerting pressure in wild conquest, who will ultimately invade Roman territory." Secundus leaned forward. "They call it the Great Migration. Did you hear something like that before?"

Volkert had, but he was careful not to show that. Instead, he frowned in surprise and shook his head. "What else did you hear?" he encouraged Secundus, who nodded, quite pleased with himself.

"It will be a strong reconnaissance troop, advancing into the East, and mounted, in order to find out how far the Huns have penetrated and where their path could best be blocked. It seems that the Emperor would prefer to beat them outside the Roman frontiers in order to relieve the pressure. I personally think all that is absurd nonsense. But I'm only a lowly decurion."

Volkert nodded, but his mind raced. He was unable to escape the logic of this plan. In his own past, the Empire would, even if all the necessary information would've been available, not been able to put this kind of campaign on its feet. However, with the reform of the whole apparatus in full swing and with the superior technology that was now introduced piecemeal by the crew of the *Saarbrücken*, it might succeed. When the Huns could actually be pacified somewhere in Eastern Europe, a key reason for the collapse of Rome would be eliminated. The originally settled nations of that area would see no reason to push westward. Rome would have received an important historical respite. This plan smelled like Captain Rheinberg, so bold and far reaching as it was. There was no other explanation.

"You know more," Volkert said.

Secundus smiled. It was clear that he needed additional motivation to come out with the rest.

Volkert didn't hesitate. "You're broke, my friend!" he said flatly, grinning knowingly. "You lost at dice yesterday, half the legion knows about it."

The face of his comrade became long. Obviously Volkert had hit the mark. "It was scamming," Secundus hastened to say, the usual excuse of the luckless. The decurion was a passionate player, and as fast he sometimes managed to make a small fortune from the pay of the less fortunate, as quickly he lost it again because he never knew when it was time to quit. Last night must have been particularly bitter. Decurion Secundus was broke, and at the same time full of ambition to enact his revenge on those responsible for this predicament. Volkert was sure that he would be able to get satisfaction – there were examples for his accomplishments in this area. Everything the decurion needed was some seed money.

"I'll lend you something," the German said. "Just a few coins, but enough to enter the game this evening."

"You'll get it back tomorrow. With interest!" Secundus assured radiantly.

"I'm not interested in interest," Volkert parried. "Tell me the rest of the news. You're still holding something back!"

Secundus smiled and nodded. "This will make you very happy."

Volkert was fighting for his patience.

"You're on the list."

"What list?"

"The list of soldiers the general intends to send to the imperial court. *Thou shalt be with the great expedition.*"

Volkert looked at Secundus with wide eyes. The horror that threatened to overwhelm him was hard to control. A trip to the East, on a fact-finding mission? It could take months, perhaps even years, and it meant that he had to forego all hope to see Julia in the foreseeable future. In his head, fatalism and resignation alternated with rebellion, even anger. Should he desert again? Then there was definitely no place left where he was safe. Should he ask to be excluded from the selection? On what grounds? All this seemed hopeless.

Secundus wasn't able to interpret the feelings that were evident in Volkert's face correctly. "Hey, I gave you more news! You stick to your word, right? You'll give me a few coins for tonight?"

Volkert nodded and turned without a word. He trudged to his people, took one of the spades lying around and began to participate in the work. This or the wine, he thought, but he had to numb his mind and wanted nothing more than total exhaustion.

3

Martinus Caius, the son of a rich trader, was disgusting.

There are many ways to describe a person. One can hold forth on his character, describing his appearance, analyze his relationships with other people. The way he moved or spoke as well as important attributes such as his body odor. Preferences, vices and habits might help to illustrate someone in his entirety so that even a third party had a picture of him. Then it depends on the observer how he – after looking at all these aspects related to each other – comes to a final evaluation.

Martinus Caius was corpulent, with pale skin and watery eyes. His hair was a fading reddish-blond although he wasn't even 30 years old. He moved slowly, almost sluggishly, and his sausage-like fingers resembled whitish maggots of considerable size that peeped under the edges of his robe. Marcus Caius, the father, sent caravans and ships to all corners of the Roman Empire and held considerable shares in two other companies who sailed the Mediterranean with their ships. The biggest problem was that Martinus was the only natural son of his father and thus sole heir and basis of all the hopes and ambitions of his parents. He was spoiled, he was greedy, he drank like a fish, he knew every whore in Ravenna, he splashed his father's money all over the place, and while he came from a prestigious house, his friends were the dregs of Roman society. In his few sober moments, Martinus' favorite activity was to avoid any work and to escape the snares of his father who desperately wanted him in his offices to learn his craft and to increase the company's fortunes. When his escape successfull, he celebrated his spectacular feat with more wine, more disreputable friends, and even more easily available women. He was, at least in the eyes of Julia, the daughter of Senator Marcellus and his wife Lucia, really disgusting.

The worst thing about all this was that she was engaged to him.

While Caius the Elder sat with Senator Marcellus sharing the latest rumors from the imperial court in the courtyard of the senatorial villa, Julia remained with her sister Drusilla and her mother Lucia at a table in the dining room, staring gloomily into her beverage. She found it hard to maintain a friendly and noncommittal mask, because aside from the members of her own family said Martinus also was present, already with wine stains on the festive toga, as well as his mother Claudia. Claudia, the wife of older Caius, was the exact opposite of Lucia. Where Julia's mother was as wide as high and her massive body radiated with the dignity and arrogance of a queen, Claudia was a withered skeleton that threatened to disappear in the vastness of her clothing. Where Lucia left no doubt that her husband, senator or not, ultimately did what he has been told to do, Claudia remained submissive, very submissive, and was ready to be the lowest slave to her husband's wishes.

The connection between Martinus and Julia was a family agreement. Lucia was determined to ensure that her daughter never again wasted any thought to a scandalous connection with this strange time traveler who was now hunted as a deserter throughout the Empire – although probably with relatively modest zeal, as she had to admit. The elder Caius hoped that the marriage would lead Martinus to a better way of life, and he was furthermore not lost to consider their own social advancement through connection to a senatorial family, not least the chance that once a purified Martinus would have a chance to be appointed senator. So it seemed like an agreement that would lead to everybody's satisfaction. And while Martinus didn't even pretend to be pleased with the connection, Julia's duty as a daughter of the house was not to show her feelings in public.

This was difficult for her, because the predominant emotion in her aimed to add blood from the idiot's broken nose to his wine stains.

"You are charming, honorable Lucia," Martinus looked unsteadily and with watery eyes at Julia's mother, while his thick lips twisted into a false smile.

Lucia did not seem to recognize the hypocrisy of her future son.

Eager to avoid a fate that would leave her daughter without family, money and influence, she returned the smile of the young man with her own falsity, and consequently they both piled layers of lies and deceit on each other until they formed such a dense mass that it could hardly be distinguished from reality. "Dear Martin, you're too lenient with an old woman," Lucia said and threw Claudia a grateful look. "A well-bred son you have there, my dear!"

Claudia raised an intimidated look as if she couldn't quite believe what has just been claimed about the completely misbegotten fruit of her loins. She tried a tentative smile and said nothing, the tense skeletal fingers woven into the folds of her gown.

"What are your plans once we have married?" Lucia wanted to know from Martinus, who already threw longing looks toward the slave with the wine jug, though the young man had already emptied two well-filled goblets. That he, in spite of these amounts, didn't show any deficits nor seemed to develop a particularly good mood worried Julia.

"I ... I shall be soon working in my father's companies, I assume," Martinus said a bit clumsily, like he didn't really believe what he said. "My father has high hopes for the new economic reforms of the emperor. Trade will intensify, he says. I have to be ready, he says."

"And what do you say, my dear fiance," Julia rasped her own licorice. "What are your ambitions, Martinus?" She smiled coquettishly. "I'm used to a good family and a certain standard. You know – clothing, jewelry, servants, amusements. Have you ever held games in the Circus Maximus?"

Martinus looked slightly distressed at her, but struggled to maintain his composure. "Not yet," he managed. "But our wedding should be the occasion to organize them."

Julia looked at Martinus in mock, but convincing indignation. "We are a Christian household! We disclaim games as a barbaric act and do not wish to be brought into connection with any!"

Her tone left no doubt about her deep aversion, and Martinus blushed. Lucia threw her daughter a sharp look. She was little thrilled that the fiancee was willing to allow her future husband to run into her extended knife.

But Julia decided to even turn the blade inside the wound. "You are also a Christian, Martinus?"

"Sure, otherwise your father wouldn't have agreed to it," the young man replied somewhat more confidently and finally managed to bring himself to wave the slave with the wine. He rushed and filled the cup to the brim. As Martinus led the drink rather hurriedly to his mouth, he added to the existing stains some more. Julia smiled sweetly while Lucia apparently could barely control herself from not rolling her eyes. Her husband had his little vices, but his desires were focused on fine confection and to a lesser extent to wine.

"I'm glad," Julia said, smiling. "I take it to be very strange that you want to hold games. Killing animals and humans for general amusement is not worthy a deed for a Christian man. Maybe the deceitful followers of Arianus would do this. Your family are Arians?"

Julia knew Martinus as only a pro forma Christian and someone who was certainly not discouraged by faith in pursuing numerous amusements. The prohibition of breaking a marriage would, it was said, make him particularly vulnerable. And that Marcellus, and thus his family, were Trinitarians was generally known, though the senator made no fuss about it. Unlike others of his coreligionists, especially Bishop Ambrosius, he wasn't of the view that a dispute over a detail should throw the whole Church into turmoil. Martinus wasn't aware of all of this. He turned red and sought desperately for a proper reply. To buy time, he took again to the wine.

Of course, Lucia had to take that last bit of joy away from her daughter. "Don't care, dear Martinus," she cooed, throwing Julia a warning look, "it is not so important. The house of Marcellus is known for its tolerance, and instead of the games we would like to host a grand banquet, which is expected to meet all tastes."

Martinus smiled gratefully and waved an affirmative gesture. Julia was sure that every banquet was acceptable to him, as long as good wine was served in sufficient quantity. She saw the young man emptying his cup with one gulp and then licking his lips. No, she corrected herself, it would be also no problem if the wine was terrible.

To distract herself from her impending fate, Julia let her gaze wander over the small crowd of invited guests. When she saw an old gentleman who despite his advanced age stood very upright and seemed to suffer from the petty gossip of society at least as much as she did, her face lit up again. Lucius Tellius Severus was not just an old general and a respected senator, he was a friend of the family of many years, and Julia had a received friendly welcome when she came to him with her concerns about the forcibly recruited Thomas Volkert. Yes, he even promised to look out for him, and maybe he had a ray of hope for her and was able to lighten the threatening clouds a bit. She apologized to her mother, gave Martinus an evil smile, whose deeper meaning the man obviously didn't understand, and rose.

Seemingly aimless, she wandered around the room until she came to a halt beside Severus, who, as her luck provided, now rested on a chair. His smile was the first genuine expression of emotion tonight, and already for that Julia was sincerely grateful to the old man.

Therefore, she didn't mind that Gunter, the dumb Germanic slave, joined them. Since Lucia had appointed him as watchdog of her daughter, he followed her every step. Since he knew virtually no Latin and spoke Greek only in pieces, Lucia could talk easily with the General.

"Well, my young pigeon, you don't seem to be very happy about the upcoming festivity," he said to her.

Julia just barely controlled herself not to spit on the floor very unladylike.

But Severus understood how she felt and shook his head indulgently. "The young people don't always understand the wisdom behind the decisions of the elders," he said half-seriously, half ironically.

Julia snorted.

Severus wiggled warningly with his finger. "I didn't say that the wisdom of the elders is always the right answer to all questions, lovely Julia. And I realize that a marriage with a miserable rascal as Martinus Caius will hardly seem to be wise." He sighed. "I have big issues with this."

“It benefits the family,” Julia said stiffly but was pleased to have found a compassionate soul in Severus. “I have to consider only the well-being of my family. My own is less of concern.”

Severus nodded. “The fate of many women. In your case it is particularly serious, since you’ve already lost your heart.”

Julia hesitated, looked around cautiously. No one seemed to care that she was chatting with one of the guests of honor. However, it wasn’t apparent that this was more than just polite conversation. Then she moved on with her question.

“Have you heard anything? Of Thomas? Where has he been abducted to?”

Severus looked blamingly at the young woman. “Although I have my reservations against the practice of forced recruitment – it seems as if the time travelers want to limit it –, we shouldn’t condone that derogatory talk about necessary measures for the protection of the Empire. You too, dear Julia, enjoy the security that these ‘abductees’ guarantee for us all.”

Julia didn’t want to argue with Severus and therefore abstained from an answer. Instead, she gave the old man a sugar-sweet smile to which he responded as desired.

“I have made discreet inquiries. It seems that your Thomas has distinguished himself in battle and has been promoted.”

Julia’s eyes sparkled. Yes, that was her lover! No notorious drunkard and wastrel, but someone who excelled even in a desperate situation. Her heart began to beat and she leaned forward. “Where is he?”

“In Noricum. I don’t know exactly where, but I take the Legio II for the most probable location.”

“Noricum?” Julia frowned and tried to remember the exact geography of the Roman Empire. Then her face lit up. “That’s not far!”

Severus nodded hesitantly. “Reached in a few days with a fast horse; by cart it takes a little longer. My child, what are your plans?”

Julia straightened herself up, as she wore a thoughtful expression.

“Don’t run away again,” the old man warned with genuine concern in his voice. “Once, everyone will accept it as folly of youth, the second time may be regarded as an offence to the family. And this can have serious consequences. Not even I might be able to help."

Julia patted his hand. "Don't worry, I know something better. Thank you, thank you so much!"

She leaned forward and blew a kiss on the forehead of the old general, a gesture he enjoyed with closed eyes. Then she turned away, looked at her father and her future husband and drew a deep breath. It was time to put a plan into action.

And this time, her mother would not stand in her way.

4

Many years before, in the future, Lieutenant Klaus von Geeren – no, Captain, as he had to remember, since he had taken the place of the fallen Becker – had some days off duty. Together with a comrade, he had gone to the old city of nearby Trier, the oldest urban settlement on German soil, for a nice outing. He had always been interested in history, and this passion would be quite satisfied there. The fact that he had at that time also a girlfriend in Trier may have also played a role.

He remembered that he had stood one evening before the *Porta Nigra*, the "Black Gate," the largest and best preserved building from Roman times. He had tried to imagine how it looked in the past – with the temples and baths, the forum and the mighty walls of the former imperial residence. Von Geeren took great effort to imagine this as realistic as possible and ultimately entered the building to get a feel for the history.

Now he was part of this history, standing before the gate which in the future would become the Porta Nigra. It wasn't a single monument but an integral part of the city's fortifications, and black it was not: freshly painted, not weathered and darkened by a thousand years of continuous existence, the building with the large gate towered in front of him, and through it wandered a lively traffic of pedestrians. As in most Roman cities, Trier also banned carts during daytime not to burden the already narrow streets and alleys. Von Geeren knew well what that meant. His room in his otherwise very ordinary accommodation in a Roman barracks, where the bodyguard for the emperor was housed, opened its window to one of these streets. In the darkness of the night, the donkey carts rumbled over the pavement to supply the shops, the markets, and above all the imperial palace, which seemed to devour vast amounts of inventories. The noise and the shouting of the donkey driver, the squeaking of the wheels, the loud conversations, all this had disturbed the young infantry officer sometimes at night, at least until he had finally become used to this kind of background noise.

He looked again up the gate building, saw the city militias, observing traffic through the open portal with sluggish interest, while their comrades downstairs sometimes stopped travelers to ask where they were staying and about their intentions. Generally, however, vigilance was not high, and the feeling of constant threat, this atmosphere of oppression, fear and almost hysterical desperation that he had experienced in Thessaloniki, didn't prevail here. Sure, Germania with his troubled tribes wasn't far, but the Emperor was in the city and with him the army of the West, camping outside the gates in two large field camps.

The German went unmolested through the gate – he was known by now – and marched toward the imperial residence. He took the way often. Seldom did he found himself in front of the Porta Nigra to look at it in silence. The guards might think he was crazy and possibly were talking behind his back about this strange behavior. The infantryman was himself not entirely sure what actually drove him here. Perhaps it was because this gate gave testimony of all the centuries it will survive up to his own time, and it provided an immediate memory of his origin, which seemed to disappear out of his memory the more he got used to this century. Far from the *Saarbrücken*, the most important symbol of "home," this city gate was his point of contact with the abyss of time and his own life before that fateful and mysterious journey. Perhaps he was coming back to make sure that it existed. The Porta Nigra was as much a time traveler as he himself, and he only paid a return visit to something he had visited in the 20th century.

An old friend, so to speak.

The young man with the lanky figure pushed the thought away. Before him, another event waited in the endless chain of meetings he had with the leading generals of the Empire, often in the presence of Gratian himself, acting on behalf of Rheinberg. It was about big plans against major threats. Today the commander of the East, the not yet proclaimed Emperor Theodosius, had arrived in Trier, interrupting the preparations of the campaign against the defiant Sarmatians. In the coming days also Rheinberg himself was expected to return. Von Geeren longed for this moment because while the discussions with professional Roman officers were quite refreshing, those endless conversations in the court of Rome, including all of their vagueness and hidden meaning, were tiresome. This place seemed like a snake pit and his complete lack of understanding of political intrigues had made him a guarded man, only saying what was essential, embarrassingly anxious not to remark anything wrong.

And since he didn't even knew what was right or wrong in most encounters, he rather preferred to say nothing.

It took half an hour before he had penetrated the multiple layers of guards and courtiers and finally stood in the meeting room, which he had grown accustomed to in recent weeks. What he liked about this room the most was the large stone fireplace whose warm flames were very welcome given the winter temperatures. On the walls, carpets with numerous ornaments hung, which also kept the temperature in the room bearable. On the ground, strewn with mosaics, a mighty wooden table stood, on it spread out a new map of the Roman Empire. It was new because it had been made by the best cartographers of the Emperor on the basis of far more accurate material from the *Saarbrücken.* The Roman maps had not always possessed the right standards and distances, and although it had proved to be difficult to identify the exact position of some of the ancient towns in the German maps, they had made progress by identifying landmarks and working from there. And so the generals now had a large, in scale with reasonably reliable distances map not only of the Empire itself, but also of all the surrounding areas. As if this had not stunned the Romans, they had ingested the existence of America with great astonishment and some disbelief. For von Geeren, it had been surprising that they had neither been excited by the existence of India nor China, although had not been fully aware of the distances, for with both territories existed, albeit sometimes in a roundabout way, trade relations. But the two major American continental halves and the large extension of Africa to the south, as well as the existence of Australia, led to heated discussions. Some daring officers had even proposed equipping an expedition to America, now that they had these new oceangoing ships; von Geeren was sure that it would ferment and mature in the mind of many an adventurous man.

And there, spanning the wall, an even larger version of this map hung, carefully drawn on finely tanned, light leather. On both maps were marks for troop locations and the names of neighboring kingdoms or peoples living there, entered accurately. Dominating on the map of the wooden table, was a large, red arrow: It symbolized the approach of the Huns to the extent it could be derived from the scientific material in Captain Rheinberg's personal collection. And that was also the subject of this meeting.

Present were the Generals Arbogast, Malobaudes and Theodosius, some less senior officers who served as a kind of general staff, as well as scribes. At the request of von Geeren, an officer of the Eastern imperial forces, had joined as well. They had met him before Thessaloniki, and Gratian seemed to think the world of him. In fact, he was an important person in the plans that they developed, because it was Richomer and himself, von Geeren, who were supposed to organize the large scouting mission.

Most of those present held a cup of warm wine in their hands. The highly diluted swill was allowed everywhere; a ban on alcohol wasn't known here. Wine was the common drink, it was like water, only more harmless. Therefore von Geeren clutched with both hands a warm cup and was more pleased with the nicely tempered hands than the tolerably savory drink.

Arbogast spoke the first words after everyone had gathered. "Well, let's see where we stand. Tribune von Geeren, give us the current status. You have received news from Ravenna?"

The officer nodded and walked over to the map. "The first of the new steamships will soon be ready. Three more are already commissioned, and the factory is busy day and night to produce steam engines, a process that still has its challenges. Nevertheless, the fleet that we need will be available in a few months." Von Geeren pointed to the map and especially the red arrow. "I think that we have discussed various strategies and agree that we haven't much choice. We need to stop the Huns and their onslaught against the borders of the Roman Empire."

"Our fleet will therefore, once prepared, embark some legions and bring them the west coast of Europe along the northern sea. Through a passage that we call the Denmark Strait, we then reach a large island called Rügen. This has never been occupied by Roman troops, therefore, it wasn't known to you until recently. We should march the legions to the East from there, along the Baltic coast of Germania, after a hopefully successful landing. From the land side, we put the legions of Pannonia in march, so we can intercept the Hun's advance in a pincer movement." Von Geeren illustrated his remarks by moving small, colored pieces of wood, symbolizing Roman units, so that all those present were given a visual impression of the plan. "We will accompany this campaign with the German legionaries, because we need advanced weaponry for this endeavour, especially weapons with long range. Some of these technologies we are trying to adapt to local modes of production right now."

"You speak of iron cannons!" Arbogast said. He was among those who witnessed a demonstration of the machine guns in Sirmium where Gratian had pitched his camp. And the effects of the cannonade of the *Saarbrücken* before Thessaloniki had visibly impressed him.

"Actually, I speak of steel guns," von Geeren corrected him. "Unfortunately, we don't produce the steel in sufficient quantities. But we are working on it. We need field artillery to control a broad front section. The Huns are extremely fast and agile; their troops consist almost entirely of cavalry. We have to adapt to this way of fighting." Von Geeren paused and took a sip of wine. He twisted his mouth, because the drink had become cold and the sour taste fully pierced his taste buds. "Our biggest problem is that we don't know exactly where the Huns reside at this time, in which direction they are moving and at what speed."

"We have spent some time to ask the Goths we've beaten before Thessaloniki, as well as their Hunnish allies. I don't know how literally we can take the testimony of these people, because they tend to describe time and distance rather vague. We also have instructed our border troops to gather information from the neighboring nations, but even here the quality of information is varying. Therefore, this big red arrow."

Von Geeren paused again. His long speech in Latin cost a lot of time, because he was still fighting with the language despite all of his studies. When his audience now and then grimaced or indulgently smiled, he knew that he had deviated once again in terms of grammar and vocabulary. On the other hand, these discussions could not wait until he had perfected his language skills.

"So we will send a fact-finding mission," he continued. "We are going to proceed as follows. Several larger units from 100 to 1,000 men advance fan-shaped into the eastern areas to explore. The largest units are reinforced with our infantrymen to probably gain tactical experience in fighting Hun riders. To ensure the protection of these men and their precious equipment, we must also send with them a significant number of legionaries. But we will all proceed as cavalrymen – our mission must be fast and mobile."

"And then?" Arbogast asked.

"From the main body of our reconnaissance teams, we will widely send single spies, so we can cover a significant territory. This is especially important if it turns out that our assumption about the position of the Huns is wrong. We must be able to find them without fail."

"Why can't we equip the entire scouting mission with your powerful firearms? I've heard that your people are already working with the artisans of the Empire to build a corresponding factory," one of the officers unknown to von Geeren asked.

"To build the factory is not the problem," he said patiently. "We have conducted experiments with a rifle, which we call 'musket'. The results are indeed very satisfactory. But the weapon is inferior to the Hunnish bow in firing speed, range and accuracy. Equipping the legionaries with these muskets wouldn't have any positive effect. Better to take a unit of experienced archers. Our people are working on an improved version, with a rifled barrel and cartridges specially manufactured, and a double-barreled version, which should be equipped with a magazine. This requires large forgings and craftsmanship, and those few men who are actually capable of doing so are simultaneously engaged with the steam engines, shipbuilding and the construction of the bombards and steam catapults that are the new ships armament."

Von Geeren made an apologetic gesture. "We are working as intensely as we can. But what we're attempting here is ultimately a revolution of a technical nature. This requires, despite all the support of the Emperor, its time. By the way, we also try to teach the Roman craftsmen and masters to become teachers themselves, so that they actually can help to kickstart production on a wider scale. But until then, a lot needs to be done. I'm sure that we will eventually be able to provide larger parts of any legion with new weapons. But that is not enough: These troops must be well-trained. New weapons require new tactics, and these are very different from those they have been accustomed to. The challenge is immense."

"The challenge is immense, indeed," Arbogast repeated nodding, "and we don't have enough time. It is the year 379. If the historical information which we have received from our friends from the future is correct, the Huns will be not long in coming. The decisive battle occurred in 451, but previously to that, various Germanic tribes will have conquered Spain and North Africa, and Gaul is in great danger, too. We know about these things, and the victory over the Goths at Thessaloniki has already established a very important deviation from history, so that we now have a different starting position. But as long as the pressure of the Huns to the various nations of the East is so massive, the only valve for fleeing peoples will be a weak Rome, and this is our end, if we don't take pressure out of the boiler." Arbogast smiled at this phrase of the Germans that he had made his own.

"Then there is agreement about our plan?" von Geeren asked. Arbogast was absolutely right when he said that time was short. Theodosius, the supreme commander of the East, had listened to the explanations in silence. Von Geeren couldn't quite make sense of the man, the Spaniard had to know that he was actually been chosen by history to become emperor. But the haunting portrayal of the devastation that had been done in Spain by the Vandals obviously had left its mark on this man. He may have his flaws, but love for his homeland he didn't lack – nor military expertise. He accepted what was needed, at least that's what the German hoped for.

"We have already started preparations," Arbogast continued. "The Emperor has given appropriate instructions. We pull the best men from all legions. We look for individuals who don't shy away from the rigors and are cunning at the same time, no stupid blockheads who cannot think. They should be young and still have combat experience but not old veterans who are no longer willing to learn something new. You must be able to ride well or be able to learn it quickly. This is an almost impossible combination, so we cannot grant voluntary assignment – everyone who is capable must go. As a reward beckons early promotion, additional pay and all the loot that can be found on the way. The goal is to break camp immediately; the snow is thawing."

Von Geeren nodded. Arbogast had invested a lot of time in this project. It was largely thanks to his support that things were developing fast, sometimes even without a formal decision of this august body.

"When will Rheinberg arrive in Treveri?" Theodosius asked.

"In a few days," von Geeren said.

"In addition to this mission, another problem appears to be very urgent," the commander of the East said. "We have to take care of Maximus and Andragathius."

Everyone looked at the Spaniard in silence. They knew the historical development as it had been reported to them by Rheinberg. The revolt of Maximus, the *Comes Britanniarum*, against Gratian. How Andragathius, Maximus' general, had fraudulently enticed Gratian behind his lines and then murdered him, only to commit suicide two years later, as Theodosius finally managed to defeat the usurper Maximus. It was for the Spaniard certainly not easy to imagine a historical course that would never happen like this, an alternative timeline, where he had played a major historical role. Nevertheless, the revolt of Maximus was no coincidence. The first signs had to be visible by now. Theodosius was almost more eager than Gratian to eliminate this danger. In that other history, he hadn't been able to prevent the death of Gratian. Whatever he thought of the decision by the young man not to appoint him Emperor of the East, and to rule the Empire alone, at least until further notice, Theodosius was still a deeply loyal man. The idea of a betrayal was foreign to him and didn't correspond to his character, at least this was what everyone said.

A quick temper with a propensity for rapid and ill-considered decisions, but nothing worse. And that was well known and the reason why many of those present were cautious with their reaction.

"The Emperor hasn't made a decision in this regard," von Geeren reminded them and was happy that he wasn't more than Rheinberg's deputy. He was able to pass on problems like this one to the Magister Militium, without having to justify it. "It seems as if he wants to give Maximus a chance. The Comes had initiated the uprising because Gratian had become increasingly unpopular, not least in the military. He had withdrawn more and more from the affairs of the Empire and had started a habit of hunting, accompanied by his Alanian archers, whose loyalty he had bought with a lot of gold but who would, at the end, betray him. Rheinberg has made Gratian aware of these mistakes very forcefully, and Ausonius, his old teacher, supported him. The Emperor has recognized where his wrongdoing would lead him and consequently renounced this course of action."

"That's right," Malobaudes replied thoughtfully. "I saw him rarely more serious and diligent. To become aware of one's possible future, even with a violent death by ignominious betrayal, can initiate profound changes in a person."

All eyes turned briefly to Theodosius, who threw a smile in the round. "My own ignominious death has quite touched me," he said, "as well as the idea that I'll be the last emperor of all of Rome – and that my dear son, the little Honorius, would be a failure on the throne. I also don't particularly appreciate this course of history, and if I can help to change it, then I'll do that. And that's why it's my goal to smother any danger right from start. If Gratian wants to give Maximus a chance to change his ways and to not to evoke the indignation that leads the Comes to revolt, that may be a solution to the problem. But I suggest being cautious and to transfer Maximus to a respectable administrative post without military power – and Andragathius right with him, for he who carries the seed of betrayal in himself, might seek its blossom irrespective of a potential leader."

Von Geeren recognized from the facial expressions and gestures of some of the officers that Theodosius' attitude quite caught on among them.

"Discuss this with Rheinberg," the Spaniard asked him in a friendly tone. "And with the Emperor, because ultimately it's his decision. We can only act within the framework of our commands." He hesitated for a moment. He wanted to add something, but he wasn't sure whether the commander or one of the others present would take that as an insult or indirect accusation. Nevertheless, he decided to say it, because it was strongly on his mind. "I need to point out something once again and would ask you not to misunderstand," he began cumbersomely. "As you know, we have details about the possible future – the future that we brought from our time – of which we haven't reported everything to everyone. Among us, we have disclosed nearly all of it, but most of the administration and the military hierarchy only knows of our concern with respect to what we call 'Völkerwanderung', our understanding of the economic problems of the Empire and our attitude in regard to religious controversy."

"That was already more than enough for good Ambrosius," Arbogast muttered.

Von Geeren nodded. Since the Germans were held in high esteem by Gratian, the bishop of Milan had kept a low profile – too low for Rheinberg's taste, who had advised his deputy at court to look especially after the cleric and to report anything suspicious immediately. "What is not generally known, and where we have insisted on an oath of silence from everyone, are the details about the role of Maximus and Andragathius. We want to avoid not only prejudice but also a panic among the population, which will certainly feel little joy for the reforms of the Emperor if they entail a possible civil war. I need you, therefore, to ask everyone again quite urgently to keep silent on this matter indefinitely."

"Tribune von Geeren," Theodosius replied immediately. "I have made this oath and will follow it. But let's be honest with each other: Too many people have already heard too much. Two of your own crew are untraceable, they disappeared after the mutiny failed. And Ambrosius ... as much as I respect him as a man of the church, it is clear that he harbors a grudge against you but also against many of the things Rheinberg has reported." He shook his head. "It wouldn't surprise me if Maximus already knows about his possible fate. It also wouldn't be surprising if he has teamed up with Ambrosius to promote his plans. I don't want to dismiss the Comes as a lost case yet, but we have to be tremendously attentive."

"My father, a faithful servant of the former emperor Valentinian, was betrayed and killed by the Empire, being the victim of a court intrigue. Once a celebrated military leader and hero, he was judged without mercy or consideration. I have carried this resentment with me for a long time and acknowledge that Gratian has recently called me up to ask for forgiveness in regard to what has been done to my family. I don't want anything like that to happen to other people as well. No person without actual sin should be prosecuted, especially not based on mere assumptions. But this is about the existence of the Empire. If we accept that those future threats exist, all the things we have just discussed, we shouldn't take any chances."

He fixed von Geeren with a steady glance, as if to hypnotize him. It was clear that the Spaniard cared about this issue, and he certainly struggled with himself, wanting to do the right thing. Von Geeren knew the story of his father, who had also been called Theodosius, and it had been tragic enough, as his son had just called into mind.

Von Geeren just nodded. "The decision of the Emperor," was his simple answer. "Explain your arguments to him. But I know Gratian now good enough that I can quite guess his answer 'Bring evidence. Bring evidence that even in this time Maximus is willing to buy the purple with violence.' Only then he will agree to release him from office or to take other action against him."

"However, I must concur with Theodosius," Malobaudes raised his voice. The Frankish noble and old general had almost been the biggest advocate for resolute action against Maximus alongside the Spaniard. "We're beating around the bush! Loyalty here, gossip there, let's be clear that the seed of betrayal grows in Maximus, whether it blossoms now or later. We have to act."

"The Emperor decides!" von Geeren repeated. "And you, General, will shortly be on your way to Nemetacum to observe possible activities in Britain."

The Frank snorted. "I cannot do much more than send agents to Britain and hope that they are not detected by Maximus or even turned by his promises. But yes, I'll have a thorough look at him. and if I recognize the slightest irregularity, then we have to grab him fast, hard and without mercy!"

The Spaniard nodded. "Well, General, very good. I'm sure that we can make the necessary preparations immediately! A force to be ready to overthrow Maximus, once we have the slightest hint ..."

"The decision is with the Emperor," von Geeren repeated again, a little tired. "The general is to keep his eyes open, yes, but Gratian is in charge of possible consequences deriving from these observations."

Theodosius raised his hands in a fatalistic gesture. It was his sense of loyalty that made him accept this statement without further discussion.

Arbogast looked around. "Then we agree. Once the list of the proposals for specific targets of our scout mission is fully available, we start immediately with the final assessment and provisioning of the troops. I myself will be in overall command as soon as the Emperor confirms me officially, and I'll make the trip to the East but not alone. Forty of our time-travelling friends will accompany us. The troops will be provided with the best horses and much supplies. We need quick results to develop a strategy against the Huns, a strategy that is consistent and rational, based on reliable information." He paused for effect and to give anyone of those present the opportunity to add something, but no one spoke. "Then we will continue this conversation when the list exists and Rheinberg has arrived in Treveri."

The meeting was officially over. Von Geeren gathered his few utensils very slowly, as it often happened that someone took him aside after the end of the official meeting to discuss a detail. But when the officers left the room, only Theodosius remained, with a cup of hot wine in one hand. He looked thoughtfully into the flames of the fireplace, which slaves had just fanned. Von Geeren also poured himself a cup and settled silently beside him.

"I wouldn't be a very good emperor," the Spaniard said abruptly. "My temper is too often in my way. I have heard of the story in Thessaloniki, in your past and my future, where I have put thousands of citizens to death, only because of a sudden anger. This casts a shadow on my character, Tribune."

"It will not become like that," soothed von Geeren. "This massacre won't happen."

Theodosius nodded. "Yes, that's true. But I cannot dismiss this. I know myself well enough to come to the conclusion that I'm well capable of this kind of atrocity. It's in me, Tribune. When I heard the story for the first time, I was neither shocked nor full of disbelief. I knew immediately that I'm that kind of person and could act like that if no one keeps me in check." Theodosius smiled thinly. "It is difficult to control an emperor, if he is sufficiently stubborn. I realize now how important it is to have advisers who are willing to express their own opinion, even if it differs from that of the ruler on important issues. When I think of the abolition of forced recruitment into the army! Free choice of occupation will be introduced and the tax exemption for Church properties is about to be abolished. The Edict is confirmed. No grinding of the Victoria altar in the Senate. A monetary reform and restructuring of government debt. The end of the exemption for the great senatorial families. Oh, the outcry! Gratian alone would never have arrived at these ideas, and I certainly would've not. I would have thought of any proposal in this direction as an absurdity."

"There are enough people who still think so," the officer reminded him.

"Yes, and I'm also not immune. I shall now accept an Arian as an equal Christian, and the dispute about the true nature of Trinity should be left to the scholars? The followers of the ancient Roman cults are to live in peace? The latter I can understand in a way, out of respect for the traditions the Empire and our ancestors. But I wasn't educated in tolerance, Tribune. It is difficult for me to jump over my own shadow sometimes."

"And yet you have obviously done so," von Geeren answered smiling. "You even warn us of Ambrosius, who in another course of history alloted you the title 'the Great'."

The Spaniard snorted. "The Great!" he said snidely. "And yet that great one shambled and handed the realm into the hands of an incompetent son, who only accelerated the decline." Theodosius sighed and looked at his reflection in the wine. "I'm glad that you time travelers have come," he admitted quietly. "You have at least opened my eyes. I'll do everything to avert the disaster. My father would've done it as well." He nodded to himself, as if to affirm the last sentence, took the last sip of wine, laid his hand shortly on von Geeren's shoulder and left the room without another word.

The infantryman remained for a moment and stared into the crackling flames of the fire. He came to the conclusion that today's meeting did actually go quite well.

5

Johann Freiherr von Klasewitz shivered a bit. Although a fire flickered in the room's fireplace, he pulled the coat, in which he had totally wrapped up, even closer to his body. He tried not to appear too annoyed; he knew like all the other attendees that this place was not particularly comfortable but possessed other attributes that made it appear very suitable for this meeting.

It was outside of the big cities. It was far from one of the garrisons. It had been prepared just for this get together. Von Klasewitz had been told that this property previously had been a ruinous heap of stone and wood. In his eyes, the state was now not much better, even though a squad of twenty silent legionaries had worked one week to prepare at least the main building. Through the walls, the icy winds of a Gallic winter blew. The roof was leaking, which meant that the snow lying thereon began to melt by the heat of the fire and dripped into the interior of the building, which in turn resulted in a humid warmth that made clothes damp. And once a breeze drove through leaky joints and cracks of the holey wall, the moisture of the clothes produced such a pervasive feeling of coldness that the nobleman didn't want to leave his place right in front of the fireplace.

He stood at the head of a rough-hewn table. Placed on it, one of the new properly scaled maps of the Roman Empire had been spread, which had been distributed to all garrisons, a visible expression of the influence Rheinberg was now exercised over the Emperor. Von Klasewitz forced himself not to think too long about his former commander. Every time he imagined Rheinberg's face, a mixture of unbridled anger and frustration seized him. Without any possibility to vent these feelings at some scapegoat, he had to control himself. Everyone present was a senior figure, which impressed the need to behave reasonably. This was extremely difficult for him. He gritted his teeth and forced Rheinberg out of his consciousness, knowing that the ensuing discussion would inevitably lead his thoughts yet again to deal with his nemesis.

No, he corrected himself. Who would be whose nemesis was to be seen. Though the nobleman was currently no more than a failed mutineer, he was working on a career as a conspirator and should everything go smoothly an adviser of the coming emperor, whose name should be Magnus Maximus, currently *Comes Britanniarum*. In von Klasewitz's own time, Magnus Maximus had been, for a while, Emperor of the West, after Gratian was sneakily assassinated, before he had been finally defeated by Theodosius the Great. After that, and for the last time in Roman history, the power of the Empire had been concentrated in the hands of one man. The influence of the Germans had meant that things went now differently – Gratian was the one and only emperor now. And Magnus Maximus was still as frustrated as and still has convinced of his cause as before.

The Comes was a tall man with a weathered face and a determined look, an unmistakable charisma that had helped him along the way, as he took care of his troops in a way that instilled great loyalty among the legionaries. Since Gratian's original sin had been, among other things, to no longer take care of the regular units of the legion, this was a great initial advantage for the Comes, because in these times the legions made the emperor – not the people, not the Senate, not the church.

Von Klasewitz' eyes fell on the oblique face of a man who sought to change this. He still saw in Ambrosius of Milan someone to worship. For the nobleman, the bishop was one the saints and one of the Fathers of the Church, an almost mythical, ethereal figure. That the actual Ambrosius, with whom he had to deal with currently, was actually aside from being a highly educated scholar primarily a shrewd and tricky politician, seeped slowly into his awareness. The Bishop of Milan, dressed in simple cloth, seemed not to worry about the cold gusts of wind or the dripping ceiling. Instead, he stared at the map with approximately the same hunger in his eyes as Maximus. Both had the same goal, which bound them, and their ambition was similar in many ways.

That von Klasewitz was for them no more than an instrument, the nobleman wouldn't and couldn't see. Since he had cut all ties with his past on the *Saarbrücken*, the former first officer had nothing left than his illusions and self-deceptions. Ensign Tennberg he had sent away on behalf of the conspirators. It was better when the impressionable young man didn't know too much.

What von Klasewitz didn't admit was the fact that without these illusions, which he nurtured for himself, his essence would melt like the snow on the roof of this little renovated homestead, some fifty kilometers north of Lyon.

In another timeline, which would probably never become a reality through the intervention of the Germans, Lyon was the city where Gratian would be betrayed and killed.

Nevertheless, it was one of the objectives of the gathered men to restore this historical detail in some way.

"Do we expect someone else?" Ambrosius asked.

A tribune, who had come with Maximus, nodded. "The envoy of the Alans," Maximus added,

"A barbarian?" Ambrosius asked and grimaced.

"We need the Alans if we are to succeed," the Comes insisted. "My legions are not sufficient. It also will help us to attract more Germans to our cause. We need all the support we can get, especially now that the rules of the game have changed."

He threw a significant look at von Klasewitz, who bowed his head. It was not least his job to regain a certain equality of arms – and quite literally so.

"Besides, noble Bishop, don't worry that a lousy barbarian with dirty breath and bad manners appears here. The Alans have long enough been allies of the Empire in order to enjoy certain advantages of our civilization. Why do you think the Alans are so eager to put their horse archers at the disposal of our beloved Emperor? It's the gold, yes, but it is also the Roman way of life. And many Alans have received high honors. They can hardly be distinguished from a real Roman." Maximus made a snorting noise. "Whatever a real Roman is today."

This time he avoided looking directly at von Klasewitz as his stance might have been too obvious if he had been staring at him. Before anyone could say anything, the door opened and flurries swirled into the room and immediately fell to the ground to form a puddle. In the doorway stood a wide-built man of imposing stature.

"Damn it, shut the door!" Maximus commanded and the man entered completely. He wore a long beard, the ends of which were intertwined. His hair, however, was neatly trimmed and cut in Roman style. When he took his coat jacket off, the attire of a typical Roman merchant came to light, and despite the snow it was evident that the man strived to maintain a neat appearance. He looked around, put the jacket to the others on a bench and stepped closer to the fire. Von Klasewitz looked him in his eyes. They were the clearest blue he had ever seen, like a mountain lake.

"That's Fabius Lecrinus, our liaison to the Alan princes," Maximus introduced him. "He doesn't only speak perfect Latin and Greek, he has also worked in the prefecture of Gaul for a long time and held a respected position there."

"Why did he abandon it to join our cause?" Ambrose asked.

"Did he?" Maximus asked and nodded toward Fabius who smiled at him knowingly.

"I'm still working in the Imperial administration, and my services are greatly appreciated in Lyon," Fabius said in a pleasant voice. "I'm not a freedom fighter. I just want more opportunities for my people in the Empire."

"Why then conspiring against Gratian?" the Bishop asked. "The Alans are held in high regard by him."

"Only those who are directly in his service and allowed to go hunting," Fabius said and the contemptuous tone was unmistakable. "But I have broader goals. I received certain promises from Maximus. That is why I am here."

"You are authorized to make binding agreements?" von Klasewitz asked in order to finally add to the discussion. The appreciative nod of the Bishop told him that he had asked the right question.

"To a certain extent, yes. Final decisions, of course, are only for the leaders I represent. That goes without saying, I guess."

"Then let us begin," Maximus said. "Tribune von Klasewitz will report first. It is about our efforts to compensate for certain disadvantages in terms of our equipment."

Ambrose frowned. This was the difference between the Bishop and Maximus. While the Comes, the professional soldier, had accepted the technical innovations and wondrous weapons of the time-travelers eagerly and sought to get them in his hands, the Bishop was apparently still not sure exactly where the boundary between advanced craftsmanship and witchcraft was to be drawn. That he didn't do more than just reacting with a sinister look, spoke for his realism.

Von Klasewitz coughed.

All the eyes were directed toward him.

"I don't have to tell you that our own efforts in regard to the production of modern weapons are endangered by unequal conditions in comparison to those of our opponents," von Klasewitz said. "The Emperor has the ship with all the workshops and the entire crew, and he supports Rheinberg with all the resources available to him. We have now built a small base in Britain, not far from Londinium, and started with our work there. Maximus and I have therefore decided to focus our efforts on a single goal – the production of field artillery. Cannons. Once we have a functional artillery, we can compensate for many of the advantages of our opponents. The challenges are considerable, as you can imagine."

He looked around. No, most people here couldn't imagine that. Even Maximus, who had his little weapons technology development center close by and followed the efforts made, didn't understand most of it. The production of black powder especially presented a major problem. But von Klasewitz was well aware of the fact that the elaboration of technical details would bore nearly everyone here.

"Nevertheless," he continued, "I assume that a number of pieces will be available to us in the spring. It will be bronze cannons without rifled barrel, but it is the first step. I am already working intensively on a successor design with greater range and better accuracy. Perhaps we will hammer that out very quickly, but I don't want to promise too much."

"What about the fire tubes for our legionaries?" Ambrosius asked.

Von Klasewitz shook his head. "In the short term, impossible. As our informants tell us, even our enemies shy away from arming the legions of the Emperor accordingly. We call the first stage of these *tubes* muskets, and they are not worth too much militarily. But I want to arm the troops with something else. It bears the name *grenade*, and I aspire to a very simplified construction."

Also, von Klasewitz only added in his thoughts, for muskets he needed gunpowder – and in substantial quantities.

"These grenades will help in the fight man against man?" the Alan asked.

"Against riders as well as foot soldiers alike," the nobleman replied. "Its only drawback is that each man will only be able to carry a limited number with him and that it can be dangerous if you don't know how to properly handle the weapon. The men will need proper training."

"What about the Alan horsemen?" Fabius asked. "Will we receive any of the advanced weapons?"

Von Klasewitz exchanged a quick glance with Maximus. Here the conversation left his jurisdiction. It was about politics, no longer about military strategy. Fabius noticed the silent exchange and looked invitingly at the commander. "An important question, which is linked ultimately to the number of these weapons we'll be able to produce," Von Klasewitz said. "I cannot assure it now. But there is certainly no fundamental reason to the contrary."

That was an outright lie, as von Klasewitz knew. Of course there were fundamental reasons not to give means of that power into the hands of barbarian tribes. Even among them, talented and studious craftsmen could be found, with a good grasp of the underlying principles of certain constructions. One couldn't allow the Alans to hurl grenades against legions as the barbarians could very likely become an enemy thereafter. Maximus could, of course, not say so, but von Klasewitz wasn't sure whether Fabius, educated man he undoubtedly was, couldn't guess by himself. The facial expression of the Alan remained opaque. He decided to keep his thoughts to himself, however, and seemed to be ready to accept the reply, at least for now.

"We need to cover some political options before we go into the details of the military planning which I must leave you to," Ambrosius said in false modesty. The Bishop deceived no one with his presumed ignorance. He might not be a soldier, but also he wasn't an unworldly clergyman. Yet he attracted full attention. Even Maximus seemed startled. Apparently the bishop had another surprise in store.

There was a general and unspoken agreement that the goal of the whole conspiracy was to make Maximus the new emperor. It wasn't yet clear whether he would operate as a pan-Roman Emperor or ultimately be limited to the West by the appointment of a new emperor in the East, but if he had Gratian overthrown, he would be the only man wearing the purple. Von Klasewitz had received assurances that Maximus would make him the captain of the *Saarbrücken* and an admiral of the fleet, as well as a senator. That was, as von Klasewitz surmised, not too bad. For a start.

Ambrosius' ambitions were actually crystal clear. He wanted to eradicate both the Arian heresy as well as the ancient Roman cults in order to raise the Trinitarian variant as the only recognized state church. In the timeline of which von Klasewitz came, he had succeeded in this, thanks mainly to slavishly acting emperors, first the young Gratian and afterwards Theodosius, although that one with a little less enthusiasm. But Gratian, it seemed, was now pursuing another church policy, inspired by Rheinberg liberal ideas, and Theodosius was not even Emperor and might never be. Just because Ambrosius knew what he had achieved in that other timeline, the intervention of the time-travelers must have hurt him particularly.

The bishop with the oblique face – one eye was slightly higher than the other – rose and spread his arms. Von Klasewitz saw that one of the two priests who had accompanied him to the meeting left the room silently.

"Of course, it is our common goal to overthrow Gratian and to make the noble Maximus emperor. Gratian's unlimited power is currently based not only on the fact that the Germans support him, but also that since the battle of Adrianople he alone is the legitimate ruler of the Empire after the death of Valens – as long as he doesn't appoint a successor to his deceased uncle."

“He won’t too soon,” Maximus said, narrowing suspicious eyes. “Even Theodosius turned to formally swear his loyalty.”

“Yes,” Ambrosius said, nodding. “He won’t help us in this crisis. We may even need him to be eliminated if there is time, despite the fact that I despise the notion. But there another development has emerged.” The bishop paused for effect. “A few days ago, I received a visitor. A very strange visitor. He didn’t come directly to Milan; instead, I received a message that led me to a meeting place, not unlike our present whereabouts. There I was confronted by two men. I will show you.”

As if on cue, the door opened again. Snow swirled in, and then two hooded men trudged into the room, followed closely by Ambrosius’ companion, who had led them here. Even with the hoods on, one of the men was obviously young, moved powerfully and confidently. The other seemed older, looked clumsy, and was held by the younger’s arm, as if he had problems with orientation.

Then the younger one threw the hood backwards. A striking face, adorned with a beard, a penetrating look, which seemed to dissect all present. He didn’t say anything.

“May I introduce you to the Gothic nobleman Godegisel?” Ambrosius intoned now almost solemnly. “It is one of those who fought in Thessaloniki, where he and his men opened the gates. He is a confidant of Judge Fritigern and in some ways his emissary.”

“What do the Goths want?” Maximus asked, who clearly showed his suspicions now.

“We bring a gift and demand nothing,” the young Goth replied in clearly accented Greek. He turned to his still masked companion and pulled the hood from his head.

Von Klasewitz didn’t recognize the sunken, tired and disoriented face. But Maximus and his officers drew their breath audibly and then seemed petrified.

“For those of you who don’t know this man, let me introduce him: Welcome Flavius Julius Valens, uncle of Gratian, Emperor of the East.”

Von Klasewitz stared at the older man in disbelief. Valens had died, fallen before Adrianople – in his timeline as well as in this!

Which mysterious powers of fate ever had thrown the *Saarbrücken* into the past, this incident seemed to have led to more than just the appearance of the Germans. Valens had survived and fell obviously into the captivity of the Goths.

Maximus stepped forward. "How can we know that this is the real Valens? I admit, he resembles the Emperor very much, but ..."

"He carries the imperial seal with him," Ambrosius interrupted. "He knows things that only the emperor of the East can be aware of. Ask him once he feels better."

"Better?"

"He was seriously injured and his mind has, for the moment, escaped into a dream once he realized the magnitude of the defeat he had to answer. He is ..."

"Crazy!" Maximus interrupted and now seemed to be completely relaxed. "Crazy and thus not capable of governing. Even his survival is pointless, because as insane as he seems, he must resign or be removed from office."

Ambrosius smiled softly. "You may call him crazy, Comes. I call him ... docile."

Maximus eyes narrowed again. "What is your intention, Bishop?" he asked.

Ambrosius' smile widened. "I procured you an unexpected degree of legitimacy, Maximus. Like Valens has approved the appointment of Gratian as Emperor of the West after the death of Valentinian, he will now confirm you as worthy of the purple – in public and to the testimony of each and everyone."

Silence reigned the room.

Then Maximus smiled.

6

"The normal way, if you want to go by ship, is through the Eritrean Sea," Aurelius Africanus explained, pointing to what Köhler knew as the "Red Sea." "The new maps have helped to determine the geographic elements in more detail, but it was still difficult to guess the actual position of towns and cities and the exact line of the coasts. Köhler had to realize that in a thousand years some areas silted while other areas have been reclaimed from the sea, so that the German maps, while basically very helpful, differed in important details. After Köhler and Behrens had persuaded Captain Rheinberg to attempt the expedition with the *Valentinian*, he had ordered them, among other things, to record any deviation from the maps accurately and, where possible, to take measurements, even if they might not be absolutely perfect."

"That would be easily done in our time," Köhler commented on the proposal of the Trierarch and frowned. "We have a channel, called the Suez Canal. It connects the Mediterranean with the Red Sea, which you call the Eritrean. We could go to Egypt, cross the channel and then ... where is Adulis exactly?"

"Here!" Aurelius pointed to a spot where there was also a marker labeled by a Roman cartographer. Adulis was on the east coast of the Horn of Africa. In his time, the corporal remembered, this was the Empire of Ethiopia, which traced his own roots back to Aksum. "It is the largest seaport of the kingdom of Aksum, the most important trading center. From there goes a road into the interior, directly to the capital itself. If we can't find what we seek in Adulis, then we'll get it in Aksum. There is an embassy of the Emperor there which is largely occupied with trade issues. Some of our priests are active as the Empire has opened itself to christianity for a long time. But the Aksumite are not trinitarians, and therefore the relations are in this respect somewhat ... well, cold."

"Well, we can't use the ship all the way to Adulis, since there is no channel," Köhler came back to the actual subject.

"Oh, it's there," Aurelius corrected him. "It may be that this is a large structure in your time, but already the Egyptian pharaohs have dug such a channel hundreds of years ago. The Persians have expanded it, and I must confess to my shame that it silted up, despite the efforts of Emperor Traian, for the most part now."

Köhler shook his head, less in regard to his deficient faith, but more about himself. "I have to apologize again, my friend," he said. He went to the window, which gave him a good look at the new shipyard facility, one he took in for a moment. From here he could not only see, gently swaying, the *Valentinian* at her pier, but also not far away, the moored *Saarbrücken.* If he turned his head slightly to the right, the seemingly endless row of slaves was to be seen, who labored with shovels and buckets to excavate the major drydock, which belonged to the core of the port facility. There the light cruiser was to be placed, due in a few weeks. The waters of the Mediterranean attacked the iron hull with special aggressiveness, and Dahms scrutinized the ever-spreading rust with great concern. It was high time to give the ship a fresh paint job.

Köhler also knew that it was Rheinberg's plan to buy all the slaves whenever enough gold was available, and to release them immediately thereafter. Already now they were treated as employees, not as property, as the captain had ordered.

Then his eyes fell back to the cruiser. What would happen if they ran out of the special color needed to protect the hull from salty water Köhler didn't want to imagine. One of the reasons why Rheinberg supported the development of wooden steamships, manufactured by the Romans, was not least the fear that the life and operability of the *Saarbrücken* was limited and they had to have alternative means of naval power available.

Inevitably, at a certain date, the cruiser would be only a rusting wreck.

Köhler didn't want to be reminded. He broke away from this image and turned back to Africanus, who had watched him smiling.

"So there is a channel, but we cannot use it anyway, because it wasn't properly protected against silting up."

Africanus shrugged. "It is on the list."

Köhler shook his head. He had heard this response in recent weeks quite often. The fabled list had been drawn up by Rheinberg and Dahms. It contained all the measures that they tried to take, "once time permitted." The reconstruction of the channel was certainly one of them, as well as some other construction projects. Now that they had proved that it was possible to build a functional, though not particularly efficient steam engine from bronze, even more ambitious things were on the plate like covering the Roman Empire with a railway network. This would bring benefits for trade but also for defense – and it was now, at least in theory, technically feasible. If someone asked when they would take care of it – as many other challenges too –, the answer was, *It is on the list.* As if by that, half of the work was already done.

To get coffee had been on the list, its need especially clear as the coffee bean was apparently not known yet, despite access to Aksum. It was thanks to Köhler's and Behrens' initiative that this item had been removed from the list to be actually implemented. Rheinberg called it his "feel-good-project" – the attempt to prove the critics that the arrival of the Germans didn't only have advantages because the Empire now could efficiently kill its enemies. Köhler was the motivating force that had persuaded the captain to authorize the expedition.

All of them wanted to drink real coffee again.

"So we won't go to Adulis. What is the alternative?" the NCO asked.

"Not so fast, my friend. We can, of course, travel to Alexandria, then by river boat up the Nile and afterwards across the southern border of the Egyptian province overland to Aksum. But this trip will last much longer, even though it is the most direct route, because it is difficult and the weather very hot. We can also move only relatively few trade goods by cart. But if we want the Negusa

Nagast's permission to search his country for the wild coffee bean – or even muster his active support for this mission –, we have to offer something in exchange."

Africanus bent over the map.

"We will therefore instead take the *Valentinian* to Alexandria, then travel the Nile to the channel close to Clysma in order to equip a coastal sailor who will take us directly to Adulis. At sea, we will be much faster and we can adequately carry with us merchandise that we'll acquire in Egypt."

"But from Adulis onwards ..."

"Most goods we'll sell in the port, directly to the royal merchant, so the Aksumite emperor will know soon if he has made a good deal. With a selection of precious jewels and some gold coins from the stock of the *Saarbrücken*, we'll travel over land to Aksum. There we will pay our respect to the Negusa Nagast, prepared and introduced by the local Roman representative. He should put great interest in our plans since they would earn well on a lucrative trade. We have already sent messengers ahead and announced our expedition."

"The news of the arrival of the time-travelers has spread to Aksum already?" Köhler asked.

"We don't know. But experience shows that important information travels fast around the Mediterranean. It wouldn't surprise me if the agents of the Aksumite emperor in Syria or Egypt or Palestine are very well informed about what is happening in the Empire. Aksum is a powerful state in itself – and with ambitions. These ambitions are aimed fortunately not against Rome, but to the east, to Arabia. Given our relationship with the Parthians, we are in favor of anyone who acts decisively in the East. Aksum and Rome are not allied but benevolent friends, and that should help us."

"Then we travel as you proposed," Köhler said with a nod. "The *Valentinian* is equipped, and we have a proper crew. Besides Behrens and I, two infantrymen, two sailors and a machinist of the *Saarbrücken* will join us. The rest of the crew consists, if I have understood you correctly, of veterans of the *Scipio*."

The *Scipio* had been Africanus' last command, a Roman trireme, which he had led in an equally heroic and senseless attack against the just appeared *Saarbrücken* in the Mediterranean. A hit from a naval gun of the cruiser had sent the trireme to the seabed, but a good part of the crew had been rescued. The *Valentinian* required fewer men than the great rowers, so Africanus was able to completely run the ship with the rest of his men. He liked working with people he knew and on who he could rely upon.

"I'm training consistently with the whole crew," Africanus confirmed. "We need to be familiar with a very unusual type of navigation and try to understand the weaponry properly. But once it is spring, we can safely go to sea and start our expedition."

Köhler nodded. He would soon begin his own training session on the *Saarbrücken*; currently it was his task to explain to a group of Roman sailors the basics of instrumentation. He thought of his students, who were trying to process this with a mixture of disbelief, astonishment and snide arrogance of experienced sailors refusing to learn something new, as a third man stepped into the room. It was Dr. Hans Neumann, Navy Medical Corps, and he looked unexpectedly happy.

Köhler guessed the news that the doctor brought and frowned. "Sir!" he greeted the doctor respectfully.

"Köhler, I was looking for you!" Neumann boomed and settled into a chair with a groan. "What a day, damn. For six hours I tried to teach the best healers of Ravenna and their assistants what a blessing it would be if they'd boil their surgical instruments prior to use and that it makes sense to throw away rusty instruments, rather than to continue to use them endlessly. Damn, one of the men had dirt under his fingernails and boasted that they he had already carried out operations on the open skull! They make me completely insane!"

Köhler grinned. Neumann had to air his exasperation at regular intervals, otherwise he wouldn't bear the management of his newly minted School of Medicine for long. In fact, he spoke mostly very favorably about the traditional knowledge of his students, whose manual abilities were often higher than he had imagined. The Gallic medicine schools were famous throughout the Empire, and his students were all graduates from there, complemented by some

Egyptians who also referred to a long medical tradition. Still, some issues which had to be discussed came up again and again. Hygiene during treatment – during each treatment – was one of the necessities that wasn't always easy to convey. Fortunately, the Romans were commonly very clean people, so that the basic idea of cleanliness had a certain social acceptance. Had they stranded a few hundred years later, one would have assigned exaggerated cleanliness in a man as a weakness and mocked him accordingly.

"How is progress generally?" Köhler asked. He knew that von Neumann's efforts were of utmost importance. They needed qualified physicians, at least more highly trained paramedics, and a local production of medical supplies like bandages and simple medication. The cabinets in the small hospital of *Saarbrücken* were well filled, but that wouldn't last forever, and the more the Germans would distribute themselves over the Empire, the harder it was for a single doctor to treat everyone.

Neumann sighed. He took out his empty pipe, looked at it wistfully and stuck it in his mouth, in a desperate effort to catch some of the tobacco flavor in the wood. He had smoked his last crumb some weeks ago. It was a frustration that he shared with many men of the *Saarbrücken*.

"It's actually quite good. The initial two-month course is over, and I started purposedly with experienced field surgeons of the Roman forces. These are very pragmatic men, used to both frustration as well as improvisation. Eight of them I have intensively trained, and I want to assume that they'd already be capable to act as a nurse in our time. For this era, they can be regarded as highly trained physicians. And I learned a lot about local medicines from them. For both sides, exchanging knowledge was a good thing. One of them stays with us and will help in future courses. Two will henceforth continue to work on the *Saarbrücken* in the hospital, along with my medical assistants. The remaining five go back to the legions. I have told them to train at least two of their assistants as thoroughly as possible, as I have done with them, and they have promised me to do so. With luck, the new expertise will spread quickly and become general knowledge soon."

Neumann sighed again. “Rome needs these experts.”

Africanus abstained from any comment. Although he felt, like many others who worked closely with the Germans, great admiration for some of the engineering marvels from the future, he had also developed the same, subtle inferiority complex like many intelligent and educated Romans. Not everyone showed it. Some compensated with particular eagerness to prove that they weren’t too stupid to learn and improve and would quickly catch up. But others had big problems with the knowledge gap, although Rheinberg was carefully anxious to show the necessary respect while displaying their knowledge. For some, this inferiority complex gave way to rejection, sometimes even pure hatred. This issue remained to be difficult.

Africanus wasn’t immune to these feelings, but he was confident about his own qualities. His knowledge of the Mediterranean and his familiarity with the regions of the Empire made him a valuable source of knowledge the Germans couldn’t easily replace. So the Trierarch never had the feeling not to be equal or not to be respected. Neumann’s last remark was silent but revealed that he was not entirely free of reservations himself.

“But you are surely not here in order to report about the progress of medical education,” Köhler turned the topic back to the topic on hand. “Unless you want to tell us in person who of your graduates will accompany us on the *Valentinian*.”

Neumann’s eyes flashed. He grinned broadly.

“No,” he said simply.

“No? But I thought ...”

“I’ll come myself!”

Köhler raised his eyebrows, but was careful not to show too much surprise. Neumann had probably foreseen this doubt and nodded friendly toward the man.

“I spoke with Rheinberg shortly before his departure to Trier about this,” he said. “Of course, I’m particularly interested in the medical knowledge in Egypt and Aksum and want to learn from it. Moreover, I am the only member of the crew who has certain botanical knowledge, quite useful for the purpose of our endeavor, I presume. The most important thing is that I no longer can endure it here, and I've told Rheinberg that he either gives me better things to do than playing the professor of medicine, or I leave the service, open a practice in Rome, buy me a fat villa and marry a senator's daughter with huge tits!"

Köhler smiled. Neumann was and remained to be the officer with the laxest attitude toward proper soldiering. No wonder that he got along so well with the man. "And the captain has accepted your ultimatum?"

Neumann was still grinning. "Naturally! You have helped me!"

"I did?"

"You and Behrens and your tavern in Ravenna, poisoning the Empire with brandy. Other crew members also began to develop ideas. Rheinberg will have more and more trouble holding the men together. If I disappear, the dam will break. No, he has every interest to keep me happy."

Köhler saw that the doctor was enjoying himself royally.

No, he corrected himself: imperially.

He grinned back and welcomed Neumann in his crew.

It would be fun.

7

Julia thought of how to endure all this, and it wasn't easy. Her parents, as well as her estranged fiance and soon happily wed spouse, had insisted on a public ceremony – and quickly, before the defiant Julia could think of something to subvert this union. Since their families were both Christian, they had waived the traditional Roman marriage formalities. The church itself hadn't developed any guidelines on how they had to get married – not yet, anyway –, and therefore the families had agreed to make it a proper but also conveniently fast ceremony. The primary goal of this event was less to delight the newlyweds than to show the public of high ranking guests that several problems had been solved – Julia, who had previously been in serious danger to become a spinster, was finally supplied with a husband, Martinus Caius, who so far had been very familiar with all the anatomical details of local prostitutes, was shown the right path, and two important families of nobility and money had joined, which was also of political importance. Something to be sealed with a lot of attendance, something which had to be festively celebrated and adequately witnessed by other worthy families – and therefore they had invited all of them.

And no one refused to honor the invitation.

As the villa of the family was unable to cope with such a crowd, no expense had been spared. Before the walls of the city, two giant marquees with waterproof tarpaulins had been erected on a specially built wooden structure. Countless slaves also had to build a kitchen to prepare the necessary food, and many armchairs and benches were either bought or rented to offer all guests the necessary comfort.

Julia's mother had formally presided over the preparations. As a commander, she had the legions of staff to conduct and planned the entire festivity with military precision. The only contribution her father had to make – apart from handing personal invitations to particularly important guests of honor – was to dig deep into his pockets and to produce golden *denarii* in large quantities. The fact that the immensely wealthy father of the groom also contributed a small amount potentiated the pomp and luxury of this celebration. The best wine in Italy was brought in cartloads of amphorae. That was the particular aspect of the festival for which Martinus Caius finally had shown some interest. Otherwise, he tried to endure the hustle stoically. The fact that he had applied attention to this important event only for a second, spoke for his attitude. That it was Lucia, two hours before the actual ceremony, who strictly forbade the slaves to proffer the groom any alcohol, and pointed out who intended to call the shots in the future, especially with respect to the newly established union between their families.

At least, Gunter, the stupid Germanic slave, was now out of the game. The minder's massive physique had barely concealed the fact that he had the mental capacity of a loaf of bread. At first, Julia had felt a certain pleasure to trick him in order to escape his vigilance but abandoned the scheme after a short while; it was just too easy. And so Gunter had accompanied her at every step, until today, until such time as the useless son of a powerful man would take her under his wing.

Julia was ready to endure it all.

It was her plan which gave her strength. It was the fact that both her parents and the groom had granted the wishes of a spoiled and difficult bride, all of them very happy that these two were actually to be married. Julia had milked this relief, as best as she could, and she was very satisfied with the result.

Now she only had to survive this ceremony and make the best of a game whose rules she didn't care for. While slaves still plucked at her wedding clothes, she looked to the other side of the marquee. There stood Martinus Caius, almost lost and pitiable in the festive toga he had donned. He didn't seek eye contact with his future bride, his obvious interest was solely focussed on the delicacies that were served on the longitudinal wall of the tent in order to be consumed quickly by the festive congregation. Someone rolled a handcart with six massive amphorae filled with the best wine, followed intensely by Martinus' eyes. Julia had a pretty good idea of what would happen in her wedding night, and that gave her good reason to worry. Less because she hoped that her new husband would fulfill his marital duties in a particularly excellent way but because it was necessary, indeed essential and quite pressing that despite all the disgust she felt that he did his duty.

Julia was pregnant.

The father was Thomas Volkert, the fruit grew since that night at the inn, the first and only night together before he had been "recruited into the armed forces." Julia knew it for a long time because her bleeding had stopped and she felt violent nausea in the morning, a condition she had been able to keep a secret before her family. A gentle convexity was increasingly difficult to disguise. How good that both families had unanimously waived the farce of testing her virginity. Everyone knew about her past passion for the German.

It was necessary, and for Martinus not least, that everyone assumed that this child would be a legitimate offspring of this marriage. And there had to be a wedding night. It was ultimately a good thing that the wedding took place as soon as possible, before the pregnancy would be too obvious.

At worst, Martinus was either sober enough to actually want to do the job, or so drunk that no one would think him able of performing anymore. Julia had already conducted a highly enjoyable conversation with her mother in this regard, who had been very happy about the sudden aspiration of her daughter to fulfill her marital obligations to the fullest. She had immediately taken up the task to ensure that Martinus was supplied with wine only in moderation. Julia left it to her mother. She was an expert at manipulating other people.

Nevertheless, Julia had decided to keep an eye on Martinus. She could well combine this task with showing her apparent desire regarding the consummation of their marriage, and this would help in legitimizing the sudden fertility of the senator's daughter. For a while, Julia was ready to live with this lie, hoping to inform

Thomas about their child later and develop a plan to move away from this hateful marriage – even if she had to ask to the Emperor for help.

Julia took a deep breath. Her dress was perfect. Already, she wore the ring she had received on her finger, a token collected with the engagement promise of Martinus. This belonged to ancient pagan rituals, but it seemed as if the church was willing to accept this kind of symbolism. Volkert had told her that the tradition of the ring still existed in his time, a time in which there was also a firmly established wedding ceremony of the church, which wasn't yet available.

Julia's eyes scanned the room. She found the two priests, confidantes of her father, who would unite the pair with the senator's blessing, in a dignified, but not too formalized manner. Ultimately Senator Marcellus would give his daughter to marry the son, because with this step Julia left her parental family and belonged to that of her husband.

Since she would thus also leave the immediate sphere of influence of her mother, Julia was actually quite excited about this prospect.

Her father waved. The central part of the ceremony would begin soon; apparently all the important guests had arrived. The large wood stoves spread a pleasant warmth despite the winter temperatures. Julia sighed, and everyone saw this as the usual nervousness of the bride. That the reason lay much deeper, she had to keep to herself until further notice.

Senator Michellus took her arm and led her to the small podium that had been set up at the head end of the tent. Martinus, rather lethargic, also had been directed to the front by his father. The aqueous look of the groom, with whom he greeted Julia, made the prospect of a "real" wedding night even more uncomfortable. The man had definitely drunk enough wine to develop both desire and potential memory loss at the same time. Julia made a mental note to take that into consideration meticulously.

She smiled.

And smiled.

And smiled through the whole, relatively short ceremony. She smiled, as her hands were placed in those of Martinus. She smiled as the priest stepped forward and loudly intoned the blessing. She smiled as Senator Michellus declared them married and asked the audience to celebrate this special event with him. All responded with loud applause, it rained congratulations, pats, handshakes, good advice and suggestive remarks.

Julia smiled.

She imagined that the man at her side was not the pudgy drunkard but the young officer from a foreign and strange world to whom she had so quickly lost her heart, but the image didn't last for long. For only a brief moment she sensed what she would probably feel once the day would come when she would marry the man who was the only one with a right to a wedding night with her.

Would feel. Would feel. Julia intended to fight to her last breath for what she had vowed to herself, as her allegiance to Martinus was nothing but a lie.

She smiled. And smiled.

As the crowd rushed to the buffet, and the celebration was immersed in smacking, tasting and shuffling noises, the oh so happy bride, still smiling, stood in a corner, took a cup of wine to ease her tense facial muscles, drank small sips, and watched as her husband, the beacon of her life, emptied a large cup with deep, thirsty gulps and refilled at once. Martinus was well on the way to stupor, and he had to be stopped at the right time. When Julia saw that her mother had the situation closely in view, she felt strangely calm, a feeling that she rarely felt regarding her mother.

Then a man in strange attire stood in front of her, bowed, raised his cup in greeting, and said in unformed Latin, "I congratulate you on your marriage and bring you the best wishes of the Master Militium. The noble Rheinberg must unfortunately apologize because he travels in important affairs of state to Treveri."

Julia returned the bow. The man was one of the time wanderers, who had also been invited to this festivity. Senator Michellus belonged, beside Symmachus, to the closest allies of the Germans in the Roman Senate, and Rheinberg was known personally to him. It was certainly the least that the new Supreme Commander had sent a deputy.

The man bowed again. “I haven’t introduced myself. I’m Lieutenant Joergensen of the *Saravica*. Always at your service.”

Julia smiled, this time quite by heart, and glanced left and right. No one of significance was in earshot. “Say, Lieutenant, are you aware where your deserter has vanished to?”

The young man grimaced for a split second before covering his expressions with a mask of politeness. “Who are you referring to exactly, Julia? Unfortunately, we had quite a few lately, our former first officer among them.”

“Yes, a shame, and how good things didn’t turn out worse. No, I mean that young ensign … that’s the right word, right? … the man, because of whom my parents hurried me to marry me this one over there.” Julia remained of perfect courtesy and showed no bitterness. It was also the lack of understanding on the side of Rheinberg that had led to this escalation. She hoped to be able to properly control her emotions. Joergensen, however, was less controlled. When she asked her question, a shadow had fallen over his eyes. He was not even angry or upset like when he had mentioned von Klasewitz. For Julia, it seemed as if the officer was a bit more … sad.

An interesting discovery.

“We haven’t heard of him,” the man finally said after some hesitation. “He’s disappeared from our view.”

“But you’re still looking for him?”

Joergensen shrugged. “The Roman administration was instructed to look for him, but one man in the Empire … it will probably be a coincidence if we find him.”

Julia frowned. “But you also seem not to put too much emphasis on the search.”

“That’s not entirely wrong,” the German admitted. “Thomas Volkert has made a mistake, but he’s young and maybe a little impetuous. Now as I see you as a radiant bride before me, I can understand that certain feelings can cloud one’s judgment.”

Julia offered him a beaming smile for the compliment. She wanted him to go on.

“Captain – pardon, *Magister Militium* – Rheinberg lost men during the mutiny, and although our efforts are progressing in regard to the training of Roman sailors, we need every experienced man. Nevertheless, desertion is a very serious offense. We cannot just ignore it. And on the Roman side … it's clear to us that an overly rapid pardon of Volkert would also be politically inopportune. Clear rules have to be enforced, especially considering the fact that he wanted to kidnap a senator's daughter."

A unique interpretation of reality, Julia thought to herself but kept her smile. In doing so she was by now very proficient.

"… So we hope that, as we say, grass will grow over the matter. But the fact is that he is now in danger of being found and executed by the Roman authorities. Rheinberg is quite prepared to consider clemency, but on the other side circumstances require from him to set an example, showing that he treats his own people like any Roman soldier. Something we cannot change until further notice. And therefore … Thomas … well …" Joergensen hesitated, as if struggling for words. "… might try to contact you. Should he do that, he should be informed that he currently can't hope for mercy. He has to keep hiding. However, I think he's probably punished enough by this marriage, if you allow me this remark."

Julia held steadfastly to her smile, even if now it threatened to become sour. But the man was of course quite right. This marriage was a punishment for Volkert and for herself. And for that reason alone, it wouldn't last. "I'll remember that and should he actually contact me, I will certainly convey the message to him," she said softly. "He is a reasonable man and will make the right decision."

If Joergensen wasn't sure how he had to interpret this response, he kept his discomfort for himself. He chatted for a few minutes over trivialities, but by then a queue of other guests who also wanted to pay the bride their respects had formed in a polite distance. Joergensen said goodbye, as obviously his message had been received, undoubtedly the ultimate reason why he had been sent to this celebration, and disappeared into the crowd.

Julia didn't expect him to remain for a long time. She could have told him that she had a pretty good idea where Volkert was staying and that the Roman authorities would probably be able to find out where he was, if they were seriously looking for him. But for now Volkert remained in a no man's land, not pardoned, threatened by death, but also not so high on the priority list that he was in imminent danger. She also could have told the officer that she would leave shortly after the end of the celebrations with her husband to a prolonged honeymoon, to Noricum, a place she "had always wanted to visit." Because Volkert was there.

Finally, she would devise a plan to flee with him and to have the kind of union she really dreamed of.

This time Julia was better prepared. A casket with golden coins and trinkets she had already set aside. They wouldn't suffer.

Then she turned to the next guest, an elderly matron, friend of her mother, and like her a champion of old Roman customs. She was pleased with Julia's wedding as much as Lucia, and that alone was reason enough to dislike her profoundly.

"My love! How adorable! How charming! How ..."

How terrible.

Julia smiled.

8

"The Emperor is waiting for you!"

Should the servant have had any opinion about the upstart who had acquired the right to join and leave the court as he wished, and whose origin was at least doubtful, then he kept it for himself. His expression was clearly laid out as a perfect mask of strict homage, and his movements were completely rehearsed, from the bow to the indication toward the wide wooden door, behind which the current chambers of the Emperor were situated. Rheinberg knew Trier was indeed capital of the Empire, but that was a quite vague concept. Capital was where the emperor was. And since a Roman emperor as a rule governed from the front, the official name of the capital was, if not irrelevant, quite secondary. Nevertheless, there had to be a place for the imperial administration to reside, at least that part which didn't travel along once the emperor moved his army, and at this time it was Trier. There were already plans to relocate headquarters to Ravenna, certainly in the historical development Rheinberg was aware of. In fact, there was an argument to actually implement these plans, especially now that Gratian was ruler of the entire Empire and not only the West.

Rheinberg followed the path pointed out to him, and entered the room he now knew quite well. It resembled a study. The young Emperor, who had been sitting behind a large, marble desk and signed papers, rose at once as Rheinberg came in, and smiled pleased. He wasn't alone. Captain von Geeren was also present; he had apparently been waiting on a sofa, a cup of wine in his hand. He, too, came immediately to his feet when the servant ushered in Rheinberg. Also, Elevius was present, the personal servant of the Emperor, who cared for him since childhood and shared, as Rheinberg knew,

Gratian's secrets. The old man poured hot wine into a cup, as the captain of the *Saarbrücken* stepped closer, and handed it over with a slight bow.

"The trip was uneventful, I hope?" Gratian opened the conversation, after they had made their welcome. "The roads are safe?"

"As safe as one would expect if accompanied by forty cavalrymen," Rheinberg said, smiling. "But in general, the situation is not bad. Even the Sarmatians are holding back, as I heard. The news of the victory at Thessaloniki seems to have duly impressed many barbarians and their leaders to prefer waiting a bit."

"Let's sit down!"

The men took place, and in the first few minutes the conversation turned to vanities. Rheinberg felt relaxed. The warm wine certainly made his contribution, but he came more and more to the belief that one could work well with the young Emperor. He still had something fickle and jumpy to him and sometimes seemed to have difficulties to hold to an opinion, but now that he managed the entire Empire, the increased responsibility had a positive effect on him. The fact that he had an advisor like Rheinberg who tried to confront the Emperor with the potential realities of history in all their brutality certainly had an impact as well.

Gratian took a long look at Rheinberg before speaking. "General, your reforms get me in trouble."

Rheinberg nodded. He knew that at this point no comment was expected from his side.

"First, there are the decisions regarding religion. I almost think those are the most harmless. I get support from those with whom I have the least trouble anyway: Symmachus and the group of traditionalists who still cling to the old cults. The confirmation of the Edict has played into their hands. Even the reduction of alimony for temples and priests has been accepted grudgingly."

"That was the price they had to pay," Rheinberg interjected. "The powerful and richest of the ancient cults are going to establish an organization that raises funds for the supporters to sustain the temples. They have to organize themselves."

"It has, after all, helped me to reduce the innumerable exemptions from tax for church properties. We have agreed on reduced charges, more or less. Not all of them pay."

"Teething problems."

Gratian frowned. "Yes, perhaps. Hopefully. But the financial aspect is only one side of the issue. Christians rail against the confirmation of the Edict and the trinitarians against the recognition of the arians and vice versa. This makes them almost more angry than my tolerance to Jupiter, Hera and Venus."

"We have expected that. But it is still better than to prefer any side by the state and thus spending valuable resources on a conflict that doesn't help us in dealing with the actual problem."

"Yes," the Emperor said. He sounded convinced enough, but Rheinberg knew what he had to overcome. Gratian had been brought up as a very devout trinitarian. It was hard to jump over one's own shadow.

"Then the whole tax reform," the Emperor complained. "The elimination of numerous tax privileges. That was a howl. There is still howling. The administration moans. I don't even know how to collect the entire tax properly!"

"For this, however, the tax rates were lowered," Rheinberg added. "More people must now pay, but individually less."

"That would be okay for many traders or craftsmen, but all those who were previously exempted? I have to struggle with some powerful men here, Rheinberg."

"I understand." Rheinberg tried to put a certain amount of sympathy in his voice. In fact, the reforms weren't even sufficient in his eyes, how radical they may appear to some. "But it's about the very survival of the Empire."

Gratian nodded thoughtfully. He sighed, then continued.

"The abolishment of the obligation to choose only the profession of one's father has caused little outcry. The conversion of guilds and other associations in purely voluntary associations has been more difficult. But I had the feeling that a lot of those affected saw it as a liberation. It increases the competition, because the professions are now keen to attract the best talent."

"That's good and as intended," Rheinberg said. "We need quality, especially if we want to introduce technical innovations throughout the Empire."

Gratian scratched his head. "The biggest chunk, however, is the administration of slavery. A regular fee to be paid for each adult slave in private property, a one-time charge for each infant born into slavery and a tax credit for anyone who has released slaves into freedom. A sales tax of twenty percent on the slave trade." He fixed Rheinberg with his eyes. "We both know that this is tantamount, Rheinberg. I am a Christian and have a very fundamental problem with slavery. We seem to share this proviso. The law will make slavery very expensive – more expensive than free and salaried labor, because in addition to the fees the owner has to provide food and shelter."

"Slavery is an important factor inhibiting the progress of Rome!" Rheinberg repeated an old argument, with which he had convinced Gratian of the new tax system. "If an economic system can rely on a cheap and large workforce, it doesn't have to trouble itself with inventing new technologies that improve, simplify and speed up production. And if we want to export our new innovations from the future through the width of the Empire, people won't accept it. They will say, 'Why all this? Slaves can do that! There are enough of them!' Remember the outcry we had at Thessaloniki once we entered into a settlement agreement with the Goths rather than to subjugate 50,000 new slaves! So there is certainly a moral argument, but there is also an economic one. Imperator, we need to abolish slavery in order to make Rome stronger!"

"I know, I know," Gratian said. "But probably I have to be convinced repeatedly. Half the Senate cursed me because of this thing. All the big landowners!"

"Tell them that every freedman is a potential recruit for the legions," suggested Rheinberg. "Slaves cannot be soldiers, and we need soldiers. If we set the slaves free, some might feel the call of the arms themselves. Especially now that we have changed the pay structure – and not touched the tax privileges of veterans."

Acute shortages of soldiers in the armed forces and the massive difficulties in finding volunteers for military service were the biggest challenges Rheinberg had faced after his appointment as commander-in-chief. Rapid reforms had been necessary – but a colossus like the Roman Empire moved only very slowly.

That was Gratian's problem. In the original timeline, he had died because he had forgotten what it meant to be an emperor. The endless hunting trips with his Alanian riders, neglecting the needs of the armed forces and the fact that he couldn't meet the high expectations invested in the son of the great Valentinian. The arrival of the time travelers and the confrontation with this fate had triggered a profound transformation process in Gratian. Now he wanted to be an emperor and to take care of the right things, make good decisions and ensure that his realm held together. But ironically, this new determination made his situation more and more uncertain.

Rheinberg's goal had been to prevent the long civil war that followed the death of Gratian and to prepare for the onslaught of the Huns and all those peoples who were pushed away in their wake. But now it looked as if the internal resistance in the Empire became so strong that an explosion was almost impossible to avoid. The captain had to admit that it wasn't easy to do things and to communicate them properly, especially if you didn't understand how the very people you tried to help thought and felt. Rheinberg had to consider that, despite his personal feelings, the question about the nature of Jesus Christ, whether he was mortal son of God or God himself, did entice the fervor of Romans and drove them to fanatical action and thought. But this wasn't his time, and he fought every day to understand how everything that seemed to him so obvious from the study of history, was in reality so different, and could prove to be a serious challenge.

Sometimes he wanted to despair. But he had chosen this path, and many people believed in his vision of a better, a victorious and an Empire based on a solid foundation. There were not too many, but the number grew, and the influx of curious, adventurous young people as well as accomplished scholars to the "German village" near Ravenna also spoke that there was a potential with which one could work.

He didn't add anything for while, and Gratian looked at him quizzically.

Rheinberg smiled weakly. "I was thinking," he apologized.

"I find myself doing that a lot lately. I don't always come to a conclusion."

"I wish I had a solution for everything. But I can act only on the basis of what I know. We must try to set a new course."

"And hope that the ship is not too decayed and will still be able to reach port," Gratian completed the analogy. Dealing with Rheinberg had helped him to a dry humor, which he had never shown so openly. Not every member of the extensive court had been too happy about it.

"We will now pull the troops together we'll send to explore the exact location of the Huns," Rheinberg said, switching to the most important issue. "We improve the weapons and the training of the legions and renew the fortifications, especially along the expected route of invasion. And if we do get some time, only a year or two, then we can march a new type of legion to the east and stop the Huns before they get anywhere near the frontiers. No later than then, Your Majesty, we can completely focus on the renewal of the Empire as well as the solution of ecclesiastical conflicts. Then it will be possible for broad sections of the people, commerce and trade, to benefit from the technical innovations we have to offer."

Gratian nodded. "If we have this time, I'll be happy. But although Maximus as well as other potential troublemakers behave very quiet and I have dealt with the details of your future knowledge in strict confidence, I'm afraid that I must either take immediate action against a potential traitor, or this kind of dissatisfaction will nevertheless lead to revolt and rebellion."

"We cannot arrest Maximus only because he might be a rebel in the future," Rheinberg said. "That would be a witch hunt and will cause constant fear among all notables and military. Arbitrariness would be dangerous, because with our knowledge of the future, any measure could be justified. No, we must continue to do everything possible in oder to act according to law and order. Maximus is a loyal and capable commander of troops in Britain, and before we don't gather any hard evidence that he is already planning the usurpation, we need to leave him alone."

"Yes, that may be. I'm just afraid that once we know with certainty, the rebellious soldiers will already be on our doorstep."

Rheinberg sighed. "Then we have to be prepared for that eventuality as best as we can."

It was obvious that Gratian didn't like that answer. He, however, seemed to be willing to accept Rheinberg's argument, at least for the moment. Rheinberg knew it was boiling among the "insiders". There were some who didn't want to wait longer, willing to march with open eyes into a potential disaster. Von Geeren had reported the same and he was aware that he did walk on a tightrope. It all depended on to what extent Gratian was ready to hold back, and hoping that his authority was big enough to encourage his men to do the same.

Gratian nodded. "And the new ship, the *Valentinian*, will leave for Egypt?"

Rheinberg was grateful for the change of subject. As always, if there was much to do, the conversation quickly grew tiring. He was a naval officer, not a politician. And von Geeren, sitting quietly, was no help. "Yes, I'm assuming that it has already put to sea," he said. "The expedition will not only help to demonstrate the new naval capabilities of Rome in the Mediterranean but also establish important economic connections."

Gratian proffered a weak smile. "Now, with the new ... what's the stuff? Spirits? ... you already had a great success. Your men have sold the technology all over the Empire. Rome is drunk."

"Rome was already drunk, only this time it's faster," Rheinberg corrected, also smiling.

"I want to reiterate that the idea of the alcohol monopoly is still on the table," the Emperor reminded him.

"I already have communicated this to my men very gently. Both are willing to concentrate, at least for a start, on their newly acquired Taverna, mainly because they have no time for great commitment on business matters. Both will participate on the trip with the

Valentinian to Aksum. I think that we can agree on this: A percentage of the revenue from the monopoly goes directly into our research and training center in order to secure an income and to relieve the general state budget. Then it should be no problem if Rome will help replenish the budget with the help of the drunk."

Gratian nodded.

"What my people are now looking for will help the drunk to become sober," Rheinberg added, again smiling. "The trip to Aksum is of great importance."

"Then I'm curious. Coffee you call it?"

"Yes, and it's very versatile. Most importantly, it is served as brew with hot water. Depending on your taste, milk or sugar can be added. Very invigorating. We miss it badly because our own stocks are already depleted. When brandy was a success, coffee will be a sensation. And if we do it as we have discussed it – set up a strict state monopoly for an inaugural period – then the gold coins will just be flowing into the treasury. It will take a while, but I'm firmly convinced of it. And not even our worst critics are able to say no to a cup of coffee."

"That is, after all, a good prospect," Gratian said. He spoke in a silent, withdrawn tone.

Rheinberg took a deep breath. "Your Majesty, Rome has indeed a good future," he said firmly. "We are facing major challenges, but don't you notice the difference? Not so long ago you have only sensed the great dangers and the impending doom without clear knowledge! But now we know where we want to go and what we must do. There'll be stumbling blocks on this path, I have no doubt. We'll even occasionally fall down and get bloody knees – but we are in a unique position that'll give us a lot of strength and the power to face all challenges. A secure Empire that prospers economically. An Empire in which there is inner peace. An Empire that earns the respect of its neighbors and that fears no one. An Empire that is driven to new heights by new technologies and scientific innovation. And all this, Your Majesty, will be inextricably linked to your name. Please don't lose sight of that prospect. It's always the ruler who will be praised and remembered first."

Gratian's smile widened. "Don't underestimate your part in it. The mere fact of time travel will make you and your ship immortal."

"We didn't do it on purpose. We are victims of a fateful event. We have searched the sea thoroughly for similar signs, reached the point at which we have arrived, over and over again. For all of us, it is clear that the process doesn't seem to repeat itself. It is not influenced by us, and its origin remains a mystery. This historic event will surely stay in everyone's consciousness forever, yes. But what we – what you – will make of it, that is of real historical significance!"

Gratian nodded, as if to confirm this to himself. Elevius, who had silently stood on the side, handed him a new cup of wine. "Let us dedicate ourselves to the details now," the young Emperor finally said, pointing to a series of documentary records. "We've got a tiring afternoon ahead of us."

And so it was.

9

"The ship looks totally like shit!"

The fact that seaman Hannes Weinkamp uttered this sentence with a proud tone stopped Köhler in his impulse to tell him his opinion. Since his statement was also made in German, so that the Roman crew of the *Valentinian* perceived only the tone and the satisfied smile Weinkamp's, there was no apparent need to reprimand him.

In addition, Köhler wasn't hardly in any position to contradict the four sailors of the *Saarbrücken* who he took on the maiden voyage of the steam sailing ship. No one aboard the *Saarbrücken* was an expert in ship design – especially not in regard to steam-sailors made of wood. The *Valentinian* was a mixture of theory from books and the shipbuilding experience of Roman shipyards. The carpenters there knew exactly how to built a trireme or any of the large freighters, with which the grain from Egypt was taken to Italy. They could also build smaller sailboats, fishing boats or coastal vessels that transported the news and some freight from seaport to seaport. The idea of the time-travelers building a modern sailing ship that combined the advantages of a schooner or brig of the 19th century with the independence of a steamer had been a challenge to implement. Since it had been under time pressure, some kind of compromise had emerged – a slightly slimmer traditional freighter with new rigging, two masts, pre- and main sails, as they were actually much later used in the time of the caravels, with a keel that made the ship more seaworthy, and a high rail to resist the Mediterranean storms – and a compartment containing a steam engine made of bronze and iron. It was the first of its kind put into service in the Roman navy, fired with charcoal. Stoker Karl Forstmann, a silent, lanky man of Dahms's staff, had been assigned to take care of it. He had accepted the work in a laconic and taciturn approach, but left no doubt that he considered the investment into steam engines made from bronze as premature and ultimately dangerous. He not only made sure from the beginning that the "engine room" had more than enough water at the ready in case of a fire, but looked visibly pleased that the *Valentinian* would start its journey under sails. Even in ideal conditions, the steam engine would accelerate the Roman warship with its simple propeller not faster than to 6 to 7 knots. That might prove useful in the case of adverse winds, but it wasn't a great speed advantage over other ships.

Köhler's searching glance slid off the high, iron chimney sticking out of the afterdeck down to the two bombards, which were lashed right and left on the middle deck. These were the very first cannons from Dahms's armory, far removed from the steel guns of which the engineer dreamed. As a direct way to that goal, they had preferred bombards to the originally planned steam catapults, which had been removed accordingly. While stoker Forstmann was already confident of his machine, the crude condition of the two guns had shocked Hannes Weinkamp. They had no rifled barrel, although the barrels had been poured with the utmost care and were certainly no worse than the guns with which battles of the Thirty Years War had been fought. They fired no bullets, but a kind of iron shot, pressed together in thin cloth sacks. The bombards were not supposed to sink ships but to ward off pirates or other enemies by mowing them down and then to disturb grappling attempts. Weinkamp had fired some test shots causing both enthusiastic and frightened sympathy by the Roman crew and had been able to discover that aiming and hitting constituted too difficult to target properly. But as the guns rang loud and smoked properly, the psychological effect on potential opponents wasn't easily dismissed.

All in all, the *Valentinian* was a ship that had been built as efficiently as possible in the short time available. This didn't make the new pride of the Roman fleet pleasant to look at – Weinkamp wasn't wrong in his judgment, at least from a purely aesthetic point of view – but hopefully, it would be so impressive that the littoral of the Mediterranean would realize that, in a figurative sense, a fresh wind blew. Even if it consisted of the smelly exhaust of a steam engine.

"Weinkamp, control yourself! We're being watched," Köhler said. Indeed, the harbor was full of onlookers and on a wooden grandstand, sheltered by a canopy, sat notables of the Empire. Naval officers, the Prefect Renna, a good friend of the Germans, high city officials, and some senators. A group of musicians played on, and servants offered snacks; it was almost like a carnival. With so many spectators, the start of *Valentinian*'s voyage was not allowed to have any blemish, and the hope in that regard was mainly directed below deck, where the crew had started to fire the steam engine for a good half hour, and now, at least, some smoke was visible. Given the fact that today was an overcast winter day, windless, with gentle rain, the new technology was particularly important, because otherwise the ship would have to be rowed out to sea by the waiting triremes.

And that would guarantee a good number of sneers from those who had always known that this was insane.

Aurelius Africanus, officially the captain of *Valentinian*, felt itchy. His years of seafaring experience didn't help much because this ship was unusual for him. There had been a few shipyard sea trials that the Trierarch had embarked on to familiarize himself with the seaworthiness of this unusual construction, but it was this maiden voyage on which the ship and hence the commander had to prove themselves for the first time.

Africanus could rely on Köhler's support, as the NCO held the exalted post of first officer. Nevertheless, the German was not allowed to put himself too much on display, for that would probably undermine Africanus's authority. It had been a conscious decision to make a Roman captain of the new ship. The inferiority complex of those who realized how far the technological development of the time-travelers was ahead of the Empire had to be actively attacked so that the Germans and their role found widespread acceptance. Africanus was the representative of all the Roman navy captains, and great expectations had been laid on his shoulders. Everyone who knew him was aware of this pressure, saw immediately that something was bothering him deep under his seemingly self-controlled appearance. Köhler wasn't irritated. He had always been of the opinion that a good officer needed some solid acting talent, as he had to manage to instill confidence and stamina in the crew even under adverse circumstances. Merely leaving the port with no wind should belong to the smaller exercises.

"Cast off!" Africanus bellowed hoarsely.

"Ropes are free!" a polyphonic answer came both from the pier as well as the crew of the ship. With a barely perceptible movement, the steamboat left the wall. Köhler kept a close eye on the process but saw no reason to intervene.

Africanus sighed, heard only by those who stood with him on the upper deck. The old *gubernator* of Africanus' sunken trireme was also responsible for the steering of this ship and had become familiar with the far more comfortable mechanism. The Trierarch pulled the mouthpiece of the communication tube toward his mouth, blew through and ordered: "Engine – quarter speed ahead!"

Köhler could imagine how Forstmann grimaced. Quarter speed with a bronze steam engine that couldn't build up proper pressure was a ridiculously low acceleration.

But the stoker obeyed the command without further grumbling. The steam rose rhythmically from the chimney, and the upper deck, located right above the plant, began to shake gently with the movement of the drive shaft. Köhler closed his eyes and felt how the steamboat began to gather its strength.

The *Valentinian* awoke.

Meanwhile, the crew had pushed the ship with long sticks away from the harbor wall. The helmsman didn't need any instructions to do his job. He spun the wheel once he felt, just like Köhler, that the ship began to respond to the rudder. The bow of the steamer swung toward the center of the dock. The ship slid gently through the smooth water.

Viewers watched the process with reverent silence. Even the musicians had stopped playing. The notables had risen from their seats under the canopy. Some of them had already seen the *Saarbrücken* in action, but this was something special. No marvel of an abstract, distant time, but the work of Roman naval workmanship – with some help, yes, but a ship they could understand more easily than the metal colossus of the light cruiser.

This ship really belonged to them. A Roman, one of theirs, was in command, and another one steered it. That it was a German mechanic who made sure that inside the ship the steam engine worked properly couldn't be seen and was properly hidden from many onlookers. Köhler allowed himself a smile. Rheinberg's decision to allow the *Valentinian*'s immediate passage with a predominantly Roman crew and Africanus as a commander had been spot on. The spectators on the walls of the harbor radiated pride and admiration, where they had been looking at the *Saarbrücken* rather with fear and intimidation.

Triremes and small sailing-boats swarmed the *Valentinian*, escorted the ship from the dock and gave her an escort. Colorful flags and pennants hung from the poles and on the ropes, people waved enthusiastically. Köhler heard a joyful cry, and he looked at the young Marcellus, the first Roman member of the *Saarbrücken*'s crew, who excitedly stood at the rail and bounced on his toes while he waved vigorously. Köhler took a step forward and realized that among the many ships that accompanied the *Valentinian* was also the fishing boat of Marcellus' father, who had given his son with obvious pride in the care of Chief Engineer Dahms to become more than a fisherman. Dahms took the job very seriously, and the almost 13-year-old boy had begun to moan quickly about the intensity of lessons. But since he had become something like a ship's mascot, not least because of the role he had played in the failed mutiny, he had been selected for his first real assignment. His first big trip as an assistant to Forstmann was a reward and a test at the same time. Dahms had actually slightly moist eyes after he had agreed that Marcellus was allowed to go on board. Of course, this was only due to eye irritation, as he had assured everyone. No one had believed him.

Dahms had left a family behind, a wife and a son he would probably never see again, living in the distant future. Everyone knew that he treated young Marcellus with the benevolent sincerity of a father and less with the ruthless discipline of a superior, and no one had ever scolded him for that.

Köhler had to promise twice to take care of Marcellus. It was clear that he would remain on board the steamer and wouldn't join them to Aksum, although the boy still hoped otherwise. Dahms himself had given him multiple warnings along the way, and the small bag that he had given him to bring his belongings on board was a gift. Marcellus had received it with obvious pride. The chief engineer of the *Saarbrücken* had added a number of exquisite Roman sweets to it, something Marcellus would probably only notice once he opened the bag on board. No, this was far removed from the strict discipline of a supervisor and instructor. But Köhler enjoyed these small gestures that warmed his heart, like a few days ago, when they had given the assembled slaves in the tavern their freedom, an enterprise whose shares Behrens and he had bought and taken full control before their departure. All former slaves had received an offer of paid employment. Everyone had accepted.

There had been wet eyes. Köhler felt that things changed, and that he could achieve more than he could have ever imagined in his life. He touched the lives of many people and did things differently. Better. Just as Dahms had touched the lives of fisher-boy Marcellus, who was jumping up and down at the railing and waving to his father, bursting with pride.

He would take care of him, he promised Dahms in silence for a third time.

"Full speed ahead!" Africanus ordered, and Köhler could imagine vividly how stoker Forstmann heartily laughed in the belly of the *Valentinian*. But the man did his duty, increased the pressure, and the pounding noise of the machine became clearly audible through the wooden planks. The light breeze that had started wasn't sufficient for the sailing boats to keep up with the steamer, and Köhler heard the noise from the two Roman triremes as they were dipping the oars into the water, trying to match the speed of the steamboat.

Africanus waved from his position beside the helmsman at the triremes. For a short time, the rowers could keep the acceleration with their experienced, muscular movements, especially now that the sea was as smooth as glass. But it took only another five minutes until the trierarchs decided to let the oarsmen rest, and the triremes disappeared slowly out of sight to the *Valentinian*'s rear. Finally, they turned away to return to port. If anything proved the superiority of even such a crude steam engine, then it was this maneuver, and the returnees would report in Ravenna how the new Roman warship reliantly entered the open sea, without sail or oars, and increasingly far from the coast, like no trierarch who was of his right mind would dare. It was a new quality of seafaring, there was no doubt. Köhler smiled contentedly, and his eyes met with Africanus, discerning an enthusiastic glimmer. The other Roman crewmen aboard quacked like little girls, beating themselves on their shoulders, and joking in their excited and boisterous state. Africanus apparently didn't intend to that, and there was no need for it anyway. The hazy but quiet morning didn't offer any further challenges in store, and the *Valentinian* now headed westward, directly to Alexandria. The large, round compass was the birthday gift of the *Saarbrücken*, although the men of Dahms were already busy manufacturing similar equipment. But the chief engineer had personally taken the device, covered by a sheet of glass and installed it next to the big steering-wheel. In addition, quite accurate maps were available, Roman as well as copies of the German ones, as well as a spare sextant from the light cruiser. Dahms had it placed on his list of priorities to manufacture sextants with and had been happy to learn that the quality of Roman ironwork was quite sufficient to provide what was desired, once one had told the craftsmen what was expected of them. But the production had just started, so their instrument had been plundered from the inventories of the light cruiser.

The haze lifted, and a radiant but unfortunately not too warm winter sun blazed. As the sea roughened up, the *Valentinian* moved stronger, but held up well in the water. Köhler nodded toward Africanus.

"We should relieve Forstmann of his misery," he said to the commander. "Ten minutes at full power and he surely fears for his life."

Africanus grinned and gave the order to reduce the machine to half speed. Forstmann's confirmation came suspiciously quickly and held undoubtedly a relieved tone.

"We start with the maneuvers!" Africanus ordered. "We need to know what this ship can do!" He fixed Sepidus, the old gubernator with the weathered face, clutching the steering wheel with almost childlike enthusiasm and looking back at him expectantly. "Toward starboard, and hardly!"

Sepidus let the wheel twirl. The steamboat creaked. Africanus really wanted to test its limits.

"Oh shit!" Weinkamp muttered.

10

Freiherr von Klasewitz groaned ostentatiously. The foreman, nominally head of the factory, looked at him with a steady gaze. Certainly, the time traveler was in his right to give him orders, and he was therefore willing to endure a certain amount of moodiness. But this on one side so knowledgeable, on the other side quite unbearable man strained his patience and his nerves to extremes. The Roman was convinced that they would come to the expected results more quickly if that man would keep his distance and let him do his work. He had even toyed with the idea of complaining to Maximus about the German, but the Comes seemed to think the world of the stranger. And he didn't want to offend Maximus, as sincere admiration was all the foreman felt for him – the leader who was responsible for all of their future, the one to become emperor. So he had no choice but to endure von Klasewitz and his moods.

And he actually learned a lot once you put all the tirades, unjust rage, and arrogant remarks aside. The science that the nobleman called "ballistics" he found particularly fascinating. Not that it was too strange for him – the foreman was very experienced in building catapults, onagers and other long-range weapons for many years – but the manner in how von Klasewitz described new materials, new manufacturing techniques, and how to properly calculate their operation, all linked to each other, and were indeed thrilling.

Very promising also. If they would only succeed in their plan that at least one of the pieces could shoot without breaking into parts or cracking and could fire a shot with some accuracy. The foreman, Bulbius by name, had to admit that there was still room for improvement with respect to these aspects.

That von Klasewitz called him and his men repeatedly barbaric, incompetent morons, however, didn't particularly help with the needed development.

The nobleman had clearly not improved his personal skills during the last weeks. On the contrary. For him, based on his viewpoint, this was all beneath him. A necessary evil, a duty he had to fulfill to achieve a higher goal.

He stared at the gun barrel, a compact, elongated form of good five feet in length, made of cast bronze. While the Empire still had difficulties building a suitable furnace for steelmaking, it was known to von Klasewitz that Dahms and his men had already proceeded relatively far, and the production of iron and the first puddle furnace would soon begin operation. For von Klasewitz, these challenges were so much higher. He could not utilize the diverse skills and resources of the crew of the light cruiser. The ensign who had escaped with him had been given another task. Von Klasewitz was quite knowledgable as an artillery officer, with expertise in ballistics and the technical parameters of modern naval guns. But everything else, especially the production of the guns and the necessary tools and skills he had to painstakingly piece together from his memory, and often even that wasn't sufficient.

The gun barrel in front of him was telling example of his dilemma. The fine, barely visible hairline crack would be fatal when firing the first shot and would tear the metal, making the cannon already now totally useless.

"Melt it down," he said hoarsely. "Melt it down and repeat!"

The foreman bowed his head. He found that his men were making progress. The last two attempts before had been complete failures, where everyone realized at first glance that the experiment had failed. With this one they had to do further examination and for a while even assumed that they had been able to produce a working cannon. But the nobleman was apparently in no mood to acknowledge this progress and to praise anyone for it.

Actually, he was never in the mood to do that.

Bulbius nodded again and turned without a word. He let von Klasewitz alone, immersed himself in the hot and noisy factory floor of this top-secret facility near London, to do exactly what he had been assigned to. It took a minute, then three strong workers came and rolled away the useless pipe under the scowl of the nobleman on a handcart, directly to the oven, to be melted down. The fact that they were in a hurry, because the artillery was supposed to be ready for the big attack, was something they were all well aware of. Nobody wanted to disappoint the Comes.

Von Klasewitz turned away, climbed a wooden staircase at the edge of the factory floor, and entered the study he had set up. It consisted of two rooms, separated by a wooden wall – a combined work room and meeting room in which he tried to produce meaningful design drawings, and a living room, which, on his insistence, had its own small latrine. The notion to have contact with hundreds of talkative Roman workers using the big facility just outside the factory had instilled horror in the nobleman.

He longingly glanced at the door to the living room, which he had, as far as it was possible, tastefully decorated, with thick carpets, some statuettes, a large fireplace, several couches, and of course a wide bed, covered with skins and blankets. He enjoyed that luxury, which in some ways surpassed even the way of life on board of the *Saarbrücken*. And unlike Rheinberg and his followers, he was also of the opinion that to abolish slavery wasn't that urgent. The fact that Maximus himself had graced him with two Scythian girls, just 16 years old, to fulfill uncomplainingly their role as servants and playmates, had convinced Klasewitz of the fact that there were simply some people who had to be served, and those who were born to serve. What else should these illiterate creatures, conversing in a strange gibberish, do with their lives? The face of the man showed a glimpse of anticipation. Currently, the slaves were held in the appropriate quarters. The workers on the factory floor were almost all free men, many of them soldiers, and only simple, manual labor was left to the few slaves. The other work, cooking, washing clothes and, as von Klasewitz relished, the more relaxing moments were reserved for slaves. He was aware that even formerly convinced Roman slave owners, inspired by Christianity, started to reject the use of female slaves for carnal appetites and held morality very high. But von Klasewitz, despite the fact that he surely supported the unity of the Church and the elimination of apostates, allowed himself a certain amount of liberal attitudes. This was booty from Roman attacks beyond Hadrian's Wall. In the end, the barbarians were little more than animals and would never play a role anywhere in the world.

So being engrossed in these thoughts, he had at first completely overlooked the figure who sat in a chair in front of his desk. A man who rose now and unfolded to considerable size. Maximus, the Comes, had come to see himself how things progressed. Von Klasewitz straightened. He wasn't always sure how he should behave in the presence of the future emperor. The Comes was an important, influential man, and he was the one to whom von Klasewitz had to be thankful for his position. But he also was, in his eyes, not more than many others in this time: barbaric savages who didn't deserve to benefit from his knowledge.

But well considered … an interesting train of thoughts unfolded suddenly in the consciousness of the nobleman. He paused imperceptibly, gave Maximus a noncommittal smile. His gaze went for a moment into the void.

If events moved the right way, they should actually let him, von Klasewitz, as the superior mind from a superior time, take command and initiative. The nobleman had to concede that this was currently unlikely. Nevertheless, deep in his heart he knew that ultimately only things could go well if he took the lead, and in these days that could only mean …

Von Klasewitz breathed heavily, ignoring the questioning look of the Comes.

It could only mean, yes, ultimately, that he wore the purple himself. This idea, so inappropriate and unreasonable, appeared in view of the presence of another man who currently had much greater chances to gain this office, but he forced him to think in sudden clarity. He smiled broadly, and although Maximus clearly interpreted that smile as directed toward him, he would have reacted angrily if he had guessed the real reason for the nobleman's joy. The German exilant, here, at this moment, in a room of a factory building near London, no more than a glorified engineer with dubious success, suddenly felt that he was planning the right steps and everything seemed to make sense, to become the logic of his existence. Ultimately, the failed mutiny had been a good thing, he thought as he reached for Maximus's arm in greeting. Having failed as captain of the *Saarbrücken*, he would succeed triumphantly as Emperor of Rome, someone before who Rheinberg would bend his knee.

The smile of the baron widened.

"Good progress?" Maximus's question interrupted his thoughts.

He composed himself quickly. Now that he knew where his fate should lead him to, any kindness, yes subservience wasn't incompatible with his zeal, but only necessary means to an end. Servility, tended by determination. "Progress, yes, but we are still behind schedule," he said. Some time ago the former officer had learned that it made little sense to lie to Maximus. The general was a man who had many confidants, people who were devoted to him unconditionally. He was always well informed about everything. Probably the reports sent to him by von Klasewitz now and then were largely superfluous. Maximus knew about all the details of their work.

"The cannon I saw looked quite good," the Comes remarked. He had the scene on the factory floor undoubtedly regarded through the windows of the study, which allowed a generous view of the events in the hall.

"It was a step in the right direction but unfortunately still unusable. A fine crack. The first firing would have burst it and probably injured, if not killed, the operating crew. But we are getting closer."

"The guns are an important part of our plan," Maximus reminded him.

"I know that."

"I'm counting on your success."

"You may depend on me."

Maximus' expression didn't indicate whether he gave faith to this assurance or not. "We need twenty pieces, at least," he insisted.

Von Klasewitz didn't flinch. Not too long ago, other quantities had been discussed. Maximus seemed not to particularly care about yesterday's talk.

“Twenty then, with the necessary ammunition,” said von Klasewitz, trying to act as confidently as possible. In fact, the tactics of the insurgents depended decidedly on having not only numerical superiority in battle, but also to be able to use the power of artillery as effectively as possible.

“Thirty would be better,” continued Maximus.

“Thirty are possible, but not likely,” was the nobleman’s reply. It didn’t help to give to someone like the Comes promises he subsequently was unable to fulfill. The man seemed satisfied. He probably didn’t expect any different answer.

“What about the other weapons? What was the name – arquebuses? Hand grenades?”

Klasewitz nodded. “Yes. Simple guns that can be used by strong men. I still hope to be able to equip a centuria with these weapons, despite my misgivings. The progress here is encouraging. The production is simpler, because the load is not as strong. In addition, your efforts have meant that we now have a sufficient amount of gunpowder. Hand grenades are simple. We have designed a workable variant. We are able to produce several hundred, as long as we have enough gunpowder available.”

“That’s good news. It is a dangerous undertaking. Before long, these things can no longer be kept secret. Something will eventually seep through. Rome already looks suspiciously in my direction. I know that there are men at the court who are out to kill me, because they have learned about your history – my future. They don’t know that I took you in but are pretty convinced that what I have accomplished in your time might repeat itself. Certainly, some errors I won’t repeat. I have already directed things in ways that are different from what has happened in your version of the story.”

“You spoke of a second plan,” von Klasewitz remarked with curiosity.

“I have spoken of a complement to our military approach,” the Comes corrected. It seemed to amuse him to discuss these matters. “We cannot build solely on our military successes; we must strike elsewhere as well.”

"You don't want to tell me," von Klasewitz said and couldn't completely hide his disappointment. At the same time, this fact sparked anger in him. He didn't seem to belong to the inner circle of the conspiracy. That would change. Everything would change. Now he saw a clearly delineated path. Maximus liked to keep him at bay, but it was obvious that fate had some surprises in store.

Maximus patted von Klasewitz's shoulder with false camaraderie. "It's better if you don't know everything. Some things flourish more in secret. And in this matter, absolute secrecy is of great importance."

Freiherr von Klasewitz knew exactly how the Comes had meant that. Oh yeah, once a traitor, always a traitor, those were the unspoken words behind this joviality. He couldn't be trusted. Grim determination filled the German. Yes, he would prove to the Comes that he was certainly correct in his assessment. The purple would, if at all, only rest for a short time on his shoulders.

Von Klasewitz smiled and lowered his head submissively.

Now wasn't his time.

Maximus glanced at the drawings on the worktable.

"Explain to me again the principle of those guns the *Saarbrücken* has," he demanded. "I need to know what to expect in the worst case."

Klasewitz suppressed a sigh.

Now wasn't his time.

But soon. Soon enough.

11

It was a pleasure to see the suffering face of her husband. It was her revenge for the fact that he hadn't been drunk enough on their wedding night and she had to help out. A bitter and yet so sweet revenge. As the cart rumbled through a pothole and was shaken back and forth, Julia remained on her soft cushions well protected and comfortable. She had no eyes for the beautiful scenery, she stared solely on the slumped figure of Martinus Caius, who was sitting a few meters in front of her, the reins in his hand.

Julia had insisted.

The road was long, full of dangers.

And Martinus, son of a trader, was a man of experience, grew up on the streets and roads of the Empire. He had absorbed, with the milk of his mother's breasts, the sweat of the horses, the creaking of the axles, the curses of the muleteers. A man of the streets, a sage of the way, a hero of transportation. Julia had called him all this, with shiny eyes and adoring posturing, obviously to be seen by his father and mother, and unexpected, indeed incredulous pride had appeared on the face of the older Caius. So it was only logical, yes manly, that Martinus, the faithful husband of his lovely wife, while traveling toward their anticipated honeymoon, to take the reins into his own hands. For this, he had to sit on the hard wagon seat, and of course he wasn't allowed any wine – or worse, the new Germanic spirits. His eagle eye was on the way, his searching gaze looking for potential hazards, and all this for the protection and convenience of his, oh what a blessing, pregnant wife.

Julia reached into a bowl of fruit and shoved some grapes in her mouth. Somewhere in the Empire, any fruit always flourished, and the advantage of a marriage with the son of a rich man was that his father could easily procure all these delicacies. A slave who traveled in their cart gave Julia a cup of diluted wine. Outside, it was cool and getting colder the farther they advanced northwards. But Julia's cart, surrounded by a thick tarpaulin and padded with carpets, was relatively well-tempered.

Poor Martinus Caius, heroically suppressing his curses and his desire to warm up with a good drink, pulled his coat tighter around himself. Julia let fall the tarp so she could no longer scrutinize the sufferings of her husband, before it became too cold for her.

All of this would have been half as difficult for the younger Caius, if his father hadn't insisted that the other two carts, full of provisions, clothing and other essentials, should be headed by a highly experienced and familiar foreman from his staff. He would report any dereliction of duty by his son immediately to his boss, and Martinus Caius, quite pleased with the sudden, positive attention in the eyes of his father, would return to appear to be the old weakling.

No, Julia had half-approvingly, half-incredulously accepted that somewhere in her unloved husband some pride was left. Pride perhaps of his unborn son – of course, Julia "felt" it would be a boy – whose creation he found difficult to recall in all details. His wife had told him about his manhood in so many words, but he himself barely remembered that he probably undressed and had demanded the same of his wife, and afterwards ...

Julia remembered better. German spirits had their advantages. The drunken but horny Caius had needed no further exhortation than to drink a large glass of it. He was gasping asleep after a miserably failed attempt to entice the small Martinus to perform his duties, still lying in her arms.

That went very well, Julia had to admit. And since then, her husband had not approached her. Once, one morning, he had tried, but Julia had expressedly vomited before his eyes. With dedication.

Since then, he left her alone.

Julia took a critical look at the wine. That was no need to simulate the vomiting; it came from the heart. Her pregnancy was now noticeable.

The car rumbled again. It was a long journey but quite comfortable. Martinus' father had mustered his best cart, and eight armed men as escort, four of them of strong build and carrying powerful clubs so that nobody would approach them. During the nights, they would be safe. Not in hostels, as did ordinary travelers, but always with family friends, in an appropriate environment, in safety and with luxury. Julia knew that news preceded her journey to dissuade the friendly hosts with explicit references to not grant the younger Caius free access to the cellars of the house, as he was taken with his new serious, manly, and, yes, truly Roman obligations. Wife and son, certainly an heir, had to be safe in his hands, and the newly awakened sense of responsibility was cherished by his new wife, at least in public.

Martinus Caius had since the beginning of their journey a bad mood and almost, but only *almost*, Julia felt a little bit sorry for him.

She consoled herself with the thought that once she had disappeared from direct access of their in-laws, she had turned out to be a bad bitch, and Martinus Caius finally had an excuse to indulge his favorite vices, and his portrayal of the suffering dupe might even solicit sympathy from his family.

Apart from the shaking of the carriage and her delight in the suffering of Martinus, there was nothing to bother about. Her journey was relatively easy because they had to simply follow the military road. From Ravenna they went directly to Aquilea, and from there along the Via Julia Augusta to the north toward the provincial center Virunum, the capital of Noricum Mediterraneum. From there, the road led to Noreia and up to Lauriacum, the city in which Thomas Volkert's legion had been stationed.

If her information proved to be accurate.

If he was still in Noricum.

Julia didn't want to think about it. At worst, she would spend simply a boring spring in a completely uninteresting garrison town, far away from the comforts even of the provincial Virunum. She would eventually return to Ravenna and bring a child into the world that would carry the surname Caius, at least until she could find out where Thomas was staying.

Or until he found her.

One or the other would happen, she was quite sure of it.

The car rocked again violently. A suppressed curse from her husband caused Julia to smile.

"The journey pleases you, mistress," the slave tried in conversation. Julia wanted to reply angrily, but then she remembered what Thomas Volkert had said about slavery, as they had discussed the subject briefly. In his house, so he had said with a certainty that was new to her, there would be no slaves, only free servants, properly paid and well-treated. And if there would be no money for staff, well, even better – then he would serve Julia and respond to her every whim.

He had been so sweet. Of course, Julia didn't believe the latter for a second. Of course, they would lead a simpler life, but she had taken precautions. A casket with jewelry and a belt with golden coins sewn in, a bag of silver and copper coins, most of it easy to carry on the body. Enough to buy a small piece of land, perhaps a few animals, and certainly a few slaves.

No, she corrected herself. No slaves. And it was only befitting to accept the explicit wishes of her true husband. Slaves were human. And they were to be freed. Julia was a Christian and had understood this notion thoroughly, at least theoretically.

So she took a breath and smiled at the slave.

"Your name is Claudia, isn't it?" she said warmly.

"Yes, mistress."

"You're born into slavery?"

The young woman lowered her head. "Yes, mistress."

"Were you previously well treated by your master?"

"I'm happy, my lady."

The answer came a little hesitant, sounded more polite than honest. What should Claudia possibly reveal of their previous work? She had been one of the servants of Martinus Caius' mother. No prominent position, but the work of a personal slave, directly under her command. It was told that all the male members of the family tended to temper. It was also said that the elder Caius, fatigued by his unsightly woman, jumped on every woman that couldn't escape in time.

Slaves usually had no chance to escape anywhere.

Julia decided to change the direction of the conversation. Claudia was now apparently intended as their personal slave, and she made a mental note not to make the live of that young woman unnecessarily difficult.

Once they arrived in Noricum, she would make off with Thomas Volkert, and Claudia was probably exposed to the whims of her "husband." On the other hand, she wouldn't have to worry about a lot from him. Julia had ensured that in one of the two cars a barrel of the new German brandy was carried. Once they had arrived in Lauriacum, she would hand it over her husband as a kind gift from a caring wife.

And disappear.

Martinus Caius would get drunk deep into unconsciousness, for which no special incentive was needed. And as soon as he would learn of her escape, he would simply continue.

Julia didn't care. She was done with Martinus once she left.

Apparently encouraged by Julia's willingness to converse, Claudia turned back to her.

"I know that it is insubordinate to ask you to do something for me, mistress, especially as I serve you only since recently ..."

Julia smiled encouragingly. "Speak."

"As soon as we are in Lauriacum, mistress, and the accommodation and everything is properly prepared, may I then, for a half or full day, have the freedom to visit my brother?"

"Your brother lives in Lauriacum?"

"He is a slave in a wealthy patrician's house," Claudia said now very eagerly. "He was sold four years ago to that place, because he can write well and read, and works as a clerk. Sometimes he sends me a letter, but I cannot read or write, and must always find someone who reads it to me and can rarely respond. Writers are expensive, and so far I have received very little money."

If there was a beautiful case for Thomas' insistence on properly paid staff, then probably this was.

"I wish to see him again. We are very close," Claudia added, half-shy, half-hopeful. "Just recently, he sent me a letter."

Julia nodded. "Of course, this will be possible," she said generously, and rejoiced when Claudia replied with a grateful smile. "And some money you shall also have, now that you are in my service. Every person, whether slave or free, should have a few coins in his pocket."

The joyful expression of the slave was even more intense. She tilted her head, probably to hide a tear in the corner of his eye.

"Say, what does your brother write about the conditions in Lauriacum? He will have already told you the usual gossip and the most important news from the area?"

Claudia nodded eagerly. "He writes a lot and likes it, the good Remius. Apparently legions have moved to the city from across the country. The taverns are full of soldiers from all corners of the Empire."

Julia frowned. An uneasy feeling crept over her. "Did he write about the reason? A new campaign against the Germans? The Sarmatians have become rebellious, yes?"

Claudia shrugged. "He knows nothing in detail. It is said that an important military expedition to the East is going to happen. And that it's ultimately only a relatively small force, all on horseback, and that some time travelers would accompany them. That's all. We'll soon learn more once we'll arrive, milady!"

Julia nodded absently. A sudden chill went through her and she pulled the cloak around her shoulders tightly. A nasty idea crept up, an idea which had no rational basis, but easily entered her thoughts and didn't let go.

"When ... when is this expedition to commence?" she finally managed the next question.

"I don't know, milady. But normally as soon as the weather is good enough, and progress of preparations is fast. On the other hand, if all are riders ... they could be on their way already. The letter is now more than two months old,Milady."

If Claudia was surprised at the sudden interest of her mistress in Roman troop movements, she didn't show it. She was just glad that there was hope of being able to meet her brother – and to be allowed to keep a few coins in her hand. Therefore, she was more than willing to answer any strange question.

Julia said nothing more, staring at the plane of the carriage, her thoughts in sudden turmoil. Of course, it could mean nothing, she reassured herself. Thomas Volkert was freshly squeezed into the service. He mastered the horse, yes, that he had once told her, but also that didn't mean anything yet. They took men, apparently of special qualifications, from all over the Empire, and Lauriacum was only the collection point. Thomas would probably just look interestingly at the bustle, not be part of the action.

Definitely not.

Certainly.

Yet the thought gnawed at Julia that her Thomas, due to a wild twist of fate, had been able to attract the attention of his superiors and now also belonged to that expedition. After all, he had been promoted ...

And the expedition was probably already on its way.

Her trip to Noricum came perhaps too late.

Fear overcame Julia, fear of futility of her endeavor, in which she had placed so much hope. The cart lurched. Her spouse cursed. Julia didn't care.

She was in a hurry now.

Very much so.

12

Bertius was actually too small for a legionary.

But since they now took almost everyone, soldiers of his height were no longer an exception in the Roman forces. He was among the few who had volunteered and had spent more than ten years in the legion. During this time, in spite of all challenges, his belly had grown bigger, his hair thinner, and his eyes thicker and somewhat watery. The former was due to his fondness for candied fruit, in which he invested part of his pay, the second was due to his age and his tendency to baldness, and the last was due to his fondness for wine, in which he invested the remaining part of his pay. The fact that he hadn't been promoted above the rank of a simple soldier in spite of his ten years of service had a lot to do with the fact that Bertius had developed an excellent instinct of avoiding potentially lethal activities. Narrowly below insubordination, he always found someone he could blame for his own negligence, always ready to hide when it came to the crunch behind the backs of others, which his short stature was helpful to a considerable extent. But he gladly and often talked about his alleged glorious deeds, especially if someone else bought him booze. His simple Germanic descent from a village near the Lahn he embellished mostly with large-scale epics in which he was an outcast prince's son, who had found refuge within the borders of the Roman Empire, driven by his many enemies.

In short, Bertius, the Teuton, was a talker and a quitter, and Thomas Volkert had the joy to stand guard with him for the night. For a decurion that was a little bit more comfortable – he had to make the rounds and check all duty soldiers, whether they slept or otherwise neglected their duties. Once he found a man doing so, the legion called for draconian punishments, which could lead to the death of the unwary. Since Bertius refused to die – in fact, he had wanted to prevent this throughout his military career with great zeal – he was vigilant and, unfortunately, also required the attention of his superiors. The moment Decurion Volkert arrived during his nightly round at his post, the more solid figure of the legionary stretched, a shining glow crossed Bertius' face, and he began to annoy Volkert with all sorts of speculation, rumors and stories. He did this primarily to escape the deadly and soporific monotony of guard, and Volkert was quite aware of that. This monotony was exacerbated by the fact that here, in the middle of a garrison town, nothing of note was expected to happen despite the proximity to the border. The biggest challenge might be legionaries who wanted access to camp after a bout of drinking in the city, although the gates were closed at sunset.

That night, not even that happened, and therefore Bertius was full of desire to communicate interesting topics he had heard somewhere. Volkert either had listened to these a dozen times or he simply wasn't interested.

Rank had its privileges, so he could snub the legionary and march on, hoping that ultimately fatigue would conquer Bertius, and he would fall silent during their next encounter. Volkert told himself that he wouldn't even punish the man for dozing off, if he could just shut up.

But Bertius had much to say.

As Volkert passed him the third time that night, shortly after one in the morning, the chubby soldier was obviously awake. And before the Decurion could tell him to keep quiet and simply carry on with his vigilance, he had started to address him. The enthusiasm with which Bertius followed his urge to communicate made for someone of a generally friendly disposition like Volkert difficult to interrupt.

"You know, Decurion," Bertius began eagerly, as kneading his sausage fingers. "I heard that the great expedition will go to the East. I heard tomorrow the troops will be mustered for the last time."

Volkert couldn't help but to listen. That the scouting mission was to leave for the East he was well aware of as, he had been assigned to participate. And the fact that a troop of German infantrymen would accompany them bothered him since he had learned of it. But had Bertius actually for once snapped an important information?

The portly fellow seemed to notice Volkert's sudden interest and hastened immediately to exploit the opportunity.

"It is true, Decurion," Volkert said with a portentous tone. "Tomorrow we will all meet the time travelers. A demonstration of their thunder-weapons is planned to help the soldiers who march out with them to get used to them. And then, a few days later, the expedition will begin."

Bertius lowered his voice almost conspiratorially. "I've heard you'll join as well, Decurion!"

Volkert nodded absently. He already pondered how he could wriggle himself out of the expected quandary. Sure, they didn't know him here under his real name. He had grown large arched whiskers and the months with the legion had certainly changed his appearance in many other ways, so none of the infantrymen would recognize him at first glance. Fortunately, he had only superficial contacts with them while he was still on the *Saarbrücken*. He only interacted regularly with Captain Becker.

Who, as the rumors had it, was dead.

With luck, he could hide the fact that he spoke German. With luck, he would be able to stay as far as possible away from the infantry. Volkert threw Bertius a searching look. Perhaps he could even learn something from this specimen about hiding.

Bertius interpreted the Decurion's glance wrongly and took a step back. "Of course," he stammered, "it would be a great honor to be selected for this glorious and very important mission. But I'm really unworthy. Experienced men, who represent the spirit of Rome much better than I, should be preferred in my place, to ensure the endeavor's success."

Volkert grinned.

"Believe me, o Lord," Bertius misinterpreted Volkert's facial expression again. "I'd be a burden. Look at me! I drag myself through my duties in my desperate attempt to make a pitiful contribution to saving glorious Rome. Don't get me wrong – the idea that I protect the peacefully resting children of the Empire gives me great satisfaction, and it's not that the prospect of a perilous mission in which I would fail without a doubt makes me very afraid – but the idea that I won't do justice to Rome and shame my ancestors does indeed."

Volkert shook his head. Bertius' years of practice as a quitter had trained his rhetorical talents quite impressively. "Your ancestors are but wild Germans, who would be happy about every threat Rome has to endure," Volkert considered.

Bertius paused for a moment, then he licked his lips to gain some time. "That's true, but German bravery and decency prevail and the desire to serve the legitimate sovereign with utmost loyalty ..."

"That reminds me: Didn't you tell me that in your escape from the captors who wanted to kill you after the murder of your glorious father, you rode for days and nights until you found safety in the Empire's borders?"

Bertius swallowed. "Um, well, I was still young and full of despair. Afterwards and getting older, I surely slipped in my efforts to keep certain abilities, if you know what I mean, noble Decurion."

"The noble Decurion will ensure that you are tested on a horse tomorrow, o brave Bertius," Volkert announced. The slightly stern undertone of his statement signaled to the legionary that this wasn't part of any jocular banter. Volkert had much understanding for the peculiarities of his fellow soldiers and left them in peace in this harsh surroundings as much as it was possible. But Bertius overdid it with his attitude to perform his duties within the armed forces by making it a cozy life. And what was aggravating the issue: He was a volunteer. Volkert knew that those pressed into the service did their duty with less than the required motivation, and understandably so – but a volunteer with ten years experience under his belt?

Bertius said nothing, turned and stared into the darkness, like he expected to be attacked by wild Sarmatians at any moment.

Volkert continued his tour. The conversation with Bertius had distracted him from his real problem long enough to regain some inner peace. To keep a cool head was the real challenge now.

He felt a certain sadness when he thought of the infantrymen who would arrive tomorrow. They represented a piece of home. They were actually like him. But he couldn't reveal himself to them. The risk was too great that he would be arrested and brought to Ravenna in shackles. The death sentence would surely follow.

He couldn't allow that, not for his own sake and not because of his love for Julia, which had become for him a constant reminder of his existence and purpose. He didn't want to and wouldn't give up hope.

And if it meant to ride against the Huns, then it should be.

As Volkert returned to the guard fire, two other officers joined him; like him, that had been doing laps to other sections of the large fort to oversee the area. Volkert knew them only by sight, as they served in other parts of the legion, with which his own unit had rarely anything to do. Silently, they sat by the flickering fire, enjoyed the short break, which allowed them to warm up.

An amphora with *pesca* made the rounds, water mixed with vinegar water, the standard drink of the Roman soldiers. During the guard service, any form of alcohol, even the usually highly diluted wine, was absolutely forbidden. Pesca tasted as could be expected, sourly to inedible, but the water, most likely infected with germs, was only made palatable by adding the vinegar. Volkert had initially had his difficulties getting used to the drink but had to concede that it was refreshing, even if the refreshment was the result of having a shiver of revulsion driving through the body. For nighttime, there was the usual meal, the *puls* or porridge. Although this certainly was available in different variations – and in the one the men had cooked for the night pieces of beef had been added – Volkert had never developed a great passion for it. Many of Rome's enemies called the legionaries "porridge-eaters," an insult accepted with equanimity. Porridge was easy to make, the ingredients were easily procured also during a march, and it quickly saturated even the worst hunger. The meal, as Volkert knew by now, was especially helpful to provide the necessary energy needed by the men during marches, and therefore meat dishes were mostly reserved for camp life when the replenishment worked reasonably. Here, in a garrison town, the choice was of course much greater, and the fact that the watchkeeping officers had carried a pot of porridge without much discussion showed that this was a habit deeply ingrained in all legionaries. Ultimately, Volkert couldn't help himself, after he scooped a plate of the warm mash, to appreciate the pleasant feeling of a properly filled stomach and the energy that this feed gave him. Fortunately, gaurum wasn't inflicted in puls. He wouldn't enjoy this form of seasoning throughout his life, that he was sure of.

So the night passed. As Volkert had resumed his round again and observed Bertius, the man appeared to be busy, his view always directed toward any possible area of approach, spooning cold puls from a plate. The best way to end the comprehensive presentations of the legionary was, as Volkert knew, to give him something to eat. That Bertius was only allowed to drink pesca was a real ordeal, but he was enduring it with pride. The joy and the zeal with which he stuffed the cold porridge in his mouth and the sound of cracking once he encountered not properly mashed grains with his teeth, showed his determination. This night, Volkert was sure, wouldn't transform Bertius into a slim and presentable first-class soldier.

A multi-week ride, on the other hand, could do miracles.

Volkert smiled, as he went on.

He hadn't forgotten his announcement. Tomorrow Bertius would sit on a horse. And then they shall see.

13

There were several reasons why the *Valentinian* had set course in late winter. An important reason was the fact that this time of year the navy largely came to a standstill on the Mediterranean; in general, the authorities banned even the trips of larger vessels in the period between November and March. The heavy seas of an already unpredictable Mediterranean constituted a major challenge for vessels of the Late Antiquity, but here the steamboat had two important advantages. Firstly, they wouldn't even come across cheeky pirates, because also for them this time of year was for hibernation, and secondly, because being outside the regular season, their passage to Alexandria would be a public event of outstanding proportions, thus reinforcing the propaganda effect that they intended to achieve with the trip.

In addition, since a constant, fresh northern wind came up shortly after their departure, the ship was progressing well even without the use of the steam engine. The strong wind resulted in a stormy sea, which would have been the undoing for any rowing boat, and also many of the antique sailing vessels would have had massive problems – especially those who intended to travel from south to north, as to intersect in the wind was still a largely unknown procedure. The upstanding and very stable *Valentinian* with its mighty keel made the face of trierarch Africanus glow radiantly, which showed that he was more than satisfied with her behavior at sea. For the captain, this was a completely new experience of navigation, an unimagined security and stability, felt by all of the ship's officers and even without using steam power. Once the wind died and turned for a short time, the joy was even greater as the *Valentinian* slowly, but with great persistence, steamed against upwind and was not to be driven back toward the Italic coast.

Despite the disparaging opinion of stoker Forstmann, the steam engine, made of good bronze, worked properly and reliably. The young Marcellus helped below deck in servicing the technical marvel, and as Köhler learned, his understanding of the mechanics of the machine grew with every hour he spent with it. Any superstition, every timid fear that might still be felt by other crew member of the steam sailor was completely alien to the boy. He absorbed the fascinating technical knowledge like a sponge. Perhaps Dahms's desire to make the boy Rome's first real engineer would actually come true.

Another crew member, who replaced every fear and apprehension with almost childlike joy, was old Sepidus. For the gubernator, Köhler felt a strong kinship, as he was unwilling to retire from his duties, slept only sparingly, and took over the helm at every opportunity. As a gubernator, who had grown up with cumbersome and shaky triremes, the *Valentinian* had to be something like a revelation to him. He was probably more excited about the new toy than Africanus, and the trierarch was already grinning like a cheshire cat.

And so the *Valentinian* made good progress. With a good wind, they made eight to ten knots, in adverse conditions still four to five, driven by the tireless and charcoal-fired steam engine. Köhler was pleased that the winds were generally gracious, as charcoal wasn't half as effective as coal, and although they had the steamboat filled to the brim with inventories, the NCO doubted that the ship could have reached Alexandria with continuously running machine at full power. Coal, he knew, was on the list of priorities of commodities to be procured, not least because the inventories of the *Saarbrücken* were almost depleted and the light cruiser threatened to become immobile.

For the trip to Alexandria, they needed about seven days at their current speed. Köhler had been able to calculate the distance, given the experience of Africanus and their quite accurate maps. The coastline was different in the 20th century, as some parts had been conquered from the Mediterranean over the centuries. A freshwater lake, which was far from the coast inland and currently Alexandria's largest water reservoir, still existed in the 20th century but was linked to the sea and therefore salty. And there were some additional changes, although these ultimately were only of marginal nature. It was one of the tasks of the *Valentinian* to explore how far the German maps differed from the reality of today.

Time passed without major incidents. The sea was rough, and the wind moody, but they were spared from a real winter storm, and it became warmer by the day. At the end of the sixth day, as a starry sky stretched over the crew of the steamer, Marcellus recognized with open eyes a glow in the south.

"That," Africanus said, "is the lighthouse of Alexandria, the Pharos. It is one of the wonders of the world." Köhler, despite a rather limited formal education, knew that his time the lighthouse lived only in legends and drawings, as it had been destroyed long ago.

The night passed quickly. The light of the Pharos was, in a clear night, visible from up to fifty kilometers, and the *Valentinian* had reduced her speed to arrive in the harbor at dawn. As the sun rose, the whole splendor of Alexandria unfolded in front of the crew, and Africanus observed with amusement that the Germans, just as Marcellus, enjoyed the sight with open mouths. There was of course the lighthouse, stretching more than 130 meters upwards, at least by Köhler's conservative estimate, divided into three floors. They also realized that the famous and impressive lighthouse wasn't alone. A smaller one faced the sea, sitting on a cape, and was, as Africanus explained, called the Pharillon. It was a little less massive than the symbol of Alexandria, but offered, at night and during fog, a clear demarcation of the harbor entrance. Now, at this fresh and sunny morning, they stood there as stony witnesses of an ancient building technology, impressing everyone. Africanus and Sepidus, who both already had been here several times, didn't disturb the prayerful stare of the observers. For Africanus, this was a homecoming, as his family hailed from a fellahin village further south along the Nile.

The *Valentinian* entered the port from the west. When they had left the lighthouses behind, on the port side, the impressive panorama of the sun palaces could be seen, shining in many colors. Here, in the vast buildings near the sea and away from the stench of the metropolis, lived the rich and highly placed, the powerful shipping families of the city, the merchants, high officials of the Empire, or simply those who were of old money. This city, founded by the legendary Alexander, had been even before the Roman conquest an economic and administrative center, and many of the Greek and Egyptian families who were still living here today could trace back their pedigrees and their influence on the fortunes of Alexandria many hundreds of years. There were plenty of wealthy inhabitants who lived from what their ancestors had accomplished, and their pleasant existence was made very evident by the grand palazzos.

The closer they got to the actual landing, the more the breathtaking splendor of the city unfolded before their eyes. Even those who've already been there several times couldn't help but look up from their work and devote a few moments to the sight. Directly in before them, the great theater of the city towered, built close to the shore, with its own pier, so that the rich and famous could reach it without having to endure the dusty and busy streets of the city, and on the nearby water rowing competitions were held in the evenings. Situated next to the Grand Theatre, the actual port area stretched with its piers, numerous shipyards and a large market area with warehouses and open storage areas on which, despite that during this season barely any vessels arrived, a lot of activity prevailed. Once the *Valentinian* had passed the beacons, the instruction had been given, although not really necessary, to fire up the steam engine, to achieve the desired propaganda effect. The loud puffing of the machine echoed across the wide dock and broke at the high and imposing buildings on the shore, and it wasn't long until a good quantity of onlookers had assembled to witness the majestic approach. Köhler felt reassured as rapidly a cohort of port guards appeared who shut off the berth and began to repel too inquisitive spectators.

Köhler took his eyes from the panorama of the city. He would still have plenty of opportunity to look at the temples and churches across the large squares. But he already knew that his help wasn't needed: Africanus had everything under control. As the steam engine died and the ship was pushed with a gentle, almost unnoticeable movement toward the quay, the ropes flew and the *Valentinian* was moored, her maiden voyage officially over. It was clear that the new design had proved to be excellent.

At the wharf, a delegation of the city's notables had gathered in addition to the onlookers, local officials who would dominate the first round of welcome. Of course, there would be a reception by the governor in this part of Africa, before they could make the trip inland to arrive as quickly as possible at the Red Sea and from there onward Aksum.

Once the *Valentinian* was firmly lashed, Marcellus approached the railing and looked expectantly at Köhler and Africanus.

"Can I explore the city?" he asked eagerly.

Köhler threw Africanus a look. "We are both busy with the officials for a while, and we must certainly leave a small guard – but I see no problem in granting the rest of the crew shore leave for the day."

"Especially you time travelers," Africanus added. "You know not more than Ravenna and Thessaloniki so far. You must make yourself familiar with the Empire. A Roman and a Greek city are in many ways different than Alexandria."

"What is the difference?"

Africanus smiled. "Alexandria is Alexandria. Here you find all of them, from around the world, from all regions of the Empire. Here you find all Christian churches and all other religions, the most noble scholarship side by side with fanatical stupidity. There is no city like Alexandria."

The Trierarch looked around, then waved to Sepidus. "My old friend here," he said, as the man with the weathered face joined them, "has been here many times in his life. He once even had a steady girlfriend. Laviria was her name, right?"

The older man rolled his eyes. "Do you have to warm up the old stories, Africanus?"

"She had fire!"

"Oh, yes, but not under her stove. Every time I had to bring her to a tavern and spend my meagre pay for meals she ate almost on her own. And after the third year, there was clear evidence for the results of her appetite!"

Africanus grinned as Sepidus, who with masterly fashion, put on a suffering face. "Sepidus was at that time secutor on a trireme, which belonged to the Alexandrian quota," he told Köhler. "Shortly thereafter, he was transferred to Ravenna."

"One of the great strokes of luck of my life. Laviria suddenly spoke of marriage!"

"Yes, the Emperor's wisdom is unfathomable, and he watches with kindness on those who serve him!" Africanus replied. "Anyway: Sepidus knows his stuff. Call your men, Köhler, and the young Marcellus here, and I'll give them my mate as a guide. Look around in the city and return before dark. You yourself, my friend, will have to accompany me, though."

Köhler glanced at Behrens, who looked with shiny eyes toward the shore. It was the first time for him to step foot on another continent – in both eras. It was clear that he wanted to join to the small group of those who were given the guided tour.

"Then I'll meet with Africanus and Dr. Neumann to do the honors," he said, trying to copy Sepidus' suffering face with similar intensity. He didn't quite succeed.

A few minutes later, two groups left the ship. The larger of them, consisting of the five Germans and Marcellus, disembarked expectantly under the direction of Sepidus. The other, consisting of Africanus, Köhler and Proreta Lucius, would welcome the waiting notables and probably provide a guided tour of the ship for any visitors interested in the technological marvels. In addition to those who joined only out of politeness, Köhler expected that some with serious technical and professional curiosity would appear – shipowners, shipyard managers, trierarchs of other vessels. Rheinberg's statement had been very clear: The blueprints of the *Valentinian* were no secret – down to an exact plan of the steam engine, which they should distribute among Alexandrian scholars upon request. It was as pointless as counterproductive to keep all this a secret. Only when such innovations quickly spread and became common knowledge they could help improve the situation in the Empire. This was another reason why the captain had endorsed the trip to Alexandria: Although the heyday of the city was over, the metropolis was still considered a center of knowledge. This feature could turn out to be useful.

The first group plunged enthusiastically into a dazzling city, crowded with pilgrims and travelers from around the world. Sepidus led them to the width of road, the main artery of the city, which was, as they were soon to learn, built strictly symmetrical, like a chess board. It seemed, if kept one important monuments in clear view, that it would be absolutely impossible to get lost in this place, and also Marcellus seemed very impressed, but far from lost. Among the important buildings was, in the west of the city, the Moon Gate, and one of the most magnificent churches of Alexandria, the Theonas Church, formerly the seat of the bishop of Alexandria. On the way, Sepidus explained that there was hardly a city in the whole Empire where the religious divisions of the realm unfolded more distinctively. Alexandria was both the city of the Arians as well the Trinitarians, as powerful bishops like Gregory or the famous Athanasius left their mark on the population. In addition, many other faiths were apparent, even the officially banned Manichean creed from the Orient, which had been established here trying to find a gateway into the Roman Empire.

In the city center, there was another large church, whose construction was completed not too long ago – the Imperial Church, which was the current seat of the bishop. To all this, the visitors devoted some time, and the pleasure of discovery got to them, as at every street corner something new was to be admired. Temples and other places of worship, partly of great architecture, lined up against each other. The racecourse was one of the meeting points of the city, and as Sepidus told them, the Alexandrians were crazy about the races – if something like a national sport existed, this was it. They visited the square of Alexander, named after the former much less mythical but very real founder of the city. Once, the Sema had been located there, the tomb of Alexander, which later relocated to the newly built palaces of the Ptolemaic kings and was even later, under the reign of Aurelian, destroyed.

Again and again, they returned to the width of road that divided the metropolis exactly in the middle. In addition to the coastal region whose palaces they had been able to admire from the sea, this was another preferred residential area for those who were well off. It was loud and hectic, because activities persisted along the busy boulevard day and night.

Sepidus had of course dutifully explained the pleasures of the city's nightlife, as Alexandria was particularly known for it. The numerous localities in which to drink, dance and indulge in yet other pleasures were apparently well known to the old gubernator, and it was Behrens who ended his enthusiastic and increasingly detailed descriptions with a silent nod toward Marcellus. The boy had developed a very intense interest for this exposition and seemed a little disappointed that Sepidus promised Behrens to use another outing to inspect personally the attractions described.

The end of their hour-long round tour was the Serapeum, the most impressive of Alexandria's pagan temples. Dedicated to the city deity Serapis, the building was of gigantic proportions; its colonnades and columns shone with an almost blinding white, while the numerous paintings exhibited vibrant colors. Before they had left for Alexandria, Behrens had Captain Rheinberg explain to him what could be found in the few books about Alexandria, including the fact that in the old time line just three years from now, in 391, the Emperor Theodosius would order the destruction of this unique place of worship. Now that the Spaniard wasn't considered as emperor anymore, it was quite possible that the building could be spared. As the visitors observed the architectural masterpiece and looked at each other in astonishment, the desire grew in all of them that in fact this building should persist, because it was doubtless a landmark of the metropolis, just as the Pharos lighthouse.

Köhler, Neumann and Africanus, however, didn't have the pleasure of extended sightseeing. It was characteristic of the local leaders, who had certainly heard of the technical achievements from the future, that the esteemed guests were immediately led to be greeted in the Museion. Here, the remains of what was once considered the famous library of Alexandria could be found. This largest collection of ancient knowledge had been partially destroyed during Caesar's invasion of Egypt, only to be restored and to fall victim to fires repeatedly. The latest bloodletting was only a few years back, again at the time of turmoil under Emperor Aurelian, as apart from the destruction of the residential neighborhood and other parts, a great quantity of the scrolls had been annihilated. Nevertheless, visitors could convince themselves that the collection was still considerable and that until that day scholars of world renown used the papers for their own research. Scientists even received public scholarships to work on their projects. The Museion was closest to what one might consider a research institute, at least until the arrival of the *Saarbrücken*. And the current chairman of the institution, a mathematician named Theon, welcomed the time travelers with an enthusiasm that was based solely on the eagerness of a scholar wishing to learn new things.

Of course, all curiosity aside, once a number of scholars was gathered who formed the welcoming committee led by Theon, the usual envy of the accomplished scientist aroused and the need to demonstrate everyone's ingenuity. It was therefore inevitable that – aside from the expressed desire to visit the *Valentinian* and especially the steam engine – a young Greek scholar, who called himself Dionos and announced himself to be a student of the great Heron of Alexandria, couldn't wait to demonstrate to the visitors that not all the marvels of the future were as marvelous as expected.

And since the time travelers had created a stir with their steam engine, it was understandable that Dionos appeared well prepared for the visit and presented his own apparition.

It was evident that Köhler and Neumann were duly impressed. Stoker Forstmann would've fit well in this group, but he had chosen to become familiar with the city.

They entered a light-flooded room with circular and large windows. On the ceiling were beautiful paintings that pointed clearly to the Greek goddess Athena. Much more importantly, a metal structure stood in the middle of the room. Next to them were two other young men, apparently students of Dionos, waiting for them.

"This," the scholar explained, touching his neatly trimmed whiskers and his dark brown eyes shining with pride, "is the Aeolipile!"

Köhler and Neumann considered the apparatus curiously. It consisted of a vessel, a simple sphere, arranged to rotate on its axis, having oppositely curved nozzles projecting from it, like tipjets. Dionos started immediately to present its functionality. When the vessel was pressurized with steam, the steam expelled through the nozzles, which generated thrust. Once the nozzles, pointing in different directions, produced forces along different lines of action perpendicular to the axis, the thrusts combined to result in a rotational moment, causing the sphere to spin about its axis. The water was heated in a simple boiler that formed part of a stand for the rotating vessel, connected to the rotating chamber by a pair of pipes that also served as the pivots. A simple, but ingenious device.

It worked perfectly.

The sphere spun.

"This invention of the great Heron is using, as I may say, the very same principle of your machine that drives the ship and was used to come to Alexandria," Dionos explained with a mixture of pride, arrogance and self-confidence that couldn't quite cover an undoubtedly aroused inferiority complex.

Neumann and Köhler exchanged glances. That was precisely the very thing Rheinberg had warned them about. Avoid any hubris. These people had to be taken seriously. Never even remotely suggest that the time travelers were techonologically far superior to them. Arrogance was fatal.

"Dear Dionos," Neumann said, "You surely have impressed and surprised me. I wouldn't have thought any of this possible. Alexandria is truly a great place of knowledge and learning. I recognize that over the centuries up to that time we come from, so much seems to have been lost, so much that what we had to regain laboriously. Heron must have been a genius. Is he alive? Can we talk to him?"

The young Dionos seemed to be very pleased by the physician's response, because he smiled broadly and bowed slightly.

"Heron is dead for over 200 years," he informed Neumann. "I consider myself as his student on the basis of his studies, who I intend to continue and refine." He hesitated for a brief moment. "Maybe I can use your engine as a way of inspiration."

"Perhaps, but surely we won't teach you anything of the underlying principles anymore, because you have obviously been inspired by your teacher and have internalized them perfectly. Maybe you are even able to improve upon our machine on some important aspects of craftsmanship. To this end, we will be just happy to help."

Dionos nodded happily.

Africanus spoke. "Dear Sirs, I would like to thank everyone on behalf of the Roman fleet for this highly instructive hour. We leave this place inspired and encouraged in the knowledge that as long as the Empire has learning of this kind available, we can overcome any storm – quite literally. But we visit this beautiful city only as a transit station. Our route takes us further into the realm of Aksum. We need to start immediately with the necessary travel arrangements. Apologies therefore that we will, for he foreseeable future, not be able to benefit from your knowledge anymore."

Was it due to Africanus' friendly words or the fact that the scholars had proved themselves sufficiently to the strangers, the parting with their visitors wasn't delayed. With many polite phrases, many bows and expressions of mutual esteem, the men were released and returned to the *Valentinian*.

The evening bound all crew members as guests of the city's notables who had invited them to a feast in their honor. For the next day several guides would show interested visitors around, while the ship's officers would start the preparations for their trip to Aksum. There was also a meeting with the local governor scheduled, with whom they wanted to discuss plans for the establishment of a modern shipyard facility. Since they were officially commissioned by the Emperor, they got all the support of the local authorities they could ask for. In Adulis, the port city of the African Empire, they were already expected by a Roman trade envoy, who officially represented only the economic interests of the Empire, but in many cases also conducted diplomatic tasks. Everything was, as far as they could see, going very well.

Until Marcellus disappeared.

14

Ambrosius, Bishop of Milan, was in a bad mood. He secretly asked the Lord to forgive him his thoughts, but the unflattering words about his fellow travelers that conquered his mind, the travel conditions and the hopeful end of his journey, simply didn't disappear from his consciousness. The cart in which he traveled by road to Treveri was badly sprung and his companions, all priests of his closest circle, showed their bad mood to each other, rather than bear the difficult conditions with humility and, may God grant it, finally shut up. The weather was cold, and they didn't advance very rapidly. Ambrosius would've preferred to travel on horseback, which would be faster and ultimately more pleasant, but couldn't refuse his brothers "to assist him," as they called it.

Ambrosius was able to cope very well without this kind of assistance. Nevertheless, it was necessary to observe certain conventions. He was on his way to the Emperor to ask him questions that would test his orthodoxy. For this, he needed witnesses, and the brothers he took along with him were supposed to perform this function. He also wanted to re-enter into the dispute with the new General Rheinberg, who was close to the Emperor and doubtlessly had continued his heretical whisperings during recent weeks. Ambrosius knew that he had already entered a dangerous path because of his covert support for Maximus, so he had to protect himself and be careful in his subsequent decisions. And the more the news spread in the leadership of the Church that the once pious and orthodox Gratian had succumbed to the dictates of the witch from the future, the more the Church hierarchy would keep quiet when Maximus seized the purple by force and reversed the so-called "reforms" the Emperor enacted with worrisome speed.

At least that was Ambrosius' hope. He wasn't so sure that Maximus would actually deliver on that promise quickly. Too many of the actions of the young Emperor, and even the bishop had to acknowledge that with grudging respect, made sense. Among those was certainly not the explicit confirmation of the Edict of Tolerance made by Galerius and thus tolerating heretical trends in the Church – but so much else wasn't that stupid, and a Maximus, once confronted with the requirements of government, would recognize the logic and benefits of some measures very well. Ambrosius accepted that, as long as the new emperor would meet his key demands: to make the Trinitarian strand of Christendom the only valid state church; and to burn all other sects, cults, religions, including the ancient Roman state gods, on the pyres of history. This was Ambrosius' will, to be accomplished, if necessary, with sword and fire.

They were not far from Trier and would reach the city in the late afternoon, in time before sunset, when the guards shut the gates and allowed no more traffic. Ambrosius thought to make representations to the Emperor at once, who, also one of the positive changes the bishop didn't like to consider too much, worked long hours every day, sometimes from very early until midnight. Previously, as Ambrosius knew well, Gratian used to go hunting quite often and had given up duties to subordinates who then had made decisions sometimes more, sometimes less according to his wishes. What magical influence Rheinberg ever had on the young Emperor, it helped Gratian to reach a new level of seriousness and self-discipline.

The Bishop looked in his heart to find regret, as he tried to extinguish this life soon, but he found only sincere conviction that it was for the good of the Church and thus, ultimately, the right thing for the whole world. There were sometimes victims and the Lord would assess this properly once judgment was upon them, and Ambrose was willing to pray for those who died and were innocent.

But he wouldn't spare anyone who stood in his way.

Thus prepared internally, the Bishop was able to endure the annoying chatter of his travel companions quite unmoved. His already stony facial expression prevented each of them to direct the word at him, so he didn't have to worry about being drawn into this sea of trivialities. It was a hardship, but then, through the haze of drizzle that had accompanied them throughout the day with leaden heaviness, he recognized the walls of Treveri. New optimism filled the Bishop, as the cart rumbled in the twilight before the gates, and they got stepped of the vehicle, stretched and yawned, then crossed the threshold to the city by foot. At once, the commander of the city watch provided for rapid escort to finally reach the Emperor's residence.

Ambrosius wasn't just anyone. It wasn't long until he was led into the palace Gratian inhabited. When he entered the large atrium, where guests were waiting for an audience with the Emperor, he saw craftsmen busy under the light of numerous oil lamps, working to beautify the floor of the hall with a new, large mosaic. Barriers stopped the few guests from stepping on the building site. Three men knelt on cushions in front of large boxes with colored stones, in addition to drawings lying around that represented the proposed design of the mosaic. An elderly man with a long, gray-white beard stood by and seemed to oversee the work. Perhaps he was even the artist of the draft. Now and then he murmured instructions to the kneeling men who carried them out at once. With little hammers, they added the colored stones side by side, connected by tiny layers of a special clay, which dried out quickly and would give the mosaic the necessary strength. It was a long and delicate endeavor, and required a high degree of attention, experience and craftsmanship. Ambrosius realized that the artisans knew their work, for their economical and precise movements was obvious. Even their warden seemed satisfied with the work, as he uttered now and then an affirmative grunt or tapped one of them approvingly on the shoulder.

There were a few people waiting, and they seemed not to be very interested in the artisans' work. Ambrosius stepped forward and looked at the display. It was basically not a surprisingly different or new image – the finished mosaic, that was completed by two-thirds already, would show Emperor Gratian how he sat on a chair and considered his council. Dignitaries, military, civil servants, all in submissive posture and identified through the objects they held in their hands, stood beside him. They were symbolic for the wisdom that was given to the Emperor by them and didn't represent specific and therefore identifiable persons. Ambrosius knew that for Gratian the court was both a menace as well as an inevitability. It was a hotbed of jealousy, envy, resentment, greed, the struggle for power and influence. Power was defined by one's proximity to the Emperor. Gratian had the various political currents well in mind and granted no one too much favor, had to remain flexible, distributed his attention, redeployed it, always looking for an escape route. A certain person, an identifiable individual in some "eternal" representation such as a mosaic would be contrary to this principle.

Then, the view of the Bishop of Milan fell on a detail that previously eluded him. He took a deep breath and tried not to show his anger, but he had to struggle for his self-control. No, also time-travelers weren't represented *in personam*. No Rheinberg, no von Geeren, nobody.

But down there, at the feet of the Emperor, the appearance of waves was recognizable. And in these waves, in the midst of Roman triremes, swam, made carefully from blue-gray stones and nicely composed, the vessel of the demons called the *Saravica*, after a village not too far from Treveri, a remote settlement on a westerly river.

The ship was clearly visible. The artisans had expertedly used very fine stone dust, inserted into the still damp clay, to mimic the rippling smoke that rose up from the chimneys of the ship. No, there was no need to represent someone as a person, because the symbolic power of the ship was more than adequate.

Ambrose stared at the unfinished work with burning eyes and felt the overwhelming desire to take a hammer and smash the still fresh artwork with a vengeance, to symbolically erase its perpetuation of influence from the memory of everyone.

He took a deep breath and took a step back. His brothers sat in a corner and continued their inconsequential conversations. They had not noticed.

The bishop turned away, now more impatient than before. He knew that Maximus still owed him another favor if, one day, he'd wear the purple.

A favor that had something to do with a big, heavy hammer.

He braced himself with patience. So unfathomable the ways of the Lord sometimes might be, so inevitable it was also that all heretics would finally be subjected to a dismal fate. It was this certainty from which Ambrosius drew his strength and confidence, and it also helped him to get his emotions under control. He even managed to perceive the good craftsmanship beyond that terrible image, which had simply been abused for a misguided message.

Nothing he could change right now.

It didn't take long and Ambrosius and two of his brothers, Lucius and Hardinus, were admitted to the Emperor. A staff member led them silently through the corridors of the palace until they arrived in Gratian's working chambers. Ambrosius walked in with all signs of respect. He didn't want to fight Gratian, at least not here and now, but give him a chance to show the strength of character which his old teacher Ausonius once taught him.

As expected, Gratian wasn't alone. The personalized anathema, Magister Militium Rheinberg, was also present. Ambrose forced a smile. He bowed to the Emperor and muttered a salutation before he straightened up and looked around.

The influence of the time traveler could be seen everywhere. And as Ambrosius previously had been contemplating, it wasn't only negative. The large map of the Roman Empire, which was mounted on the wall, was the joint work of German and Roman experts and excelled any known one in terms of scale, accuracy and detail. He found himself to feel a desire to obtain a similar map on which he would delineate episcopal responsibilities and areas of influence of the true Church with greater care and accuracy. He almost felt tempted to ask Gratian for a copy, but this would be taken as an admission of the superiority of the time travelers, something the bishop was in no way ready to express. He threw one last, half-regretful, half-envious look at the colored wall map, but then he fixed his eyes on Gratian, who seemed to have become visibly older since a few months ago, when he had met him the last time. The new seriousness of the Emperor, reported to him by various sources, showed in his whole habitus, in its economical gestures as in his dignified, but at the same exhausted posture.

Bishop Ambrosius took this with regret. To kill this man was certainly a waste. He hoped the inevitability of this decision would prove to be a mistake, but the confidential, almost friendly way Rheinberg sat next to the young Emperor spoke its own language. And the mistrust, the caution in the eyes of both men as they stared at Ambrosius wasn't lost to him either. The Bishop pushed any doubt aside.

"Honorable Augustus, I'm grateful that you have received me. May I introduce my brothers Lucius and Hardinus, loyal servants of our church who have accompanied me on the arduous journey from Milan."

"They're all welcome," said Gratian and nodded to the two priests who considered him friendly, one step behind Ambrosius. "We should all sit, especially after a long journey. I'll ask for drinks and food, so that you can regain your strength."

Ambrosius's first reflex was to emphasize his ascetic nature in order to win a point in the silent struggle, which would now inevitably begin. But his two brothers looked so thrilled by the announcement of the Emperor and sat so happily on the proffered chairs and looked so eager at the small tables carried in by servile slaves at Gratian's sign that Ambrose swallowed the rejection and asked himself again if the idea to take these two priests along could have been one of his worst.

So Ambrosius sat and waited until he had received a cup of watered wine and some cold food. He was hungry, but he didn't want to seem too grateful and contented himself to wet his throat briefly before he spoke.

"I'm well satisfied now! Urgent matters lead me to you this time of year, Augustus."

"Indeed?"

"I came to speak to you about important aspects of church politics and faith."

Ambrosius noticed how Rheinberg's eyes narrowed imperceptibly and his body tensed. Gratian, on the other hand, seemed to be nervous, playing with the cup in his hand, although he pretended this was rather an expression of serenity.

"It must be something very important for you to take the journey," Rheinberg uttered. His Latin, the Bishop had to concede, became better with each new encounter.

"It's important, indeed it's of great importance. I was motivated to travel here because complaints by some bishops came to my attention."

"Complaints about what?"

"The fact that the complete tax exemption of ecclesiastical possessions is about to be repealed and that new donations of property would only be made to the church with a tax burden previously agreed upon, a fact none of my brothers is especially pleased about. I feel compelled to join them in their grievances."

"You are aware of the financial situation of the Empire?" Gratian asked with slight impatience in his voice.

"Well, of course, in broad terms. I'm aware that after Adrianople extensive funds had to be provided for the re-establishment of the eastern army."

"And for many other things that are necessary to meet the Huns effectively," added Rheinberg.

"Then the Empire should certainly open up new sources of revenue. There are many wealthy people who are exempt from any tax. The majority of senators, many nobles, estate owners – they all pay few or no taxes but are of immense wealth."

Gratian nodded. "That's true, honorable Ambrosius. We have taken steps in that direction. All tax privileges are to be deleted, and the amount of levies are to be reduced at the same time. Nobody is exempted anymore, but the burden will be distributed fairly."

"Excellent. I agree with that."

"Nobody, Ambrosius. I repeat, no one is excluded. Eligibility for the exemption of the traditional religions of Rome is also terminated. Everyone who generates income has to give up some for our future. Give to Caesar what the Caesar's is."

Ambrosius squinted.

"But the Church should continue to be an exception. We have to play an important role."

"When Rome falls, the fulfillment of this very role will be difficult," Rheinberg considered.

The Bishop was very grateful to the man for this defensive remark because it allowed him to gently steer the discussion toward the direction of his real problem. He therefore gave the time traveler a friendly smile. "That may well be. But there are nevertheless your own traditions that prove that the Church is eternal and survives the millennia. Empires disintegrate, there are even schisms, but ultimately the Church remains, and with it the dominance of the Catholic faith, the doctrine of salvation based on Trinitarianism. Am I wrong?"

Something flickered in Rheinberg eyes, but he didn't flinch. "Yes, the Church exists and Rome is its center."

"And the commandments are followed by millions of people – in many countries at the same time, spoken in many different tongues, even without the unifying bond of an Empire."

"This is true."

"Then why should the Church, with its eternal mission stretching through millennia, deal with the needs of a specific country or Empire and shouldn't rather primarily take care of its own welfare and existence?"

"Yes, why not? Do you want war and destruction to rain down on your faithful?"

Ambrosius waved it away. "The message of Christ has survived crisis and corruption and will continue to do so. You yourselves are the best proof."

"But my responsibility," Gratian declared, "lies mainly in the care of this Empire and the welfare of its citizens."

"Salvation is surely your goal as well!" Ambrosius said with coldness in his voice.

"The Church is responsible for salvation – and every Christian is, in the ways of his character and behavior. The Empire can provide a framework for this, nothing more."

"This framework is in danger if you impose economic burdens on us," the Bishop argued.

"This framework is no longer under threat, if everyone shares the necessary burden."

Ambrosius shook his head. "We move around in a circle, Augustus. Ultimately, we have to answer one specific question: Can we, the Church, our faithful and all those who have not yet experienced the grace of the word, provide effective protection against eternal damnation, when the Empire simultaneously takes away the means to do the work of the Lord effectively and everywhere?"

Rheinberg leaned forward. "Honorable Bishop, allow me a question."

Ambrosius nodded once.

"Why are you so sure that eternal damnation awaits people if the Church doesn't endeavor to avert it?"

"Redemption can be only achieved through Christ," Ambrosius replied firmly. "How else can a mortal see God? We accept the sacrifice of the Son of God and thus we attain mercy."

Rheinberg nodded thoughtfully. "But God has created us in his image."

"That's true."

"If he did that, we are part of creation, and some would say we even claim suzerainty over it."

"Sure, we have an exalted position in the plan of creation – but also a great responsibility," Ambrosius said. He didn't want to have this discussion with Rheinberg but with the Emperor. Still, Gratian listened to the dispute quietly and attentively.

"And the God who created us with this exalted task is a merciful God?"

"That he is. He is willing to forgive us if we turn to Him. His goodness is limitless."

"I understand." Rheinberg closed his eyes. "And he gave us free will, to do what we think is right?"

"That he did. Finally, a reason for the fall from grace. God gave us the freedom to do the wrong thing as well."

"The wrong from our standpoint or from His?"

"If we follow the scriptures, then surely from His, because He gave us commandments."

"God is so predictable?"

"We can't fully grasp and understand Him. We can only approach a certain understanding."

"Is that so? So God, the eternal Kind and ever Forgiving, created us in his own image, yes, even gives us an exalted position, and yet we need to ask for forgiveness? Yet He judges us and our sins? And so He sends all those who don't recognize Him, and especially His Church, in eternal damnation? The Jews, too?"

"The Jews especially. They have murdered the savior!"

Rheinberg shook his head. "Bishop, you describe an unfathomable God, a jealous, envious, stubborn and envious God. With that, he seems to be not so much different from Jupiter, who walked around to screw virgins and threw flashes in wild anger when upset – or when Hera has annoyed him."

Ambrosius stared wildly at Rheinberg. "The rules of the church–"

"The rules of the church are already clear to me," Rheinberg interrupted. "But are the rules of the church also those of God, or not only those made by mere mortals, precisely because the true glory of God is unfathomable to them, as you have just explained yourself?"

Ambrosius felt cold anger rising in him. "Who are you to judge God's intentions and will?"

"I don't. But you do it constantly. The only thing I actually can judge upon is this: We are all mortals who exist at this location and at this time. We have found a way of life that has its strengths and weaknesses, and surely we have the mission to consolidate the strengths and tackle weaknesses. But in the definition of these properties we all have very individual interpretations as there are different views on the nature of things and the nature of God. But if God is really found in all of His creation, in its diversity, in all people who He created in His image, and if He gave us free will – who am I that I can offend God by using this freedom or don't use it in order to hinder other people expressing their's?" Rheinberg rose and took a step toward Ambrosius.

The bishop saw no anger, especially no holy anger in the face of the time traveler, only a deep-seated fatigue, despair, whose origin he could not fathom.

"And so this Empire must act as follows if it is to survive: It must create the framework for this very free will. This frame will already restrict this will to a certain degree and you yourselves have just advocated such. We humans currently don't know a better way to get along with each other. So we have to work with what we have. And as long as God doesn't revoke his promise that we have free will, he surely has a purpose giving it to us. Who knows? Maybe it's just the jumbled mess that we call our life that pleases him. Maybe he watches as we hike through the ages in order to leave here and now a notable impression."

"God does what?" Ambrosius exclaimed. "Are you claiming with your example that the Lord has sent you?"

"He has at least raised no objection."

"You're a tempter! One who is upright and faithful will instantly recognize it! I don't know from which pits of hell you emerged, but as Eve once handed Adam the apple, so you want us to taste a fruit whose consumption will lead us into a deep abyss and true damnation for the whole Empire."

"Says who?"

Gratian had asked that. Ambrosius stared at him as if he was a troublemaker in this dispute with Rheinberg, although it had been his original intention to have this theological discussion with the Emperor and not with the German. But by being so incensed through Rheinberg's words, he had already forgotten his original plan.

The Bishop ignored the Emperor, was completely focused on Rheinberg.

The officer looked at him gravely, almost regretfully. "Even if God would cherish the most ungodly idea that there would be those who don't deserve to sit at his side are not being allowed to partake of his glory after death, why shouldn't he punish those that were mistaken in his eyes much earlier – why wait for a court, a judgment, and then punishment or banishment, if God could easily wipe out each and everything who displeases him any time? God is omnipotent, right?"

"That is true."

"What dark feeling of revenge drives God if even upon eternal suffering we couldn't meet his stern criteria, a fate he could easily end immediately with a simple stroke eradicating those who failed him? God is merciful, is he?"

"Yes, but–"

"The end is near? Judgment is close?"

Ambrosius hesitated. If he had learned one thing from the existence of the time travelers then it was the fact that the final judgment would obviously be deferred for quite some time.

But Rheinberg continued his thoughts already. "And if God has given us choice, why should he punish us for this our choice?"

"He is testing us."

"Why? To guffaw, sitting on his heavenly throne, full of lust for vengeance and ready to weed out those who didn't make it and only to reward those who found recognition in his eyes? So there is no freedom of choice, but only one way to salvation? Your system lacks logic, Bishop."

"It's the system of God. He gave us the law."

"No, it's what people have made of it in their lack of understanding, with their interpretations and distortions and reinterpretations. There is judgment, Ambrosius, I'm sure, but only the one which we are preparing for ourselves, and indeed already have, here on earth, causing the fact that we live in fear and let us govern by fear."

"It is good to fear God."

"I don't like God if I have to be afraid of him. The God I believe in, the one who gave me freedom and has made me according to his picture, I don't have to fear. No fear of judgment. No fear of revenge. No fear of punishment."

"And if you will lead a depraved life filled with violence and sin because you think God didn't see and wouldn't punish you for it?"

Rheinberg frowned.

"God gave me free will. He will not punish me. If God would

demand strict subjection to certain laws, why did he admitted the possibility that we can violate these laws?"

"He gave us free will. Free will to err as well."

"What kind of a free will is it if the choice is between something that brings certain damnation and only one that means salvation? How free is my choice, if it's not really *my* will, but that of the Church which tells me what I have to do? But do you know what, dear Bishop, probably you are, in a certain way, even correct. I also think that God has given us laws."

"The commandments of the Lord."

"I think about more fundamental laws. Laws that don't dictate me what I have to do, but the consequences that define the outcome of certain attitudes or actions. I don't know if you understand. But there is a difference between consequences as consequences of our actions and mere punishment. We know these laws of causality, so we will naturally refrain from everything that is bad for us. Don't we consider this, we'd base our decisions on coincidences. Sometimes we are right, sometimes not. But I don't think we will ever be condemned by God for something we have chosen freely."

"The Church has rules by which one can judge one's actions easily," Ambrosius argued.

"Yes, and some are not even stupid. But punish the infidels, take their possessions, kill them? And those Christians who interpret the truth somewhat different, hunting them down with flaming torches, destroy their property, set fires, as we know what's right and they don't? I don't know. What I know is this: I have a free will. So I accept this in others, and their exercise of it, for who am I to contradict God in this arrangement?"

Ambrosius opened his mouth and closed it again. He knew at once that any further argument, the continuation of this dispute, may conflict with his goal to win Gratian over for his cause.

His two brothers had followed the dispute in stunned horror, a mixture of anger, disgust and incomprehension in their faces. That was good, Ambrosius knew. It was what he had hoped for.

Only it wasn't Gratian who spoke all these words but Rheinberg, from whom he had expected nothing but heresy and defeatism right from start. He wanted to dismiss these words, shouting his conviction that they couldn't be derived from true faith. Rheinberg wasn't important. He would die. He had to be extinguished. This was decided and sealed, now more than ever.

But this young Emperor. Ambrosius's eyes rested on Gratian's face, which reflected perplexity. This young Emperor ... could he be saved? Or was it possible to seal his fate in the eyes of his witnesses right here, in concurrence with the one of his Magister Militium?

Ambrosius turned directly to the Emperor. "Well, Augustus, you heard the words of your time traveling friend?"

"I did."

"Do you think and advocate along his line?"

Gratian said nothing, thinking. Then, after a few seconds, he sighed and stretched. "Ambrosius, I respect you very much."

"Thank you, Augustus."

"You're a smart man and respected by many. Your word carries weight, and often you speak true. I would've liked you standing by my side."

"I'll stand by your side, Augustus. But some of your decisions and how you choose your counselors doesn't make this easy for me." Ambrosius didn't even cast a meaningful glance at Rheinberg, as everyone knew who he meant in particular.

"Was Galerius very stupid, Bishop?"

Rheinberg knew that the Emperor referred to the co-emperor of the great Constantine, the original author of the famous edict of toleration, which afterwards was often wrongly attributed to Constantine. Suffering from terminal cancer, it had been one of the last acts of Galerius to sign the edict. That Constantine, masterful politician he had been, subsequently discovered the political potential of the Christian religion himself had made his role appear even bigger, at least from a historical viewpoint.

"Galerius was good to put an end to the persecution of Christians."

"Why then initiate new persecution?"

"It's a different time now. The message of Christ has come to the ears of many. It's now necessary to comprehend the state as an instrument of Christ. It's the great task of the Empire to help the true faith to success."

"Here our views differ," Gratian said softly. He rose, stroked his toga smoothly and looked pensively for a moment into the flames flickering in the fireplace which heated the room.

"I admit, once I've thought as you, Bishop. The state as an instrument of God. The Empire as the executor of the Christian message. Ausonius taught me this."

"Ausonius is a wise man. Listen to his words."

"I think he is wrong. The Empire has only these purposes: the perpetuation of itself, the creation of a framework of law and public order, the preservation of civilization. And that consists of more than the Church or faith. Rome is old, Ambrosius. Do you want us to forget the centuries that have brought us this far? Shall we negate and blemish the deeds of our ancestors? Is all that worth nothing?"

"It's a different time," Ambrosius insisted, as couldn't think of a better answer. Christian or not, the respect for the ancestors was dug deep in the Roman soul, and the hot-headed Bishop couldn't relieve himself from this entirely.

"It's a different time," confirmed Gratian. "The Huns don't care whether we are Christians or sacrifice to Jupiter, whether the soldier who wields the sword is praying to Mithras or Sol Invictus. Look at the Roman soldier and how he protects the safety of the Empire. He doesn't care if Christ is one with God or separated from him and whether that Council said this or this Council that. And aside from the Huns? What about the Goths, who call themselves Christians?"

"Arians," Ambrosius spat out.

"Anyway. Did the Goths strike my co-emperor Valens before Adrianople and shook the Empire to its foundations? And what about the Parthians, Bishop? If we pursue your beliefs, do we have to take care of the Parthian Empire? Did Julian the Apostate die in his fight against the Sassanids because he wasn't a Christian?"

"Yes, God has punished him!"

"He made a decision using his free will," Rheinberg murmured. "Perhaps this decision was stupid, but why would God punish him for having exercised his God-given right?"

Ambrosius ignored him.

Gratian sighed. "Bishop, the Huns don't care about all of this, just like all of our remaining enemies don't. The Empire is the Empire. If we don't exist, there is nothing left. This is the greatest responsibility, it is the highest objective. And for that I need the help of everyone, Ambrosius. The help of those who believe, just like Symmachus, in the old gods. The help of the Trinitarians. The assistance of the Arians. The support of the Manichaeans. That of the disciples of Mithras and Osiris and the Sun God. The unifying idea is Rome. That should be everyone's common ground, and if that is achieved and secured, let everyone believe whatever he wants to. Let them worship. Everyone needs to account for himself with his gods, as I do every day when I pray."

Gratian sighed again. He looked very tired, almost as tired as Rheinberg, and for a brief moment Ambrosius wanted to have pity on him.

Only a very brief moment.

He rose. It was clear that the Emperor had made his decision. The words were struggling for attention in the bishop's mind. He understood them on an abstract, rational level. But he didn't want to think about them like that, didn't want to see where they might make sense and where not. He knew his goals. It the end, it was the state church that needed to be established – the church of the state, the state of the church, both inextricably linked and both united in an effort to spread the true faith.

In and outside the Empire.

Nothing else mattered.

Nothing else was important.

And whoever stood in the way would be swept away by the power of this necessary and unavoidable process.

There were still a few exchanges of polite words. The atmosphere was cold. Both sides knew what they had to expect from each other. And while they were trading pleasantries, all of them considered what would happen now, what were the consequences and what was inevitably unavoidable. The uncertainty was certainly stronger among them than with the Bishop of Milan, who knew exactly what to do and where would it would eventually lead to, especially in regard to Gratian's and Rheinberg's fate.

God, he was certain, was on his side in this.

Ambrosius parried all the questions and comments of his indignant brothers, as he paced briskly through the palace afterwards and again arrived in the waiting-hall, which was lit by oil lamps. The artists who worked on the mosaic had made it a day, the site was abandoned for now. For a brief moment Ambrosius felt the need to tear it up violently. He knew that his brothers would've taken part in it, if only to please the Bishop.

He took a deep breath, glanced at the guards who stood silently in niches at the wall, seemingly unconcerned and inattentive – but Ambrosius knew better. He lowered his head and left with his companions toward the cool evening air.

15

Thomas Volkert turned around on his horse and looked along the column, which had taken careful preparation for the upcoming march. He had been assigned to one of the larger reconnaissance groups, almost a small legion in itself. After the German troops had arrived, the preparations for the departure had increased in intensity. Twenty-two German infantrymen – the best riders, as far as one could make that judgement after the short training – would take part in the expedition. It had been Volkert's primary concern to avoid the fellow time travelers as much as possible. He observed them from distance and was satisfied with the fact that he knew no one of the soldiers by name, didn't recall any of them in any particular way. It was therefore to be expected that he wouldn't make any impression on them either.

The biggest challenge was not to speak German. Once there had been an incident in which he had nearly betrayed himself. Two of the infantrymen had been sitting by the fire and made fun of a young Roman recruit who had vainly struggled with his luggage. Instead of helping him, they had uttered a number of very snide remarks in German, and these remarks eventually degenerated into insults of all Romans, the barbarians of this time, their primitiveness, their stench, and their disgusting eating habits. Anger about the arrogance and stupidity of his countrymen rose in Volkert. He almost went in between and would have shouted his reprimands. A sergeant had rescued him who had rebuked the two talkatives and assigned them a strenuous duty. Volkert had spoken a prayer of thanks afterwards. This was a warning to him. He had to exercise full self-control and keep facial expressions and gestures under control. A look, a pair a raised eyebrows, a grunt or sigh, all this could betray him when it struck an attentive observer. The best was to keep distance between himself and the infantrymen as much as possible.

At least in the previously outlined formation of the column he should be able to succeed in this. The German infantrymen would bring up the rear, together with the carts, where the expedition transported its supplies. There were new carts which had been brought by the Germans from Ravenna, they were sprung and had wheels with forged iron spokes that would be less likely to break. The technical innovation has been absorbed by the Roman legionaries with great interest. Instead of oxen or their own pitiful asses, powerful draft horses would pull the vehicles and their speed should increase. Thomas Volkert wouldn't face the Germans a lot as he had been assigned with his men to the front of the column.

When he turned back, Volkert overlooked Bertius, who sat like a sorry heap of meat on his horse, and whenever he believed himself unobserved, he threw Volkert angry looks. As the German had expected, the man was an excellent and skillful horseman, which had made him at once a candidate for the expedition. Since other officers shared Volkert's disapproval of lazy slackers, they were very happy, after careful deliberation, to have found a good reason for the pudgy legionnaire to receive a meaningful assignment. Perhaps they hoped that he would generate the heart of a warrior and prove himself. Maybe they wanted to get rid of him and his eternal bragging, especially those who would stay behind in Noricum.

Volkert glanced at the sky. It was late March, and unmistakably, spring was in the air. He took a deep breath and inhaled the spicy fragrance of nature awakening. The dawn of warm weather was one more reason for the relatively rapid departure. They wanted to come far today. Volkert had to be aware of the exact roadmap of his Centurion, and although they would still ride in familiar territory for the next few weeks, for a while even within the Roman frontiers, the task was ultimately to discern where the Hun's advance had reached by now. The aim was to plan a counterattack to stop the Huns outside the Roman frontiers and thus to avoid the worst.

Volkert couldn't say that he was particularly happy with this job. The fear of dying in this dangerous mission and never being allowed to see Julia again was as painful as the realization that was about to put more distance between himself and her than he ever had.

He pushed the thought away and tried to concentrate on the obvious. It was early morning and quite damp and cool. Breath rose in light clouds from his horses's nostrils, a vigorous Brown, who bore him willingly and seemed to be kind – maybe a little too good – natured for a cavalry horse, but Volkert didn't complain. Better that than being thrown in the dirt by a wild stallion at every possible opportunity.

Not that this was very likely anymore, at least not as it had been a few months ago. Along with the improved carts, the infantrymen had also brought stirrups that could be attached to the saddles easily. They would allow the German soldiers, among other things, to fire their guns from horseback. One of the machine guns was mounted on an especially sturdy cart, pulled by two stallions who made an even more relaxed impression than Volkert's animal – probably not least chosen because of that mindset, as they were potentially able to endure the rattle of machine gun.

The departure neared. There were still a few riders who had not found their units. The expedition's leader was already visible at the end of the street, he still spoke with some notables of the city. There were priests present, blessing the mission – those of ancient Roman religions as well as the Christian Church. Volkert himself had been, the night before, invited by some comrades to a church service for Mithras, the god of war.

He had refused. No one had reacted angrily.

From the nearby town, a column of a different kind was moving toward the legionaries. Onlookers gathered at this almost springlike day. It was widely known that this departure was something special, not to be compared with the usual maneuvers. Although the order had been given to keep quiet about the purpose of the mission, there were plenty of men like Bertius who wanted to earn some fame from their knowledge about this expedition and boasted with their potential adventures in the city's taverns. There were no Huns, neither far nor wide. The probability that the knowledge of this mission would spread from the city was low. And thus, it became a social event.

Walkers, people in carts, a few hawkers who wanted to quickly sell something – a lucky charm, perhaps, or an extra bag for the expected loot. A little money changed hands, but Volkert rejected the advances of the businesspeople. He had only little cash and held his meager salary together. He had to save with a possible future in mind, as one day, if fate should have it, he'd meet Julia again, and wouldn't want to be completely destitute by then.

He tried to force the thought about his beloved away, but the notion was persistent. He almost thought even to hear her voice.

"Thomas, you go crazy," he muttered to himself.

"Thomas!"

Yes, he went mad. He heard voices! That was Julia, far away, as if she would speak from the ether to him. Volkert placed his hand on his forehead, closed his eyes for a moment, used his willpower. This was a bad time to doubt his sanity! He didn't need these kind of problems right now!

"Thomas! Thomas!"

Volkert opened his eyes.

No, he wasn't crazy.

He turned his horse around, eyes wide, full of disbelief, a storm of emotions raged suddenly in his chest. Excitement, wild hope, strong, nearly uncontrollable desire, all of it together and much more.

But that couldn't be!

Volkert looked around, but he could see no familiar face among all the folks. Did his senses play him a prank?

"Thomas! Here!"

There it was.

It was Julia!

It was her indeed!

Volkert slipped from his saddle, almost stumbled, ran toward the young woman, fell into her wide open arms, pressed her to him, sank completely in the embrace. He ignored the meaningful glances of the other legionaries, didn't hear their lewd comments. His face hidden in the hair of his beloved, he breathed in her scent, couldn't get enough of it, clung to her like a drowning man to the floating piece of wood.

"Julia! For God's sake! How did you find me?"

Julia struggled for words. Then finally, after a deep sob, she was able to speak. "I had help! Oh Thomas! I've only been a few hours in the city and have only now heard of the departure of your expedition! I rushed here immediately! I suspected that they would also send you! Thomas! When will I see you again? When?"

All that desperate hope spoke in her words, the long period of separation. It bubbled out of her, the marriage with the unloved Martinus Caius, who was now sitting in a tavern pursuing his favorite activity. And then, she could, no didn't want to keep to yourself, the joyful, painful the most important news: that she would have a child. Their child.

Thomas Volkert's child.

It was almost too much for him.

For a few moments, they clung to each other, silently, because words couldn't express what they felt. Then they parted. He looked into her face, resting his thoughts. There was no time.

"We'll leave soon, Julia," Volkert managed to say. "We'll be away for long. You have to take care of our child yourself. Promise me that."

"I promise it."

"When I come back, I want to know a place where I can leave a message to you."

Julia didn't hesitate. "Here in Lauriacum is the house of one Lucius Verenicus Utellus. He is one of the city's notables and has a slave, a writer named Remius. He is well-regarded and will surely remain in his office. The sister of Remius is my personal slave, and they regularly exchange letters. When you're back, get in touch with this Remius, brother of Claudia, a slave in Ravenna. He'll be able to send a message that I get to see, without ..."

"Say it, it doesn't bother me," Volkert lied bravely.

"... my husband noticing," she whispered. "Thomas, I couldn't do anything."

"I don't blame you. It is a safe home. It helps to take care of our child. That's all that matters now. When I come back, I'll send a message. We will meet and devise a plan. Until then, have faith."

Julia nodded, trying to wipe the tears from her eyes, but new moisture appeared immediately.

"I trust you. You just have to survive. Oh, Thomas, please, this is your promise – No Hun, no illness, no accident will take you from me."

Volkert buried his face in her hair, stroked her back gently. "I swear it," he whispered in her ear. "It's my sacred oath. I'll return, and you'll hear from me."

"Then I swear to wait and to take good care of our child," she whispered back. Her voice was now a bit firmer. She pushed Volkert from her, took her scarf and put it around his neck. Then she smiled shyly. "It's a bit silly," she said, almost blushing, "but it's all I can give you. Keep it well."

Volkert touched the fabric, pressed it to his face, breathing in her familiar, sorely missed fragrance. Then he folded it carefully and put it in a bag on his belt.

"That's not silly," he said huskily. "It will be my consolation and remembrance of my oath. I praise you, Julia. With this gift, my nights will never be lonely and it will smother every despair that aims to take me."

More tears welled in Julia's eyes. She opened her mouth to say something, when suddenly the column's buglers blew in their mouthpieces. The signal to move.

Just now.

Volkert felt the lingering despair growing and didn't move from the spot, yet at the same time wanted to implore and insult fate and God and the universe. But the storm of emotions that threatened to tear him led to no miracles and no consolation. Julia saw how it tormented her beloved husband was, and she took a deep breath, stepped away from him completely, smiled, and wiped away the tears.

"Remember your promise, Thomas. I love you. Be well."

"I love you. And be well yourself."

"You will live and come back."

"You will wait for me and bring our child into the world."

Julia nodded. "Then we both know what to do."

Volkert smiled. He knew that twinkle in her eyes. When Julia, the daughter of Marcellus, had made her mind up, no one would dissuade her of it.

And for this trait he was, at that moment, very, very grateful.

He leaned forward, a last, soft kiss. He enjoyed the feeling of the velvety touch a last time, then turned without a word, mounted his horse, which had been waiting faithfully at his side, and rode back to the column.

When he finally looked around, Julia had disappeared into the crowd of onlookers. But he knew that she watched him, felt her eyes just as he felt the determination that lay behind those eyes.

Again the horn was blown.

Men reigned in the horses.

The column slowly made its way. People waved. Children pointed excited at the time-travelers' wagons, the shiny shields, the horses, the standards.

Bertius joined his Decurion. All accusation was gone from his eyes.

"Your wife?"

Volkert hesitated, then he nodded. Yes. By all the gods of the Roman Empire, she was his wife.

"You'll see her again. I have a definitely positive feeling. Never deceives me."

Volkert looked at the sturdy legionary, was surprised at the warmth in his voice, the understanding, the confidence that he suddenly radiated. "Those are very kind words for someone who is responsible for ensuring that you have to participate in this expedition."

Bertius nodded gravely. "If everyone is blameless, who is to forgive?"

Volkert said nothing. He turned his face to the front, took a deep breath.

It went east, into unknown territory and toward imminent danger.
Thomas Volkert wasn't afraid.
At least he told himself that.

16

Josaphat pointed Marcellus' attention toward that great building.

"Look here! Those we have quite a lot of in Alexandria!"

Marcellus looked at the church and nodded. He was really tired now. The idea to go on an expedition with the boy had been much more attractive an hour ago. But Josaphat, despite his ragged clothes and the fact that he wasn't only working in port, but probably also slept there behind some crates, had provided him with someone who was particularly fascinated by religious buildings – temples, churches, obelisks, religious monuments for every deity –, and Josaphat knew them all.

Marcellus had expected something more exciting, maybe churches and temples he knew from Ravenna. No, the almost thirteen-year-old boy had occupied the seafarers with stories of the "really interesting" Alexandria – not the city of the priests and administrators, traders and shipowners, but the Alexandria of ...

Well, one had to say it frankly – the naked women.

The more naked, the better.

For someone like Josaphat, who grew up in the streets of the metropolis, it seemed that this topic didn't quite have quite the charm as Marcellus had hoped. Although he guided his newfound friend with gentle firmness and repeatedly to this aspect, especially when they had reached another monument, Josaphat was apparently not going to be convinced of deviating from the theme of his tour and visit different places. In addition, it was becoming dark, Marcellus was hungry and thirsty, and the long day had made him quite tired. He was on the verge informing his friend that he intended to return to the harbor when he suddenly stopped, quite thunderstruck.

For a brief moment he had thought to have seen someone in the crowd. A familiar face. A face that he hadn't expected to see here. And that didn't belong here.

He blinked, looked closer. Before a tavern, some men sat on rickety chairs, all busy with wine and an early dinner, some dressed in the robes of scribes and officials, others were clearly identified as workers who probably earned their livelihood in the harbor.

Nothing unusual, one might surmise.

Probably he had been wrong. The shadows lengthened. Moreover, it was not possible. An absurd idea outright. Marcellus passed his hand over his forehead. Yes, he was hungry, and banqueting men reminded him only too well of that fact. An illusion, caused by his strong appetite.

Again he wanted to talk to Josaphat, who studied the eating guests with a significantly hungrier expression than Marcellus, when the man he had seen stepped into view again. Almost against his will, Marcellus turned toward him, eyes widened. A young fellow came out of the tavern, looked around, as if expecting someone for dinner, twisted his face, clearly disappointed, and went back into the tap room.

No, there was no doubt! There was no deception, no imagination, and it had nothing to do with the shadows.

The young man was well known to Marcellus. His name was Markus Tennberg, had the German rank of an ensign and had disappeared together with von Klasewitz as one of the mutineers after the uprising against Captain Rheinberg failed. He was wanted in the Empire. Rheinberg personally had put a bounty of 500 denarii on von Klasewitz and Tennberg. He was very serious about these two, Marcellus knew.

Tennberg was more than just a deserter like Thomas Volkert. He was a traitor. Marcellus remembered the words his master, Chief Engineer Dahms, had found on the subject. When he spoke about Volkert, there was regret in his voice, but also sympathy and understanding. Clemency. Willingness to forgive. But once the subject of von Klasewitz and his accomplice came up, Dahms's voice was cold. Although they had arrested and demoted the rest of the mutineers, confinement had been deferred as each man was needed on board. Still, Dahms treated those crew members with cool rejection and, where necessary, biting sharpness. Tennberg had disappeared, and the charge of sedition had followed him into exile, and therefore, he had earned nothing except Dahms's deepest contempt.

Not least because this feeling had spread to a certain extent on his eager student Marcellus, the boy took a quick decision. "I'm hungry, Jos," he said, slapping his new friend on the shoulder. "Let's get inside!"

"I have no money," Josaphat said, barely an inch shorter than Marcellus, but of recognizable stocky build, with coarse bones and strong, sinewy hands. Such a boy, Marcellus anticipated intuitively, was always hungry. And a lot.

He took a few coins from his pocket. The most revolutionary innovation in his life was that he enjoyed, as a crew member, a meager but regular salary. And because he had had little opportunity to spend his coppers in the past few months, a relatively decent amount had accumulated.

More than enough for two square meals in a not too shabby tavern.

Josaphat saw the coins with big eyes, now more than ever convinced of the value of their friendship, and raised no objection. Determined, the boys entered the tavern. Under the pretext that it was somewhat cold outside, Marcellus entered the taproom. It wasn't very crowded, with several empty tables. Marcellus recognized Tennberg immediately, he sat in a corner, staring into his cup. Marcellus chose a table at the side and pulled Josaphat along.

A female slave appeared at their table, looking at them expectantly. Marcellus stared. The girl was much older than him, but for obvious reasons clad in a fairly close-fitting garment that gave credit to her bodily merits. That was exactly what Marcellus had wanted, and perhaps even a little too much of it. He grinned candidly while Josaphat didn't seem to notice, instead frowning at the words on the whitewashed wall that offered something resembling a list of menus.

The young girl who had seen little pleasure in her lot seemed to be intimidated and fearful. When Marcellus looked at the welts on her upper arm, it became obvious that she had been beaten, and not infrequently.

No, he told himself, that wasn't what he had wanted.

To his surprise, his friend could read, and when he had identified the food offered, he babbled his order. Mindful of the handful of coins owned by his friend, he confined himself to bread, cheese, a simple fish dish, and diluted wine. When he was finished with the order, the slave turned away and headed for the kitchen. Marcellus watched her, half-regretfully, half-pitying. There were some strange viewpoints from the future, especially about slavery, that slowly began to make sense the longer he thought about it. He had won a new perspective of life in many aspects during his the time on the *Saarbrücken*.

Marcellus sat so he could watch Tennberg from the side while he chatted quietly with Josaphat about trivial things. He tried to avoid the subject of the *Saarbrücken* and the time travelers as much as possible so Tennberg wouldn't overhear something that could make him suspicious. His friend was already concentrated on other things because the scents from the kitchen seemed to keep him quite captivated. As the waitress came back only shortly afterwards and set earthenware on their table, Josaphat was totally absorbed by the display. While Marcellus counted some coins in the open hand of the slave, he had pulled a bowl toward himself, torn a piece of bread from the loaf, and grabbed the thick wooden spoon. With intense concentration, he ate through the smoked fish and the vegetables, his eyes fixed on all the food and thus completely unresponsive to any other input. Now and then he raised his eyes, nodded approvingly toward Marcellus, took a sip of diluted wine, and returned immediately to further diminish the steadily decreasing amount of food.

Someone was really hungry.

Marcellus was by no means without appetite but had to keep Tennberg in mind, who seemed to be far more interesting, and so he couldn't keep up with half of Josaphat's eating speed. When his friend was ready and tried not to throw too longing glances at Marcellus' portion, he pushed the remainders toward him. Showing all signs of gratitude, Josaphat wrapped himself around the offer. Marcellus kept only his cup of wine in his hand.

Tennberg hadn't done much more than play with his cup as well. He kept looking at the door. It was clear beyond doubt that he was waiting for someone.

Josaphat was finished eating – now really done! – when Tennberg's appointment arrived. The deserter rose, pointed to an empty chair at his table. Marcellus looked at the newcomer. He seemed to be well-dressed, shaved and coiffed neatly, a man of some means. The two men put their heads together and whispered to each other. Marcellus struggled, but he couldn't understand a word. So he had no choice but to sip his wine and to remain as inconspicuous as possible. Soon he felt the growing impatience of his friend, and decided to initiate him. In rapid words, he outlined the situation. Josaphat, with a full stomach and visibly grateful for the invitation, was immediately hooked. He promised Marcellus to help with anything that was going on, and ordered, only for camouflage, two more cups of wine that were brought shortly afterwards.

Finally, Tennberg and the man rose and left the tavern. Marcellus and Jos followed them. Outside, it was already getting dark. Marcellus realized that the men said goodbye and went their separate ways. He immediately knew who he had to pursue, and as Tennberg set off toward the harbor, the two boys rushed after him right away. Marcellus' plan was to determine the whereabouts of the deserter and to report his findings immediately afterwards to the *Valentinian*. Africanus and Köhler would know what to do.

The darkness made itself felt in the back alleys. While the main street was lit by the glow of numerous torches and lamps, there was hardly any illumination in the branching paths. Tennberg's shadow was increasingly difficult to identify, so the boys had to get closer to catch up. The fact that even in the dark Josaphat was sleepwalking through his hometown – and especially the port area – proved to be an invaluable advantage. The donated dinner, Marcellus concluded, had been an excellent investment.

Suddenly hard fists from behind grabbed his shirt. Marcellus struck involuntarily out, his little fist slapped a muscular arm, but then powerful fingers pressed painfully into his shoulders. Tears filled the boy's eyes, and he cried out.

"Scream as you wish. Nobody listens to street boys who have gone too far!"

Marcellus was whirled around, couldn't exactly make out the man, only a mighty shadow. Also Josaphat was caught, but he didn't resist, rather fell down like a wet sack. A second man bent over him, wanted to put him on his feet, as the boy started groaning.

"I feel so sick," he wailed. Marcellus saw Josaphat bowing forward, placing his right hand to the body, the outstretched forefinger stuck in his open mouth deeply and willingly, choking loudly and throwing up his dinner on the tunic of his captor with a big, powerful surge.

"Damn it! Ah! What a stink! Shit!" the man cursed and made an involuntary step backwards.

That was his mistake.

Josaphat tore himself from the weakened grip of the brute, whirled around and disappeared into the darkness. The captor, over and over covered with vomit, wanted to pursue, but realized already after a few steps that the boy had disappeared into the pitch-dark streets.

The man cursed again, violently and loudly. During all of this, the hands of the other man had been placed around Marcellus' narrow shoulders like iron. No chance of escape – and the trick with puking wouldn't work a second time, Marcellus was sure of it. Jos seemed to have experienced this kind of attack several times, as fast and slick his reaction had been.

Then the shape of a third person emerged from the dark.

Tennberg.

The young deserter looked disdainfully at Marcellus.

"It's him. He must've recognized me."

"The other boy got away, sir," the man who had been vomited on said in a submissive tone. "He has ..."

"I smell it. Clean up and then come to the shelter. This one we take along. The other boy is hiding somewhere, and no one will take his words seriously. No one listens to this rabble. And no one knows where we are hiding. To have this one is the most important thing."

"What happens to him?" the big man asked, taking Marcellus in view.

Tennberg threw the boy a contemptuous look.

"That's Dahms's little pet. We will interrogate him. Once he tells us, he will be killed. Another child's body in the sewer won't interest anyone. Then we can continue our work."

"The expedition to Aksum will depart soon. Should we still intercept them here in Alexandria?" the other man asked.

Tennberg whirled around and gave him a kick. "Idiot!" he hissed. "What's next? Want to write our plans on posters and display them everywhere? Fuck you! Now go and clean yourself; your stink makes me sick."

The dirtied man turned away silently. Marcellus felt lifted up and thrown over his massive companion's shoulder. In his stomach, he felt the icy lump of fear. He had well understood what Tennberg had said. Interrogation and death. Once more tears welled in his eyes, and he suppressed a sob. Suddenly he felt very alone and anything but adventurous. He waited and prayed fervently Jos would quickly find his way to the *Valentinian* and would be heard there. The crew surely already worried about his absence.

Weak resistance stirred in him, and he squirmed in the iron grip of the man, but Marcellus had to be beaten only once, so hard that the boy had to gasp for air, that he stopped its attempts. Without resistance, he let them carry him away, his face turned toward the man's back. Tennberg seemed to go ahead.

No one would bother. Therein the deserter was certainly right. Alexandria was full of homeless children, like in any other major metropolis of the Empire. They were under no one's protection.

Marcellus felt discouragement.

And this time he didn't suppress the sobs.

17

Godegisel hadn't expected this development.

Yes, he had brought the imprisoned ex-emperor of the East faithfully to those who were cross with Emperor Gratian, in order, as the Judge had expressed it, "To stay in the game." The young Gothic noble knew what was meant, and although the Goths were now de jure Roman citizens and settled on Roman territory, after they had been crushed resoundingly before Thessaloniki, the Judge still remained to be their leader, even if not formally in office, and eager to somehow help determine the fate of the Empire they were now a part of.

Military influence was no longer possible. The Romans had taken the Goths' weapons and widely distributed their people over the eastern half of the Empire. To have their own, closed settlements was banned, and with the population of the Empire being sparsely distributed anyway, that posed no problem: There were plenty of semi-orphaned villages and towns that were filled with the settlers. The reforms, which flooded the Empire after the arrival of the time travelers, benefited the Goths. They profited from the new freedoms and opportunities, as those who once had been homeless had to make an effort to be accepted in their new abode – and urged to prosper.

And now here he was, and acting as something resembling a bodyguard. The conspirators under the command of Maximus had treated Godegisel not too honorably; doubtlessly, the nobleman wasn't of equal rank for them. It was this strange contrast on which he pondered in his free hours of leisure of which he enjoyed too many: On the one hand, the conspirators wanted to fight Gratian and the influence the time travelers had through him, people they sometimes described as "unholy" and "demonic," sometimes simply referred to as "traitors"; on the other hand, they had a certain respect for them, as they had defeated their enemies in the East and ended their threat for now, something they couldn't deny. And every time Valens, in those phases where he was of relative good mental clarity, was able to accept the descriptions about the battle for Thessaloniki as true, the Eastern Roman Emperor was apparently not averse to recognize the blessing in the intervention of the strangers – albeit he seemed to struggle with the fact that Gratian was now Emperor of all of Rome.

Valens was a special chapter anyway.

The injury he suffered during the Battle of Adrianople was completely healed, and from the outside the Emperor – or ex-Emperor – gave a fully recovered impression. But something had left its mark on him. Although he went through times where he appeared clear and reasonable, there were other hours, sometimes days, in which he seemed to be lost somehow, uttering meaningless phrases, and he didn't seem to perceive neither Godegisel nor anyone else who spoke to him.

Valens had already been at his best what some would have called a fickle, indeed unstable character. He had always been very concerned about his reputation and had judged his nephew Gratian more as a threat than as a colleague in office. The older he got, the more irrational features had emerged in his personality. He had to rely more and more on the divinations of oracle-magicians and augurs of different origins, involving them in more and more decisions, and they had exercised great influence on the eastern court – which had not been seen by all aristocrats or military leaders with joy. Valens had surely felt this displeasure even if nobody had dared to tell him openly. He had become locked up, imperious and intolerant, and it had been getting worse with each year. His decision at Adrianople not to wait for Gratian's help, but to risk battle, had only been the culmination of many wrong and hasty assessments. He didn't want to have to share the glory with his nephew, which was generally accepted as a reason for this decision. But maybe just one of his oracles had told him the fortunes for the battle stood well.

So if one wanted to see something good in the new Valens, then that he was painfully aware of his greatest fault and in those phases where he seemed to think and speak clearly, he was able to argue and analyze. Godegisel had told him that it was he who had captured the fleeing Emperor in the ruins of a small farm far from the battlefield. Although Valens had been quite conscious, the older man couldn't remember any of it. He didn't seem to dislike the Goth for what he did, at least he didn't show it, and he accepted him willingly as an interlocutor, he sometimes even showed an interest in continued conversation.

The visits of the conspirators were of a different quality. Godegisel had quickly figured out what the men wanted from Valens: They wanted to take his shine as Emperor of the East to give the usurper Maximus some legitimacy. If after the fall of Gratian Valens would miraculously appear, formally wearing the purple of the East, and bless Maximus' violent overthrow, raise him to co-regent, and afterwards abdicate so that Emperor Maximus ruled Rome – that would be ideal. Valens, as he had been promised him, could retire in honor, of course with an appropriate entourage, a state pension, perhaps on Capri, or in Diocletian's ancient palace, or wherever he was out of the way.

Godegisel had the impression that this plan was weighed by Valens, not being in favor and not against it, and so the conspirators had so far elicited no definite answer from him. It was as if two souls lived in the man's chest: one of the new Valens, refined or humiliated by fall, injury and captivity, ready to compromise for a dignified life of old age; and the old Valens, proud, irascible, envious and ambitious, who defined himself entirely as Emperor of the East, and despite the rejection of his nephew's rise, rejecting the usurpation of the Britannic general simply for reasons of principle. On top of that, the conspirators had their religious beliefs poorly concealed, especially a radical trinitarianism and, sponsored by Ambrosius, the idea of a corresponding state church. Valens was a Christian, but he had governed in a part of the Empire in which the Arian bishops used to have the upper hand, and it seemed that he rejected the fundamentalist radicalism of Maximus for reasons Godegisel himself couldn't fully comprehend.

Anyway, the young nobleman was not sure what role he had to play in this charade. Officially, he was seen by Maximus as a link to the "gothic interests," whatever that meant. Godegisel wasn't even sure what *his* interests were. The Judge had given him no instructions, and fearing discovery, Godegisel also had sent no request to ask for further advice. In addition, loyalty or not, Fritigern was really Judge no more but only a little, privileged landowner in eastern Rome, surely respected, but without any formal power. The treaty with Rome stated in great detail that the Goths had to dissolve any semi-statehood and had to fit completely into the legal structure of the Empire. No *foederatii*, no state within a state, but full integration and assimilation in exchange for peace and full citizenship.

Godegisel wasn't sure about his personal attitude in regard to the whole issue. He considered Maximus to be a military commander of some ability who could muster and maintain loyalty, a skill that was definitely essential. But Ambrosius appeared to him dogged and fanatical in every meeting he attended, and in addition most Goths were more inclined toward the Arians – a victory of the cause of Maximus might prove to be rather negative for his people in the long run.

Godegisel had also spent much time thinking about the time travelers. The battle at Thessaloniki he had witnessed at the forefront. The arms of these men had indeed inspired fear. But the men themselves had differed only marginally from everyone else. They had been mortal, very mortal, and Godegisel himself had killed one of their leaders. But after that he had waited in vain for the revenge of the time travelers, expecting a special, individual punishment. The people never appeared to him as demons or beings with supernatural abilities. If it was true, and they were only separated from him by a large number of years in time, wouldn't it make sense to take their advice seriously and to create a future in which some errors could possibly be avoided? Godegisel found this idea very attractive. And if God had something against it, why didn't he simply make the trip of the metal vessel through the ages impossible in his omnipotence?

No, the more he thought about all these things, the more it

appeared that the help the Judge intended to render to the conspirators as a defiant gesture had not been fully thought through. And whether it were the critical comments of Valens when he was in the mood to talk to him, or his own perception of the meeting with Maximus and his comrades, both solidified Godegisel's conviction that he played the wrong role at the wrong place.

So he stood, lost in thought, not too far from the window of his residence, a simple building in the province of Britain, far from the capital. The fact that the temperatures in the new settlements of the Goths were probably far more comfortable didn't contribute to Godegisel's motivation to linger here any longer than necessary.

"Full of thoughts, young man?"

Valens's voice startled Godegisel. He turned around. The ex-Emperor sat in a chair, a cup of wine in his hand and spoke his first words for hours. They were alone.

"Lost in thoughts, yes, Augustus."

Valens made a dismissive gesture.

"Don't call me that. I may be a stupid old man who doesn't always recognize what is happening, but Augustus I surely am no longer. And even if I should return to my office, then only for a short time and by the grace of Maximus, who, it seems to me, is a thoroughly ungracious man."

Godegisel smiled. Apparently one of Valens' better phases has begun. They were mostly characterized by a healthy sarcasm.

"You haven't yet confirmed your role in the whole endeavor."

"I'm not satisfied with the assurances."

Godegisel listened up. That was a new line of thought, a new quality.

"You don't want to confirm the Emperor Maximus, once he has overthrown Gratian?"

"Nope." The man took a sip of wine and grimaced. "Vinegar," he muttered. Then he turned his gaze back to the Goth.

"I was very thoughtful, dear friend. Many weeks, even months. Often my thoughts were confused, but I've actually noticed much of what was happening around me."

Godegisel kept silent.

“I have now made a decision. I was a fool before Adrianople, and I’m a fool if I make Gratian responsible for any wrongdoing. He is young and does what he can. Had I waited for him, your men would’ve been wiped out at that time, and all these problems wouldn’t exist.”

Godegisel didn’t comment. But he couldn’t help himself but to agree with the old man. Against the united Roman army, the Goths would’ve had no chance. It would’ve been a bloody battle, but the result would’ve been utter defeat of his people.

“Maximus will tear the Empire in pieces with a civil war. My brother Valentinian has repeatedly warned of this possibility and has done everything possible to prevent this to happen. He handed me the East, knowing that his son Gratian would inherit the West. My job as Gratian’s uncle would’ve been to protect my nephew and guide him, rather than putting him in peril through my carelessness and arrogance.”

Valens shook his head sadly.

“No, Godegisel” he said softly. “I didn’t do my duty. I’m not worthy that on the day you found me, Centurion Alchimio and his men have died. I’ve betrayed them exactly as I have betrayed my nephew.”

The ex-Emperor had seen that Godegisel had stiffened at the mention of the name. Alchimio had fallen by the sword of the Goth, as any remaining soldiers of Valens’ bodyguard.

Valens raised a hand. “No complaints, young man. I told you, I take the blame. You did what had to be done. Had I been in your place and in my right mind, I wouldn’t have acted differently. Alchimio’s blood is on my hands, much more than on yours.”

Godegisel did not know what to say. He had been assured in previous conversations that the former Emperor didn’t held any grudge against him, but in this context, Valens had never confirmed that so clearly. What was the old man up to?

“Now you are asking yourself why I’m telling you this, right?,” Valens asked farsighted. “That’s is quite easy. When I recognized – and should I be wrong, then forgive me my words – that you are as little excited about Maximus’ plans as I am, I came to some conclusions. I ask you: Do you have clear instructions to follow Maximus' orders, just to sit here with the purpose of not letting an old fool die of loneliness?"

"My task was to bring you to Maximus and then be at his will, but always to act with the well-being of my people in mind. Officially, I cannot hold any function, because with the Treaty of Thessaloniki, the Gothic nation, as far as the survivors of the battle are concerned, is gone."

Valens nodded. "Yes, very clever. Loyal Roman citizens you are now, aren't you?" He let out a soft, bleating laughter.

"I'm not too clear about the level of loyalty and its direction," Godegisel admitted. Valens looked at him with narrowed eyes, pressed his lips on each other. Then he set his cup aside and leaned forward in a somewhat conspiratorial attitude.

"I thought about it. My loyalty is clear. It applies to Rome. It applies to the rightful emperor. Both I once betrayed – and myself as well. I won't make this error a second time."

"What do you have in mind?"

"I want to leave as soon as possible. We are guarded only weakly, more ... observed, I should think. It should enable us, especially in this weather, to escape under the cover of darkness, to bribe a fisherman and cross over to Gaul, to travel hastily to the court, and to inform Gratian about the objectives and the extent of the conspiracy."

"Us? We?"

Valens looked down. "I'm old and probably not at the height of my powers," he said softly. "I need help. Alone, I cannot prevail. What do you think, Goth? Do you want to go home or continue to kill time here – possibly even years, depending on when the conspirators intend to strike?"

The young man turned his gaze from Valens, staring back into the hazy, Britannic day and remembered his thoughts that he had just entertained. He realized more and more that the former Emperor's proposal was a way to solve his problems. And had the Judge not handed the prisoner over to his care? Godegisel found himself smiling at the prospect of being allowed to leave this rainy island.

Valens interpreted the smile correctly. He leaned back and clapped his hands.

"Bribe a fisherman, right?" Godegisel said, left his place by the window and sat down with Valens. "With what exactly?"

Valens smiled. "Well, I certainly have no gold on me. And since my friendly hosts cater for all my needs, they haven't found it necessary to provide me with some cash. But be honest – Your Judge sent you on a journey without money?"

"It was a long way. And my men also needed something for the way back." The fact that Godegisel had returned to his Gothic companions in Gaul had, in retrospect, probably been a mistake.

Valens nodded understandingly. "As a selfless leader, concerned with the welfare of your men, you have given them all the remaining money."

"Well ..."

"No?"

"Not quite."

"What is left you?"

"Ten denarii."

"Ah, gold. For two of them, every fisherman will be quite willing to help us to the mainland and for a third to keep his mouth shut, possibly even for a while."

Valens gave Godegisel an inquisitive look. The young man scratched his head. Then he grinned.

"Better than sitting around and being philosophical about it, isn't it?" he said.

"Philosophy leads to melancholy," Valens said firmly.

Godegisel nodded. "But who tells me that you wouldn't sink back into mental slumber shortly, becoming unapproachable, and possibly won't remember our plan?"

"I do. Even when I appeared absent, I've indeed been wide awake. And for our guards, I'd like to maintain this impression of delirium for the meantime. But secretly, let us make our preparations. Here, I start immediately: I have created a detailed plan of the locations and wake cycles of all soldiers, with whom we had to do in recent weeks."

Valens pulled out a document. Godegisel stared.

The ex-Emperor had not lied. He had been attentive and alert, more than even Godegisel would've expected. And he had planned his endeavor long beforehand.

Godegisel bent over the paper.

At least he was hooked now.

And he vowed never again to underestimate a Roman emperor ...

18

Rheinberg had a palace.

No other word occurred to him to describe it properly. This evening, at dusk, he returned to the refuge that had been assigned to him as commander-in-chief of the Empire's armed forced in Treveri. A large estate consisted of a main house and several outbuildings, insufficiently described by the naked word "urban villa," at least in Rheinberg's opinion. For him it was a palace.

It wasn't that he had been accustomed to bad accommodations in his past life. His father had brought him up in modest prosperity, and his family built a nice little house where Rheinberg, before he was sent to the military academy, had even occupied a separate room. Later, as part of his military career, and after passing the exam, he had enjoyed the privileges of an officer's accommodation, always something better and more spacious than for comrades of lesser ranks. Never luxurious and large, but always sufficient, especially for Rheinberg, who had been trained in self-discipline and modesty from early childhood.

But this was a *palace.*

The house's superintendent, the factotum, was called Felix and was an old, venerable man who organized the budget and had to ensure that his master didn't lack in anything. Rheinberg felt uncomfortable in his presence. This wasn't because of Felix himself, who was courtesy and politeness in person and of gentle demeanor, always attentive, friendly, officiously. It had nothing to do with the fact that Felix was an elderly gentleman, distinguished, with a neat, white beard, a venerable appearance, instinctively evoking respect – a respect that was also shown to him by the other, very many servants. Every time Rheinberg wasn't at home, Felix was in absolute command.

No, his apprehension was mainly attributable to the fact that Felix was a slave. Slave since birth. Owned by the state, to be precise. Rheinberg had asked him about his life and in a polite, quiet voice Felix had obliged. Born in slavery, he had come to enjoy a good education because his parents, owned by the state like him, had been scribes and tutors. He had learned mathematics and geometry and philosophy and spent some time working as a private tutor for several high government officials, especially in the training of their children. He had worked in the imperial administration, until he was assigned to the staff of the Magister Militium. As he was close to sixty years, he was granted with a more relaxed task, and all in all, according to Rheinberg's impression, the old man hadn't had a bad life so far.

But he was a slave.

Rheinberg had big problems with this fact. In the settlement of the time travelers close to Ravenna, slaves were no longer allowed. Those capable men and women who had been noticed while the dry dock was excavated, had been acquired and released immediately into freedom. The crew, especially those who were close to socialist ideas, couldn't tolerate slavery right under their noses, and Rheinberg had agreed happily to address their grievances. It was slavery that hindered, in his view, the technical and economic progress of Rome. To abolish it completely was one of the long-term goals of his reform program.

The biggest irritation was not even Felix, the old factotum who radiated a great degree of tranquility, confidence and thoughtfulness. Rheinberg treated him with respect, and never appeared to any of the staff rude or overbearing, and almost everyone was recruited from slaves. Felix seemed to appreciate his new master, his friendly manner, and his tendency to punish violations against the rules of the house with mildness. Since Rheinberg had occupied his residence, no one had been flogged or tied or otherwise tortured. The atmosphere was easy and pleasant, just what Rheinberg coveted after a long day in the snake pit of Roman politics.

The biggest irritation was Aurelia.

She was a gift.

No, not a gift from the gods, but a gift in a literal, pragmatic sense. Prefect Renna, who owed him his promotion to his exalted position, didn't miss to show some gratitude. He had acquired a perfect slave for his friend Rheinberg from one of the most respected slave traders of the Empire – beautiful, young, educated and naturally very obedient and well-behaved. Aurelia was born as a slave and in her ancestry pretty all of Rome had been represented. Her father was a slave native of Dacia and her mother a slave from Persia. The father she had never met – he had been sold even before she had been born –, but her mother had told her about her own ancestors who stemmed from even more adventurous corners of the world. Growing up in the home of a Roman officer, her intelligence and beauty had been recognized and nurtured early. When her owner was in financial difficulties, he had to sell his most prized possession to make money in order to satisfy the debt collector. Aurelia had been one of the most valuable assets and was sold accordingly, at the very moment when Renna had begun to look for "something suitable" for Rheinberg.

Aurelia's facial features showed the Persian origins of her mother – a narrow bone structure, almond-shaped brown eyes. The slender figure was well proportioned and with her twenty-two years she was indeed a good five years younger than Rheinberg, but had spent her whole live mainly with what made her so valuable, alongside with her physical features – she had studied hard.

She spoke and wrote Latin and Greek and a Persian dialect fluently, the latter coming from her mother. She excelled in numeracy and had received lessons in housekeeping and financial management. She had impressive organizational skills, which even old Felix seemed to recognize with some envy. She was commissioned with the administration of large funds right from start and had a hand for economics. In regard to the purchases for the house, she proceeded with an almost military strategy and seemed to use the available budget of her master in a way he wouldn't have been able to manage himself. Anyway, he had barely looked after finances since his arrival in this period. It seemed that this was now, with the entrance of Aurelia, not longer necessary anyway.

That in itself wasn't irritating. It was a relief. But Rheinberg didn't like to have a personal slave. Felix and the other servants of the house were owned by the state, but she belonged to him alone. Renna knew well why he had done that. Did he want to test Rheinberg's convictions? Aurelia as his possession wasn't able to resist him in anything. For all his moral and ethical beliefs, Rheinberg was still a young man. He had thanked Renna for the gift, but made clear at the same time that he intended to give the woman freedom as soon as a favorable opportunity arose so that the Prefect wouldn't be insulted. Renna had nodded understandingly and left it to him. She was indeed in his ownership, he could do to her what he thought fit.

Then the irritation began.

First Aurelia was a beauty. Secondly, she was obedient and docile. And the third was that Rheinberg caught himself beginning to postpone the decision to give her freedom again and again.

And when he thought about it, he found to his greatest irritation that the reason for this attitude was as obvious as it could only be – He didn't want to release Aurelia, because she might take that as an opportunity to leave the house.

To leave *him*.

Rheinberg thought about this problem that night as he entered his property. Every evening the same ritual: A slave took off his heavy coat, brought a tray of chilled wine, instructed him to the fact that dinner could be provided, and asked if he had any special requests. He took note of all this with the same mental absence as always, and knew that only Aurelia's presence would awaken him. This would inevitably arise once he had sat down to supper. He wasn't lying down. The Roman habit of lying in order to eat he hadn't been able to acquire. If invited, it couldn't be avoided, but this was his house, and his slaves didn't care.

He could have called her every night to greet him. His aversion to enforce his will was hardly surprising. What else would have made it clearer that he was the lord and she his possession? So he preserved the appearance of her independence so that he didn't need to constantly think about why he didn't go to the magistrate to immediately prepare the documents for her release, disbursing a generous payment to her, or, even better, offering her a reasonable position that suited her skills. And so he lied to himself. He knew it, yet he acted as helpless as all ...

... men in love.

Rheinberg lifted the cup from the tray, which was handed to him by a silent servant, and took a sip. Another slave handed him a bowl of warm water and a towel. He cleaned his hands and face. The water was pleasantly perfumed. The towel still in his hands, he strolled relaxed through the atrium to the dining room, which was dimly illuminated by oil lamps. Rheinberg remembered that Dahms worked at Ravenna on the production of electricity and the construction of arc lamps, one of many projects of the enterprising engineer. He reminded himself to inquire into the progress of this project. The oil lamps stank, and their light was weak. At least, they repelled annoying insects in the summer. Sometimes, however, they also expelled the master of the house, and that was not quite the intention.

He cleared his throat, as he sat in front of the table. In the beginning, Felix, who was always attending to his matters in the background, waited if his master had a desire to enjoy table music. Rheinberg, however, who had talked all day and listened to too many voices, being beset by a multitude of people, and having to indulge in useless conflicts, never developed a special musical interest and preferred silence. The table music had been abolished as quickly as it had appeared. It was now pleasantly quiet.

Then, out of nowhere, the graceful figure of Aurelia appeared. She bowed slightly – all slaves of the house had noticed quickly that signs of excessive servility weren't enjoyed by their new master – and began, like every night, to cut the meat on the tray to place it on Rheinberg's plate.

And like every night, Rheinberg said, "Let it be, please. Sit down and eat with me. Be my company."

"As my lord commands."

"And cease calling me *lord*."

Aurelia smiled. She developed lovely dimples when she did that. Rheinberg never knew anything more to add, and once she sat beside him and waited for him to begin his meal, he just sighed.

"You feel sorrow, my lord?"

"I'm tired."

"May I massage you? Your neck is always very tense."

Needless to say that her competent hands, unerringly tracking the knotted muscles, were also among Aurelia's qualities. Rheinberg had once allowed her to massage him and then never again. The emotions that had been triggered and his inner conflict between his desire and the realization that he could have her at any time had meant that he had imposed complete retention on himself. He wouldn't be able to look at himself in the mirror again if he'd succumbed even only slightly to this temptation. He wouldn't be better than ... than those who were not better. Those who found to slavery to be totally acceptable. Who perceived slaves as not equal to them. Those who viewed them as only pieces of furniture, fixtures and fittings.

"Thank you, no," he consequently said, like every night, polite and determined, and again Aurelia lowered her head. It was, he thought, the complete lack of argument that worried him. No one in this house argued with him. All were only too eager to serve. And the fact that he didn't know if he was really a sympathetic human being for them or whether they all just smiled and were friendly because they feared punishment or because they had resigned to their fate as slaves, was certainly one of the basic reasons for his continuous irritation. This was especially true for the slave who sat next to him, and he looked searchingly at her, hoping to discern what she was really thinking about him – without false pretenses, without their relationship as owner and slave in the background.

Rheinberg knew he could only find out once he released her, and as soon as possible. And the fear that she would take this opportunity at once to depart from Trier and go her own ways, as befitted a free Roman, was exactly what kept him from taking this step. This realization, in turn, the admission of his own moral weakness, spoiled his appetite this evening, as it did all those evenings before.

For weeks now, he ate very poorly once he came home.

Aurelia seemed not to understand that. Or she pretended that she didn't understand it. Jan Rheinberg couldn't believe that she wasn't paying attention to how he behaved – or acted. He pushed the plate of cold chicken away and wiped his mouth with the cloth. He had hardly taken a bite.

"Fruit, my lord?"

Aurelia handed him a bowl. The fruits were a real treasure in the winter, brought directly from North Africa to the imperial residence. It was an incredible luxury, and it was a sin not to take any, but Rheinberg declined.

"Just help yourself," he encouraged Aurelia, who did so, smiling gratefully.

"What's new around here?" Rheinberg asked in order not to endure too much uncomfortable silence.

Felix, who had wisely kept himself in the background, stepped forward, as he felt himself addressed. "Everything is fine, sir," he said with dignity. Rheinberg looked at the narrow face with its neat sideburns. As a slave of the state, Felix would only be granted freedom if Rheinberg's great reform goal, the abolition of slavery, was achieved. He understood well that until then things could take a while, since it was necessary to overcome all manners of opposition. And he also knew that it was inevitable to eliminate this major obstacle to all progress in the Empire. At least then Aurelia would obtain freedom, by law, without any further procedure. Indeed, the German considered dryly, a nice little excuse that helped him not to take the really long overdue decision right now.

For a moment, Jan Rheinberg stared into his goblet. What had become of him? Magister Militium was his title. But in reality he became a politician, no soldier anymore, no matter how his office was called. Had the pestilence of this existence, the intrigues at court, already taken possession of him? Was he now full of corruption, his character already infected by all those who were willing to sacrifice their principles for any slight advantage?

Rheinberg felt his face pale.

"My lord, are you all right?"

So much for Aurelia's attention. It was perfect.

“No, I’m not too well,” Rheinberg replied spontaneously.

Even Felix looked quite concerned at his master. “Shall I send for a medicus?”

“No.”

“You need something else?” Felix said.

“Yes.”

“What can I bring you?”

“Nothing that could help me. Felix, thank you. Retire for now, your day’s work is done.”

The factotum exchanged a brief, helpless look with Aurelia, then the old man bowed and withdrew.

“Can I do something for you, sir?” asked the woman.

“Yes. Tell me something.”

“What’s your question?”

“Who am I?”

Aurelia hesitated imperceptibly.

“Jan Rheinberg, Magister Militium of the Roman Empire, the second highest dignitary of the Empire, a powerful man.”

“Wherein lies my power?”

“Your office. It stems from your history. From the means available to you as time traveler.”

Rheinberg nodded, half to himself, half to confirm what the woman had just said. “But that’s just my title and what I can do. Who am *I*?”

Aurelia faltered. “Philosophers have different answers to this question. There is none that truly explains everything or claims validity for everyone equally. I cannot answer it.”

“But I can.”

Rheinberg saw Aurelia straight in the eyes. They were dark, almost black, like a deep lake in which one could immerse himself. For a moment he said nothing, but then he changed his mind, forced out the words as if he had to struggle with them before they left his mouth.

“I’m a selfish fool, Aurelia.”

The slave was neither confused nor scandalized. She looked at him calmly. That made Rheinberg almost anxious. Secretly, he had expected that she'd deny it or would protest. But nothing of the sort. And she did absolutely nothing to force him to finally say what was needed to bring this issue to an end. He took a deep breath, then felt overcome with great perplexity.

"I should have you set you free the moment Renna gave you to me as a gift," Rheinberg finally explained quietly. "I didn't do it. It was a weakness on my part, which is ultimately inexcusable. I wouldn't therefore apologize, because what I have done – or rather, where I failed , is nothing that can be redeemed."

Aurelia frowned. "I am a slave, my lord," she said. "I have always been. I have always been treated well. No master took me by force. I received a good education. I live in comfort, even luxury. I have tasks that correspond with my skills, and you, sir, are a gentle and friendly master. What exactly should you apologize for?"

Rheinberg shook his head. Oh, what a golden bridge! He could easily set foot on it, and it would take some time, maybe halfway, to notice how deeply he would already be absorbed in sweet morass. A dangerous illusion, which he all too easily would be able to indulge in.

But he had made his mind up."It's not the nature of man to belong to someone."

"What is the nature of man?"

"To make decisions for him or herself independently. As the possession of another, this may be just an illusion, limited by the arbitrariness of the master in regard to this property."

"Do you make your own decisions for yourself?"

"Yes."

"The Emperor doesn't give any commands? Or then, before your trip through time, your emperor in the distant future?"

It was remarkable how elegant Aurelia could summarize in one sentence the dialectic of time travel.

"Yes, I follow rightful orders."

"And the men of your crew? Are they not absolutely subject to your orders and disobedience will be severely punished immediately?"

"This is ..."

"Contrary to every aspect of human nature you claim to be true."

Rheinberg pressed his lips on each other. Again he shook his head.

"No, because there is an important difference."

"Which one?"

"I have the choice. I can leave the Emperor's service any time, take my leave, put some gold to the side and buy a farm somewhere or start a business as a small coastal sailor, a new life. I wouldn't have had to enter into the service of my Emperor in my past, I wasn't forced. I did it on my free will."

"You didn't do it to please your father? Were you not obey him in everything?"

This woman, Rheinberg realized, listened too well and had a good memory. He had in the course of weeks told his staff bits and pieces of his life, and apparently she hadn't forgotten a word.

How unpleasant.

"I wanted to be a dutiful son," Rheinberg admitted. "But it could have been otherwise. My sister Helga opposed the wishes of my parents and married a shipyard worker whose political views my father didn't like – to say the least."

Memories of Helga and her husband Karl met him for a moment. He missed his sister. There were even moments when he missed Karl, because he reminded him of his home. The less pleasant aspects were: What had become of the war – or would become? Rheinberg realized that he obviously had far greater problems with the dialectic of different perspectives on time than Aurelia.

"No, you won't confuse me," he continued before Aurelia wanted to raise another objection. "I always operated under constraints, but I always had the choice to withdraw from them. A slave only has the chance to run away, with the possible consequence of death, or death itself."

"One can always run away inside."

Rheinberg looked at her blankly.

"No master can control my thoughts. I can have complete freedom in my mind."

Rheinberg raised his hands. "That's sophistry," he said firmly. "An illusion as an excuse. Human freedom expresses itself in its relation to the real world, not within the realm of imagination. Freedom means that we use what the world offers us to create something that serves us – in any way whatsoever. And this attitude thus is the root of fundamental rights such as the right to property."

"I'm the property."

"But I hurt your right by owning you. You have no property. How can I have a right while withholding the same from you? That would be unethical."

Aurelia looked at Rheinberg for a moment and sighed. "What kind of consequence does my master draw from all of this?"

"Your master has to do what he should've done right away."

"He offends me?"

"What?" Rheinberg was lost for words, which, he had to admit, happened too often in Aurelia's presence. He took a deep breath. "Repudiation?"

"Yes."

"That's how you see it?"

"Yes."

"Don't you desire freedom?"

"I see no difference between freedom and slavery. I'm fine."

"But just because you previously had luck with your masters."

Aurelia nodded.

"What would have happened if you hadn't come into my possession through Renna after being sold from your former owner? Suppose a greedy old man had purchased you, am ungracious, selfish master. What if he had begun to beat you for any nullity and whenever he lusted after you ..." Rheinberg stumbled on this, he wasn't accustomed to discuss issues like that openly with a woman.

"Actually, why did you never ask me to join you in your bed?" Aurelia asked. "Am I ugly?"

"What? No!"

"Or do you prefer the company of men?"

Rheinberg felt his face redden. "No!" he replied emphatically. "I'm absolutely, I mean, there is no way ... you're very ..." His stumbling lasted forever. Rheinberg decided not to be driven into a corner anymore. He took up the real issue again. "If your new master would have been, in every respect, a repulsive, cruel man, then wouldn't you recognize the difference between freedom and slavery?"

"Certainly."

"So ..."

"But this is not the case."

Rheinberg tried not to touch his forehead in despair. This discussion turned out to be far more difficult than he had imagined. He had the sudden desire for a sip of wine, and as if Aurelia read his mind, it was poured at once.

"But it could be yet. Fate sometimes takes very unexpected turns, I'm a witness to that," Rheinberg insisted.

"Your attitude of life directly influences mine," observed Aurelia. "Your attitude reflects especially a lack of trust in God. If the Lord hadn't had no big plans for you, you wouldn't be here."

"This hubris has already become the undoing of many a man."

"Distrust and fear of their own fate, too."

"We go around in circles."

Aurelia smiled. "I'd like to dance with you, my master!"

Rheinberg rolled his eyes. "Don't call me that. And no, I'm not a particularly gifted dancer."

"The quality of a dance depends solely on the joy of those involved in it."

"Can we please go back to the real issue?"

"We never left the topic. It's about me. It's about you." She paused. "It's about us."

Rheinberg reached almost automatically to the wine goblet and drank in quick, greedy gulps. For a moment, he wanted to be back in the snake pit of the imperial court, in the company of the most annoying and unnerving courtiers. He had indeed imagined this to be much easier.

Or maybe he just had the wrong attitude.

"Aurelia, it boils down to a principle. The principle is: A person may not possess the other. Anyone who chooses freely and without pressure to serve someone or something – a person, a government, whomever – I will continue to call free."

"In the Empire, these differences are rather blurred," she said. "The son of the oh-so-free soldiers was forced also to become one. Was he free or slave?"

"Slave," Rheinberg replied immediately. "That's why it is one of the major reforms that are currently supported by the Emperor either to completely abolish this duty or to soften it at least. Surely you have noticed these efforts."

"No. I just wanted to understand what you're talking about."

Rheinberg decided not to drink any more wine.

"You are my possession. There are some laws that also protect the slave, but ultimately I can do with you what I believe is right."

Aurelia gave him a charming smile. "That reminds me of the earlier question, why do you ..."

"And so I have decided," Rheinberg cut her off just in time. "You might call it an insult or a violation, and I will not reproach you for that opinion. Your life has been determined by the knowledge of being owned by someone else. I ask you now to make yourself familiar with the idea that you don't belong to anyone but yourself. And I will give you the legal underpinning of this idea, as tomorrow I'll go to the magistrate and prepare your papers."

Aurelia closed her mouth again.

"Think about it. You're welcome. I should have done this much earlier."

"Why didn't you?"

Rheinberg had hoped to avoid this issue. Since it was convenient that at that moment she wasn't free, but still in his possession, he had every right to refuse her an answer. He rose. "I'm tired. Tomorrow I'll take you to the magistrate. You'll receive a release bonus, a generous sum, and if it's your wish, I will offer you employment, tailor-made to your abilities. Think about it in peace. I'm not going to throw you out, even if you refrain from working here. You've got nothing to worry about. I'll retire now."

Aurelia nodded, her fine face very thoughtful.

Rheinberg went.

He scrutinized his emotional reaction. Did he feel better now? Relieved? Ashamed? Wistful?

There was no clear conclusion.
He would probably drink a cup of wine to gain clarity.
Or two.

19

"This brat can't be left alone!"

Köhler uttered a curse and nudged Neumann, who was snoring in the bunk above him. They had retired late, as the search for the young Marcellus proved to be useless in the dark and had therefore decided to await the daylight of the next morning. Köhler had gone to bed angry and frustrated, and in this mood he awoke once the rough hands of the ship's guard tore him from his too-brief sleep.

"What is this bullshit?"

The Roman soldier let go of Köhler. Two hairy legs swung in front his eyes down from the bunk bed. Suppressed murmurs from above showed that the physician was evenly angry about the disturbance, but presented his anger with more chosen words.

"The Trierarch asked me to wake you," the soldier said apologetically. "There is a boy, a street boy standing on the pier, and he definitely wants to come on board. We wanted to get rid of him, but he insists. Africanus said, maybe he knows something about Marcellus, and he has been brought into his cabin. I should wake you."

Each one's anger was gone immediately. Köhler donned a shirt and stuffed it into his pants, as Neumann slid to the ground and nodded. The bosun hurried behind the soldiers to the quarterdeck of the *Valentinian* where the designers of the ship had inserted the cabin of the captain.

As they entered the room, they found Africanus, similarly tired, but with an attentive gleam in his eyes. A boy stood before him, in about Marcellus' age, one of the many homeless children living on the harbor, staying alive with odd jobs or pickpocketing. When Köhler entered, the boy fell to his knees. Köhler reached for him with one of his powerful hands and pulled him back on its feet.

"There is no kneeling her," he grumbled.

"His name is Josaphat. He wanted to talk to you, only you!" Africanus told him smiling.

"Me?" Köhler squinted. The boy was obviously at the end of his tether. Köhler drew him to a chair and sat him on it. "You know me?"

"No, yes, no – Marcellus told me about you, sir."

"Marcellus. You met him?"

"We were together. I showed him the city."

Köhler stifled a curse. Boys. He would've been even angrier if not for his recollection that he himself had done much worse at this age. "Where is Marcellus?"

And then it gushed out of the boy. Their meal in the tavern and the strange behavior of his new friend. Then, as they were in the alley, already on their way home, the incident. Josaphat had a remarkable memory for names and faces, which was probably a matter of survival in his situation. When he was finished with his description, Köhler knew more than he liked to.

"Tennberg!" Neumann, who had only witnessed the last half of Josaphat's descriptions after fetching his bag with medical supplies, uttered the name like a curse.

"What is the traitor doing here?" Africanus asked.

"He's certainly not here on his own account," Köhler mused. "He's alive; that is an important information. It means, von Klasewitz will probably be even more active. And the fact that he is in Alexandria leads me to two conclusions – either he is hiding here with his master, or he's here to cause mischief."

"If the description of the boy holds," Neumann said, "then Tennberg has men and money. This is certainly no coincidence. Something is definitely going on. They know about our trip to Aksum. And they seem to intend sabotage."

"We must not only liberate Marcellus but also take Tennberg," Africanus murmured and looking pensively out the aft windows. "We need to know if and what exactly they have planned. It can hardly be that von Klasewitz wants to prevent the import of coffee to Rome."

"Whom can we rely upon in this city?" Köhler asked. "The local authorities?"

"Yes, perhaps. The question is whether we have so much time."

Africanus looked at Josaphat. "Boy, where could they have brought Marcellus?"

"I know it exactly."

All eyes turned to him.

"I ran away from them, but once they lost me, I followed their trail. Nobody knows the harbor like I do. They disappeared in a warehouse belonging Emilius Clarus Vengetius."

Köhler knocked Josaphat on his shoulder. "Clever fellow! Well done!"

The boy swallowed. "Lord, Marcellus is a friend. I might be regarded as the city's vermin, but I take that seriously. I had to find out, otherwise you wouldn't have believed me. I'm honest."

Köhler measured him with a long look, then nodded. "Yes, I think so, too. We're talking about your future once this is over."

If Josaphat became curious by this allusion, he didn't show it. Köhler turned to Africanus.

"Vengetius is someone well-known?"

"One of the richest men in this city, an influential person with contacts throughout the Empire. He was considered a staunch partisan of Gratian's father and has become very rich under him. Since Valentinian's death he has remained politically covered, but at sea, everybody knows him. Every fourth corn ship carries his banner, and he employs many former navy soldiers. A man of considerable status."

"And he grants Tennberg and his henchmen shelter?" The distrust in Neumann's voice was palpable.

"If he knows about what is happening in his warehouse – yes! And it fits. We all know that Rheinberg's and Gratian's plans for the Empire are under scrutiny by many powerful men." Africanus sighed and sat down, could hardly suppress a yawn. "It's logical to find von Klasewitz colluding with Gratian's opponents."

"This is a very dangerous development," Köhler murmured. "Von Klasewitz was an officer, but a no-good, disgusting human being.

But he was the gunnery officer aboard the *Saarbrücken* and not without reason. He is well acquainted with cannons, damn good even. No one from his former crew would dispute this; they are very happy that he is gone."

Africanus looked at Köhler worriedly. "So it may be that he secretly works on artillery somewhere? If that's true, someone intends to use it!"

Köhler nodded. "We must liberate Marcellus and learn more about this apparent conspiracy. Rheinberg has to be informed as soon as possible. How can we send a message?"

Africanus made a comprehensive gesture. "It's winter. The sailing ships are almost completely immovable. The *Valentinian* is the fastest method. Let us assemble a squad and immediately leave to the warehouse. If we find something, we send the *Valentinian* to sea, full steam ahead and on to Ravenna. Sepidus can take over. From there, he sends a messenger. Treveri can be informed within two weeks about everything we learn here, perhaps even earlier. Faster won't be possible."

"Then it shall be so!" Köhler said and looked at Neumann, who nodded silently. Africanus jumped to his feet, now, as it was decided, full of energy.

It took less than ten minutes for them to assemble their strike force. Of course, Behrens was among, and stoker Forstmann volunteered as well. There were also six legionnaires at the ready, Roman marines, armed with sword and spear. The Germans carried handguns, but had added the battle armor of a Roman soldier, complete with a helmet and chest protector. They had to assume that Tennberg wielded a weapon. Köhler remembered vaguely to have even seen the ensign in that fateful night of the mutiny with a gun, but his memory might be deceptive. A lack of ammunition could be assumed, but one single bullet was already sufficient to kill a man. Köhler decided once he saw such a weapon, he would shoot first and ask later. The Roman sailors were quite aware of this danger, but there had been no hesitation once the Trierarch had assembled them for the task.

Then, under the cover of night, they left, wrapped in dark coats. Josaphat accompanied them. He was supposed to stay behind, as soon as they would reach the warehouse, and not to interfere, and the boy had sworn sacred oaths to that effect. Köhler didn't know if he could trust the boy, but now they had no time to lose. Youngsters like Josaphat existed in all periods of human history, and Köhler knew that they were always equipped with a very strong survival instinct.

It wasn't far to their destination, but twice they were stopped by a night patrol of the harbor guard. Since Africanus could identify himself fully, no fuss was made about it. It took some time before the said warehouse was in view, the entrance illuminated by large oil lamps. Crouched behind wooden crates, Köhler observed dimly three men loitering near the entrance. Apparently a vigil, though a significantly lax one.

"Are they probably the only ones?" Behrens whispered and squinted.

"If I would be in Tennberg's place, I'd have posted additional men on the roof, and one each, protected by darkness, on every side of the building," Köhler said. "A prearranged warning and I would be informed of any approach."

"But Tennberg is an ensign who has never learned the fight properly at land, apart from his basic training," Behrens pointed out. "And you, my friend, are only so smart because I have had a good influence on you. One day you might even become a real soldier."

Köhler grinned. "Thank you for the compliment. You are right, Tennberg isn't so smart. But who is with him? We don't want to assume that there is no experienced fighter with foresight and experience among the Romans."

"We shouldn't indeed," Africanus intervened. "I'll send two men all the way around the building. Over there, one can climb the water tower. The night is overcast. He will, if careful, go undetected. We should soon have better information."

Köhler found no fault in the proposition.

Soon the legionaries had received their orders and disappeared into the darkness. Köhler and the others remained in their coverage, scrupulously careful not to make any noise. However, the three guards discernible in the light dispensed by the lamps continued to make a not overly attentive impression. One periodically put a small amphora to his mouth, and there was no reason to suppose that the liquid inside was water. Every now and then, one of the men stood to stretch his legs, but they never ventured far into the darkness. A change of the guard didn't take place either.

Finally, the scouts, one after the other, returned and began whispering their reports. Africanus summarized the results ...

"Idiots!"

Behrens grinned, his teeth were visible dimly in the darkness.

"So nothing?"

"Nothing and nobody. Those three bums."

"One of which has already enjoyed plenty of wine," Köhler added satisfied. "We'll just have to poke him, and he'll fall over."

"I want to dispatch of those without any noise. I'd like to enter the building with the element of surprise. What about doors?" Behrens intervened.

"In addition to the main entrance, there are two side doors. But both are locked properly. Our friends here are careless and frivolous but not completely stupid."

"Can we break the locks?"

Africanus pursed his lips. "There are massive wooden doors. Many thieves in this city are on night raid. The large warehouses are solidly built and sealed with thick bolts and iron locks. The biggest enemy here is fire, but it takes too long and is hardly controllable. And we'd make quite a noise. The fire station would be alarmed immediately. The men are very attentive."

"We'll focus on the front door. Can we overpower those three without them sounding the alarm?"

"Knives!" Africanus said immediately, making the characteristic gesture from left to right across his throat.

"They will notice us. Two are obviously not drunk," Behrens pointed out.

"Then our two archers," Africanus said. Two of his men he had chosen precisely because of this talent. They kept themselves ready in the background.

"Two arrows is, at best, two dead," Behrens criticized again.

"We only attack the two sober ones. We wait until the drinker has downed his amphora. When his comrades fall, he will respond late or, with luck, wouldn't even understand what is going on. Then we'll have sufficient time to sink a few arrows in him." Africanus grinned. "The location is convenient. All three are in the light. My men can aim at rest and the targets are in an ideal range. I expect smooth execution."

"This out of the mouth of an officer, and I get the shivers every single time," Behrens mumbled barely audible.

Köhler could understand him well, but it was the best plan in regard to the current circumstances. He nodded toward Africanus.

The two archers were in position at once. They were ordered to take their time. This was convenient because the drunk one took another long swig from his amphora, held it almost vertically over his mouth. Then a loud belch reverberated all over the place and he dropped the empty vessel. As if this was the command, the archers released their two arrows.

One hit in the chest. The man wasn't even able to raise his arms to embrace the arrow in an instinctive reaction. He fell silently to the floor.

The other also hit its target – but only in the shoulder. The guard had turned at the last moment to the side. It came as it had to: He let out a long drawn-out, high cry of pain. Then the two archers had been ready for a second try: Another arrow felled the injured and finally the drunk, who apparently hadn't understood what had happened, and who died quickly.

Now they had to hurry.

They jumped to their feet as one man. No instructions were necessary, everything important had been discussed. Africanus was the first at the door, checked it. It was unlocked.

He didn't hesitate, pushed open the door, entered. Köhler followed him close behind, pulled his gun, then Forstmann, Behrens, all with weapons at the ready. It was dark in the warehouse, but one could discern that light flickered in the middle of the large room. Large crates and bound bales disguised the direct view.

In both directions.

“What’s going on, Titus?” a voice bellowed.

Africanus took a deep breath.

“I fell over a stupid box!” he yelled back.

“Idiot!” Laughter rang.

The men nodded to themselves, and pressed ahead, exploiting the cover heartily. Then Köhler caught a first glance. In an open area, three men stand with oil lamps. Some figures, wrapped in coats, were firmly asleep.

Marcellus, tied to a chair. He bled from the nose, the face was swollen. He was breathing, as one could see, but he wasn’t conscious.

Hot, overwhelming anger welled up in Köhler. He felt how his hands began to tremble, felt the temptation to kill here and now all these men with carefully aimed shots. Then Behrens put his hand on his forearm.

“Quiet,” his lips formed silently. He pointed to one of the figures. The sleeper had turned his face toward them.

Köhler gestured to Africanus. Those awake had been spotted right away. Now they were able to identify one of the sleepers. The Trierarch passed it on to his men.

Under one of the lamps, two more men sat. They had apparently played with dice, had stopped for a moment. Apparently they didn’t know whether to be vigilant and have a look or not.

Africanus took the decision for them.

He jumped into the light.

His men followed him.

The dice players whirled around, their faces masks of horror. As the sword of Trierarch drove into the first’s chest, a fountain of blood gushed, and the man collapsed with a gurgle. Behrens shot, one time. The bullet hit the second man clean in the heart, not to be missed from this distance. Without ever knowing what had killed him, he went to the ground like a felled tree.

The sleepers awakened, churning themselves out of their coats, only to face unsheathed blades. No one was brave enough to venture resistance.

Ensign Tennberg didn’t as well.

He came out of his sleep with swollen eyes. Köhler himself tore him into the vertical position, Forstmann wrested the pistol and the knife he carried from him. Recognition flickered in Tennberg's eyes, then hatred and blind rage.

Köhler lifted a stick, which had been lying beside Tennberg. Blood was visible on him, still fresh. The traitor himself had taken his turn to beat Marcellus, a shackled, helpless boy.

Again, black, wild rage boiled up in Köhler. This time no one stopped him. He took the stick and swung, let it crash with force into Tennberg's ribs. A cracking sound, a cry of pain. Köhler took measure for a second time, now his swing met a thigh. Tennberg screamed again, fell to the ground, doubled over. Anger and hatred, yes, but now fear. It was this fear that smothered Köhler's fury. Behrens, who had already raised his hands to intervene, dropped them and said nothing.

There was nothing to say.

Neumann had, however, taken care of the boy, untied him, began to examine him. While the legionaries bound the prisoners and lined them up, Tennberg among them, collected all the weapons and freed them of all cash, Köhler and Behrens leaned next to the doctor caring for the boy.

"Well, Doctor?"

Neumann couldn't be disturbed. With expert hands, he felt the body of the unconscious, measured the heart rate and breathing. As Marcellus groaned and opened his eyes, he leaned on him and gave him water from a canteen that was accepted greedily. The boy recognized the familiar faces around him and smiled. Then his face clouded. "I wasn't strong," he said softly. "I told them everything. They ... hit me. In the face."

"Easy, my son," Neumann murmured, as he rummaged in his medical bag. "It's not important. We have it all under control."

Marcellus looked around with difficulty, his smile returned. When he saw Tennberg, squatting with his head down, his limbs tied closely, he spat.

His saliva was bloody.

"Doctor!" Köhler urged.

Neumann dribbled some medical alcohol on a piece of white linen cloth and began to clean the boy's external wounds, so that he repeatedly wailed in pain. "Left arm broken," he said then. "And a couple of ribs."

In fact, Marcellus hung his left arm motionless.

"We should carry him and back on the *Valentinian* where I can provide him with supporting bandages around the thorax after re-examining everything properly," Neumann said. "Do you have some of your mixture, Behrens?"

The sergeant knew immediately what he meant. He conjured a flask, unscrewed the little lid and poured liquid into it. Neumann took it and put it to Marcellus' mouth.

"Normally, I'm not in favor of this," he said, "but one sip will help you."

Marcellus swallowed, blushed, coughed, gasped and wiped tears from the corner of his eye.

"Good. Köhler, take him."

It wasn't necessary to tell him twice. Since ribs were broken, he grappled Marcellus laterally under his shoulders and knees and lifted him. The boy moaned softly, but was comfortable in the powerful arms of the petty officer.

Neumann saw Marcellus' smile. "That's well. You are brave. Trierarch Rheinberg might even give you a medal."

Marcellus shook his head. "I have disappointed Magister Dahms. He told me, 'No adventures!' And now this."

"If Dahms gets angry, he'll hear from me," Köhler said thickly. "You've discovered Tennberg for us. That can't be measured in gold. Outstanding it was."

Marcellus nodded bravely, then looked questioningly at Köhler. "I really can't go to Aksum? I have proven myself!"

Köhler grinned. The young man was quick. "You have a more important mission. Tennberg, the other prisoners and the news attached to them, must reach Treveri as soon as possible. The *Valentinian* departs early in the morning, full steam ahead."

Forstmann couldn't control himself and snorted.

"You'll come along. Rheinberg will have questions. And you have to be healthy for that. I'll bring a present from Aksum. Do you have a special wish?"

Marcellus smiled. Fatigue, the pain and the spirits took their toll. His eyes veiled. But he opened his mouth and yet replied rather than falling asleep:

"Tortoise shell. A knife with a handle made of tortoise shell."

Köhler threw Neumann a look. "What kind of ideas did you put in this boy's head?"

The doctor smiled unabashedly. "You asked, that was the answer. He could have also asked for a pretty slave."

Köhler grunted.

With his sleeping burden in his arms, he made his way to the ship.

20

"It's time."

Godegisel's voice was difficult to hear, as he whispered to the resting Valens. A solitary sebum candle lit the face of the former Emperor only weakly. They didn't want to alert the guards at an early stage.

It was shortly after midnight, and outside, a dense fog covered the landscape. This had advantages and disadvantages, and Godegisel thought about both when he helped the older man and assisted him to prepare for their escape.

The mist would greatly limit the visibility for the guards. Godegisel dared to find the way to the street even without good visibility; he had been walking around to familiarize himself during the last few days. Marvelous stones, especially crooked trees, had impressed him. In some places, he had marked his way with white limestone markings. The road, they would certainly find.

But the fog would also carry far too much noise. A whisper appeared like a roar. A crunch like an avalanche. Out here, far from the big settlements, there were no other nocturnal noises that would cover theirs. The occasional owl, the wandering fox – but that was it. The guards were talking silently and stood steady at their positions. It wasn't for nothing that they had chosen this time for their enterprise: the time at night, in which every man would struggle most with fatigue.

Godegisel looked at his boots, tightly wrapped with strips of fabric, to conceal the sound of his steps. Valens was already working on his own. All the metal that they wore was padded. This also applied to his sword, which no one had taken from him. Nothing could rattle. They had only one chance, both men were aware of this. Even the coins in the bags had been mixed with cloth strips, so that they would not give a sound even during fast movements. They had, at least they hoped, thought of everything.

Godegisel didn't push Valens. They had to be thorough. When the former Emperor had finished, he rose and let himself be checked by the Goth. Then he repaid the favor for the young man and his clothes and equipment. Once both were satisfied that everything seemed to be well secured, they nodded. From now on, no word, only hand signals. Both men threw bags across their backs, looked out of the windows into the nightly darkness. There was a glimmer of light, where the guards stood. Apparently, no one counted on an attack by any opponent – normally the oil lamps would give away the sentries' position. But the soldiers were more interested in having it cozy. They certainly didn't expect those who had to be "guarded" to make a run, and it was precisely this fact that was the fugitive's greatest asset in this game.

They didn't use the front door. The property in which they were lodged had several exits. A door led into a stable, which was now empty, and the stable again lay on the edge of the forest near the road, which would lead them directly to the coast. They took this path.

As they entered the barn, and the cool, nightly air flushed into their lungs, they paused and listened. Somewhere, someone coughed – it wasn't possible to discern through the fog whether near or far. But no light could be seen from the semi-open stable door, and no movement could be heard. About two yards from the door, on the brick of the court, the white lump of lime lay, which Godegisel had thrown there yesterday, seemingly careless: the beginning of their escape route. Everything behind it blended into an impenetrable soup of darkness and fog.

Godegisel looked at Valens, who nodded. They pushed through the half-open door, without having to move it a single millimeter, and crept over the stones. The padded feet made absolutely no sound. Still, the Goth's breath rang in his ears, and he wished he could hold it for at least ten minutes.

They reached the limestone, and Valens followed the young man to the next road mark. Time and again, they looked around. But nothing was to be seen. When they had moved about twenty yards from the main building, they discerned a moving light, a sentry on patrol. One man yawned audibly, Godegisel heard how he scratched his beard and murmured something. The two fugitives remained as if rooted in the ground. The guards wandered past them, without even realizing their existence.

Godegisel allowed himself a careful exhalation.

They waited a few moments before the wandering light had been swallowed by the fog.

The Goth pulled Valens by the sleeve. The former Emperor was willing to follow through the darkness. They walked silently forward, always careful on their way. It wasn't long before they saw the band of the cobbled military road before them. At one of the markers, Godegisel recognized one of the white signs he had left behind. Everything had gone well. If fortune continued to hold on, their escape would remain undetected until the late morning hours, when a slave usually brought them breakfast.

They held themselves on the empty street, pulled the cloths from the boots and stuffed them into their pockets, always careful not to leave any traces. They made a strong start to make the most of their advantage. Godegisel had been able to find out a few things about the area in casual conversations. He knew that about five miles from here was a small settlement, consisting of several farms, not quite a *latifundium* but a respectable property. They would surely arrive there before dawn, and then they intended to buy horses and ride them as fast as possible toward the coast. Of course, this would be noticeable, and a potential witness would quickly identify them from the descriptions, but they'd still enjoy several hours' lead in the best case, and since they didn't have to spare their horses, this could be decisive for the success of their escape.

They marched silently, almost doggedly. Godegisel could've made it faster, but Valens was no longer the youngest and had endured not too many marches as an emperor. He had to take a break every now and then, drink a sip of water. Still, he was brave, never groaned or lamented, looking at the young Goths apologetically once he stumbled. Godegisel kept his patience because he knew that it was only their plan to reach the settlement anyway, and there was more than enough time for that.

As a matter of fact, they arrived before the dawn of the morning. They stood before the closed gate of the largest courtyard, which had a stone enclosure and from whose interior they heard the snorting of awakening horses. When the sun was visible on the horizon and cocks greeted the dawning day with loud crowing, the inhabitants of the estate also became active.

Godegisel tapped the gate forcefully, several times, for his signal was not immediately answered.

Once the gate was opened and a man's tired, distrustful face appeared, he looked at two figures dressed in thick coats, who raised their empty hands and asked for a conversation with the landlord. When they emphasized their request with a copper coin, which they pressed into the hand of the servant, it was not long before they sat at the breakfast table of the proprietor. At first, he was full of distrust, but as golden solidi flashed and the travelers offered him a good price for two less good horses, greed prevailed. They soon agreed, added two old saddles – not for nothing, but at an acceptable price –, and the travelers said goodbye within an hour. The horses, not particularly handsome or trained animals, were freshly fed and followed the commands of their new masters quite willingly, trotting forward.

Everything seemed to be going according to plan. Godegisel was very pleased with himself. They would have to be careful with their money, but the next and then the last major issue was the crossing over the canal to Gaul, where, hopefully, one would quickly find admission to Imperial officials who were not with Maximus. The former Emperor claimed to know some old followers of his brother Valentinian in Nemetacum, from where they would steer their steps to get to the imperial court as soon as possible.

As it grew brighter, the streets became populated. Once they encountered a military patrol, Godegisel became involuntarily nervous and stiffened in the saddle, even though the soldiers came from the opposite direction and couldn't possibly know anything about their escape. The fact helped that Maximus couldn't publicly announce that the former Emperor of the East, allegedly fallen before Adrianopel, had escaped from his custody, like a convict, and was immediately to be arrested. This would certainly lead to a great upheaval and would eventually be reported to the imperial court, which would ultimately have had the same effect as a personal appearance, with the only difference that if Maximus were to capture the two men, their future would be highly uncertain.

Godegisel didn't want to be recognized, and Valens, too, remained very determined to remain incognito.

And for the time being, they were lucky. No one seemed to take after them, and they rode at a brisk pace, hardly taking breaks, only once to allow the horses to drink.

They estimated that they would need two days to the canal coast. As they deliberately bypassed the capital of the province, where the news of their escape would most likely be spread early, they had to find one of the smaller villages, preferably a sleepy fishing settlement. Valens had a rough idea of the geography of Britain, a knowledge almost entirely missing for Godegisel. He had become acquainted with the immediate environment of his prison, but for the rest he was dependent on the former emperor. But Valens had never set foot on British soil before, although his father had once been Comes in Britain. It was therefore necessary, the farther they rode eastward, to ask more frequently for the way.

At the end of the second day, completely undisturbed and unmolested by anyone, they reached a wind-blown cluster of wooden huts, which could only be described with great imagination as a village. Godegisel had already pursed his lips in disgust and made the suggestion of looking for a more promising place along the coast, when Valens had pointed, without any comment, to the three masts stretching into the darkness of the sky. Fishing boats, and not even the smallest, lay on the beach. They were about six meters long, could be rowed or sailed, as each had a single mast. Fishing nets were neatly folded next to the boats. Normally two, if not three men, were part of the crew, and the boat, equipped with a deep hull, could take a not inconsiderable catch if the fishermen were lucky.

This wasn't the case too frequently, judging from the state of the neighboring settlement. The weather on the canal was often wild and unpredictable. Fishing was a dangerous profession and apparently mostly not very profitable.

That was exactly what they needed.

They approached the hut closest to the ships. Thin smoke rose from the stone chimney to the sky. Behind the closed shutters, gloomy light was visible. In front of the door, which was covered with a kind of wooden awning, the implements of a fisherman lay. It seemed no one feared thieves over here. The men looked at the equipment and rated it as poor. They looked at each other and grinned.

Godegisel knocked decidedly.

It took a moment, then a dull voice was heard. It sounded wary. "Who's there?"

"Travelers," Valens replied. "We need a passage to Gaul. We pay well."

Whether it was the last three words or general philanthropy that induced the fisherman to open the door, Godegisel didn't know. A bar was moved, and the bearded face of a man, weathered, prematurely aged, appeared. He stared at the two travelers for a few seconds. Valens and Godegisel stood still, smiled kindly, which was very difficult for them in the face of the stinging smell of fish in various degrees of decay, which arose from the hut.

It was Godegisel, after all, who brought out his purse and showed the bearded one a golden solidus. The fisherman nearly lost his eyes in the face of this sum. He opened the door and ordered the travelers gesticulating to enter.

The hut consisted of exactly one room, and the entire family of the good man seemed to be gathered together. A woman, who was also consumed and looked old, stared nervously at them, in her hands a pair of trousers, which she obviously just mended. There were two sources of light – a fireplace over the chimney and a lamp, which apparently burned fish oil. A wide bed stood in one of the corners, on which two children slept, both certainly not older than five or six years. According to Godegisel's estimate, the parents couldn't be more than in their thirtieth year, but they looked considerably older. They were poor people, although they were not living in absolute poverty. They had a house, the roof was apparently not leaking, and a boat, they had certain utensils, their clothes were old but clean, and otherwise everything seemed in place. Even if one could hardly speak of modest prosperity, their livelihood was bought with the hardship of being hard-working – hard work, which would lead them to death before their time. Godegisel glanced at the sleeping children. They would inherit all this. A perspective that wasn't too enjoyable. The reform policy of Emperor Gratian had a good thing – they were no longer forced to take over the profession of their father. Perhaps they would sell their inheritance and try to start something different. This thought felt comforting for the Goth.

"Sit down, gentlemen," the man said, pointing to an empty bench near the fire. Since his visitors were wearing good clothes and apparently had been riding horses, it was easy to regard them as distinguished personalities. Godegisel assumed that they didn't even have to offer the fisherman money. If they left him the two horses, tired, but in good condition, as payment for the crossing, he would've already earned a fortune. He would've little use for the animals, but the sale would bring him more than enough – certainly almost a year's income if Godegisel correctly assessed the hut.

"We are travelers with urgent business," Valens came to the heart of the matter. "We need to translate to Gaul speedily, best directly to Belgica, and look for a man whose boat can make a journey and who won't refuse to do us the service."

A greedy glitter sparkled in the fisherman's eyes. Everyone here earned something on the side, even if it was by occasional smuggling. At this time of the year, the weather on the canal was rough and the crossing dangerous. This would, Godegisel knew ...

"The weather is bad, gentlemen," the fisherman said, as predicted. "The sea is wild. It's a dangerous endeavor. I do not only risk my boat but also my life."

Valens sighed. "We're well aware of that. We reward you amply for your risk. In front of the hut, there are two horses with saddles.

They should be yours. You can sell them, and you'll get a decent amount."

"Yes, but there also will be many questions. Where did I suddenly get two horses? Won't there be questions from some ... interested parties?"

The fisherman obviously had a brain. He might not have a clue about the actual nature of the two "noble gentlemen" but seemed to have an idea about the nature of their journey. Godegisel suspected that nothing could be done. He exchanged a glance with Valens.

"Then the two horses and one solidus."

"Show me the coin again!"

It changed ownership, and the fisherman and his wife looked at it in the flickering light of the fire. He bit on it with his decayed teeth and nodded contentedly. "Not unnecessarily stretched with bronze, a good deal," he admitted unhappily.

"The horses. This is a good deal," Valens added.

The fisherman nodded hesitantly. "Good, I agree. But not at night, that is suicide. At sunrise, I will start. You can spend the night in my humble hut."

That sounded reasonable. Possibly, the miraculous sailors from the future could navigate at night, when the clouds covered the stars and the winds were unpredictable. But a normal fisherman would know that only daylight guaranteed a safe journey, and the two refugees also wanted to arrive in Gaul alive and dry.

They made up for an overnight camp while the fisherman took care of his newly acquired horses. The ferryman's wife looked tiredly at the travelers while she resumed her stuffing. When Godegisel took some hard bread, some cheese, and a few apples out of his bag, she rose to the cooking-place and drew something from a large, iron pot hung over it. She gave the men two wooden plates, the fish smell increased, but with a sudden pleasant note. Without further questioning, the men accepted the offered soup, in which cooked fish chops swam. After a day on the back of a horse in cold and windy weather, every warm meal was welcome. After Godegisel led his wooden spoon to his mouth, he could tell that the soup was quite tasty and constituted together with the bread a full-fledged meal. He nodded to the fisherman's wife, who smiled at him quietly and went back to repairing clothes. Godegisel had quite ascertained that while her husband was feeding the horses outside, she had concealed the solidus under her apron without her husband observing. Probably, she was responsible for the budget in every respect. Probably, the money would actually be put to good use.

It wasn't long before the men, plucked into their coats, fell into a deep, dreamless sleep. They were no longer listening when the fisherman came in, nodded to his wife and stowed away the removed saddles, which he would surely sell separately.

When they were awakened, they both felt as if they had just slumbered. The scenery had not changed; the fire flickered, the lamp burned, the wind was rustling outside, and the sea was audibly agitated.

"The sun is rising," the fisherman muttered. "Time to leave."

Their breakfast was short, but the woman packed some supplies into a bag, dried fish, and other hard bread. There was a hose with diluted wine. The well-paying guests should obviously enjoy the crossing, as far as this was possible at all in the face of the rough sea.

The children were still asleep and didn't notice their father's departure. Godegisel and Valens helped to push the big boat into the water, climbed over the rail even as their feet were already wet from the icy water. It was still quite dark, the spray was burning in their faces, but the fisherman seemed unimpressed by all this and kept silent without directing any word toward the passengers. The refugees found themselves in the wildly wavering boat, and then they had anchored the oars and began, at the order of the fisherman, to use their muscles. The boatman himself sat at the helm at the stern of the vessel, watching the two rowers critically, then the bow was directed to the sea. He ordered to stop the oars and set the little sail on the only mast, which immediately filled with wind. With aching arms, the travelers felt the natural force pushing them toward the sea, and not only Godegisel had the idea if it had been wise to consume the fish soup the night before ...

Godegisel wasn't a sailor. He mistrusted the water.

He endured the fisherman's knowing grin, as he finally bent over the edge of the ship to vomit. Even Valens, who had been on ships, was green in his face. It was a difference, whether to embark in good weather on a trip on a quietly rowing trireme or to sit in a nutshell where the waves rode up and down. Very unconciliably, he too, just a few minutes after the Goth, leaned forward and sacrificed to the gods.

The fisherman was unmoved, reached into his wife's provisions – which had obviously been seized to be used only by himself – and began to chew. The sight alone brought the two travelers back to choking. They forced themselves to look everywhere but not to the boatman, who obviously felt completely at ease.

The weather was not particularly stormy. There was a fresh wind blowing, and the waves were distinctly felt, but Godegisel could see that the fisherman wasn't concerned, so it was obviously not that bad. As the sun slowly ascended in the sky, the cloud cover broke up and springing warmth spread in the boat. The wind blew well and filled the sail, they made good progress. When Valens asked, the fisherman looked at the sky and muttered something of an hour. He didn't cross the canal at its narrowest point, but sailed south. This was in the interests of the travelers. They couldn't enjoy the ride despite the clear weather conditions. They felt too sick, and they swayed too much with every relatively harmless wave. Godegisel knew he couldn't swim. He guessed that the former Emperor was no different. He knew that many sailors deliberately didn't learn to swim, because in the event of a shipwreck, the prospect of salvation was in any case small, and one wouldn't want to unnecessarily extend his suffering. Godegisel considered this fatalistic attitude for a while, but came to the conclusion that he didn't want to make it his own. He preferred to be, in any event, floating with a piece of the wreck or to learn how to swim.

Then the journey was over. Without being asked, the fisherman landed them in a place that at first sight didn't look as if it was suitable, for it seemed to consist only of steep coast. But then they saw a tiny piece of flat land, from which a stone path led across different angles. That the fisherman didn't make this trip for the first time was clear to them. And this also spoke for the secrecy of the man, should the men of Maximus come to his village. When the boat landed with a crunch, the men jumped out and dragged it a few yards on the shore. Valens took a silver coin from his bag and gave it to the man as a bonus. The fisherman grinned broadly and raised his hand in greeting. He had done the business of his life, of that Godegisel was sure.

They helped him to push the boat back into the water. Now the wind was unfavorable. The fisherman sat undisturbed at the helm and retreated with agonizing slowness. In the face of his arm-muscles, which the strong Goth had mustered with adoring recognition, it was in fact to be expected that this work wasn't foreign to him. Using the oars, the wind not favorable, it would take more than two hours to return. But it wasn't even the noon. With a little luck, the fisherman would return as a rich man to his family before dawn. As Godegisel looked after the slowly diminishing boat, he was sure that the two horses had already found a new owner, and the proceeds rested safely under the wife's apron.

And he was sure that she would never see the silver coin that her husband had just received.

He smiled.

They made the ascent. Weakened by seasickness, it took a good hour until they were up. To their surprise, they immediately met a fortified coastal road, and they followed according to the advice of the former Emperor to the southeast.

After an hour, they came to another military road, which had a signpost. From there, it led directly to Nemetacum. And another hour along the way, they reached a small village, where their money was interesting enough for the inhabitants. For new horses, their means were no longer sufficient but for a warm meal and a ride on the donkey cart of a merchant who had some space left and only gladly rented it to payable travelers. Treveri was also located in this province, and they had thought for a moment about going there. Ultimately, however, Valens had decided that it would be better to go directly into the care of friendly men of the local military administration instead of traveling incognito through the country for any longer.

With aching feet but full stomach and generally of good mood, the two refugees settled into the cart, staring tirelessly at the backs of the two donkeys and rattling the road eastward. The nausea subsided.

They had left Britain.

21

Rheinberg was glad to leave Trier. Making a journey that was supposed to be useful increased his willingness to say farewell to the Emperor's court for a few days, and to abstain from its political stench.

Although, there was no real pleasure in his journey.

As Magister Militium, Rheinberg was no longer a private man, and as a figure of public life he had to travel in style. In this case, it meant that the "little excursion," which he carried out on urgent requests from Engineer Dahms, led to quite a convoy of men and carts. Once he had told Gratian of his plans, coupled with the request not to make a great upheaval, the young Emperor, wisened in these matters, had only smiled.

Of course, this trip had in any case some benefits. There wasn't only the fact that Dahms had arrived from Ravenna to accompany him on this trip. To be together with the engineer was a very pleasant change after weeks of political play. The clear, technical mind of the man and his focus on very tangible problems, all of which had to do with the improvements that they wanted to introduce in the Empire, were a salutary experience for Rheinberg. The engineer's interest in the political developments was relatively limited; he had become completely engrossed in a multitude of other problems, for whose solution he now needed Rheinberg's help. He did as he had been asked, because he had the feeling that the goal of their multi-day trip was of a highly symbolic nature.

The two Germans accompanied twenty horsemen from the emperor's bodyguard, handpicked of course, and with the grim determination to protect the master of the army with their lives. Not that there was any threat to expect wherever they went. When he had informed Gratian about the destination of his excursion, the reaction of the Emperor had been happy. He knew the area well – his father had had a summer palace built nearby, where the young Gratian had often stayed. In recent years, however, the building had hardly been used and was only maintained by a group of servants. Of course, it was now planned to be a place of stay for the commander-in-chief, as there was hardly anything more appropriate in the area.

Along with the twenty armed men, Rheinberg and Dahms, who at the end successfully declined the use of carts for themselves, followed three donkey carts with supplies and servants.

Aurelia wasn't with them.

On the day he had given signed her the certificate of liberation from the magistrate, he had returned to his villa in the evening and went to bed at once. When he had inquired about his former servant the following morning, he had been informed of the fact that she had packed her things, and Rheinberg had left no doubt that everything she owned was actually her property. She had disappeared from the house together with the document. He had also been reported that his order to give her a larger sum of money had been faithfully executed, and the young lady had received the purse without any comment.

Rheinberg hadn't felt well, at least at the beginning. Then he scolded himself repeatedly. Had he really assumed that the young woman, who evidently felt "offended," would stay with him voluntarily? As what? As another servant among many? What exactly had he hoped for?

Now that Rheinberg sat on his horse, which trotted along a rather bad road, all these thoughts came to his mind again. His face must have shown that he pondered not too gratifying thoughts, for Dahms looked at him frowning. Of course, he knew about the gift from Renna, but the very practical officer had never been inclined to gossip and never asked about her.

It was a while before the fresh morning drove the melancholy out of Rheinberg. That he had finally made the right decision, he was deeply convinced. As much as he obviously missed her presence, he felt in his stomach that he couldn't have delayed it any longer. She was now in charge of her life. She made her own decisions. She now belonged to herself, was young, educated and adequately endowed with funds. She would go her way wherever it would lead her.

Rheinberg raised his head, looked at Dahms, and smiled. They were already on their way, and before they reached their destination they would be traveling for a few more hours at leisurely pace. They were in no hurry, especially Rheinberg. Leaving Trier and seeing a bit of nature was already worth the trip.

Dahms also looked around eagerly, but he searched for something special, the rationale for this trip.

He needed hard coal, as much and as soon as possible. His demands quickly revealed that the Romans were aware of hard coal but didn't make much use of it. The main fuel was and remained wood or charcoal. Only in a few places in Germany, he had been told, coal would be mined as a locally used fuel – and, as chance would have it, one of these areas wasn't too far from the current Emperor's residence. And it had yet another symbolic meaning that hadn't escaped even the practical thinking of Dahms.

It was already dusk when the river became visible. The military road led directly to the bridge, which bent over the winding water. On the other side, one clearly could see a stone fort, manned with a small garrison of about two hundred men guarding the trade routes, the small localities nearby, and not least the summer palace erected by Valentinian. It was a peaceful afternoon. This was a quiet area, marked by agriculture, where the eruptions shattering the rest of the Empire had simply passed by. Rheinberg bridled his horse, and the whole column came to a standstill. Dahms looked around. From the top of the hill, they had a beautiful view of the river, which in their time was called the Saar. And there, around the fort, was the market patch close to the Saar, the Vicus Sara, Saravicus, the ancient forerunner settlement to the city which would name their ship, *Saarbrücken.* They had, in a fashion, arrived home.

Rheinberg had once visited Saarbrücken – the city of his time. It was a dynamic, growing place, in a region benefiting from the boom in coal and steel production, an industrial center of the German Reich and of great importance for the German arms industry. He had visited the castle of the Count of Saarbrücken, an open, spacious building that didn't resemble a castle, but rather a summer palace, a place of relaxation. Rheinberg turned to the left and peered down the river. Somewhere over there, the castle would be built in the future. The fort lay a little farther, at another, strategically important place close to the Saar.

Dahms cleared his throat. "Somehow everything is missing – every reference to what we know. And yet I have the feeling of ... I don't know ..."

"Endurance," Rheinberg helped. "The same thing von Geeren told me about when he looks at the city gate in Trier, which still exists in our time. It is something that can outlast everything else, something that can't be lost."

Dahms nodded. He couldn't describe it any better.

As it was slowly getting late, they would just try to reach the palace before nightfall, spend the night there, and then head for the coal mining area. They had been promised a local guide. Here, the hard coal was systematically mined from the ground, and there was also a small iron industry, which made use of these deposits – another parallel to the Saarland Rheinberg once had visited. If everything was as Dahms hoped, it would be an opportunity to start industrial coal mining and to send the proceeds to the south as quickly as possible. Dahms had great plans, and he needed fuel to realize them, quite apart from the fact that the functionality of the cruiser depended heavily on it.

They reached Valentinian's summer palace at nightfall. Slaves with torches and lamps came to meet them as the large outer gate opened and let them in. Of course, their impending arrival had been announced, and everything was well prepared. The major-domo, who immediately reminded Rheinberg strongly of Felix, approached quickly, and asked them, with repeated bows, to join him to the main house where food and drink had been prepared. Rheinberg took care that his companions were well taken care of, and he didn't miss the grateful glances of his bodyguards when he showed concern for their welfare.

It wasn't long before Dahms and Rheinberg were sitting alone in a large room, which had once served as a study for Valentinian. It had taken a while before the major-domo had been assured that everything was fine, and that they really wanted to be left alone. Rheinberg enjoyed the hubbub now.

"How are things with the *Saarbrücken*?" he asked finally, after pouring a cup of wine for his engineer. The local supplies unfortunately didn't include beer, as Dahms had to accept with a certain regret.

"All is well. Joergensen and Langenhagen have the crew well under control."

"What about the mutineers?"

"I have nothing negative to report. Most are grateful for the second chance and behave exemplary. All of the crew are doing well. Those who are somewhat intelligent have been assigned into the great training program – either they teach Romans or learn something from the officers. The Latin and Greek courses are accepted more and more, even by those who have muttered their disgust before."

Dahms grinned and took a sip. "This is due to the fact that we have been able to allow quite some shore leave because of the long time the *Saarbrücken* is lying down, and the men have obviously become interested in the local ladies. In any case, there has been some positive development." Then the smile left his face. "We have to make some important decisions, Captain. Not all of the men are wildly screwing around, only interested in their fun without commitment. There are decent fellows among them, many at home ... in our old days ... had a bride with serious intentions. They haven't suddenly become different persons. Some of the men have sincerely fallen in love and want to make it official."

"There is no marriage registration in the Empire, as we know it," Rheinberg reminded. "There is not even a formal ecclesiastical ceremony."

Dahms nodded heavily. "We thought about it. We have also discussed the matter with the Bishop of Ravenna. It seems as if he has a great interest in the liturgy we have brought from our time. The idea of a formal marriage ceremony has fallen on fertile soil. And as for the administrative act ..." Dahms shrugged. "... the captain may marry anyone according to old custom. Langenhagen and Joergensen can do it in your absence. We should find a solution that satisfies everyone. Above all, we should allow marriage, even without individual case examination. People have to settle down, if only to forget, well ... at least the pain missing those forever unattainable for us."

Dahms looked at Rheinberg with a stony face. He had left his wife and child in the Germany of the future. One of the reasons why he had plunged so hard into his work since they arrived was surely an effort to forget the notion of ever seeing them again. All those who had been stranded here without a firm attachment, like Rheinberg himself, would certainly have it easier.

For a moment, he thought of Aurelia. He corrected himself. It was simpler for those who were able to properly communicate with a woman. The new Magister Militium of Rome apparently didn't belong into this category.

He sighed. "I'm far from the shot, and it's hard to make these kinds of decisions," he finally admitted. "Get in touch with the other officers and find a solution, and have my blessing. But sooner or later will the men not want to leave the ship in order to have a proper family life?"

Dahms nodded. He poured himself some more wine and frowned at the candied fruit, which stood in a bowl on the table. "This will happen. It's not imminent, but it'll come. And we won't be able to hold anybody back. Think of Volkert."

Rheinberg grimaced. "Heard anything of him?"

"No, nothing. He has disappeared into thin air. We have evidence that he was involuntarily conscripted into the Roman army. But we lost his track and, well, we didn't particularly push the matter. It's no use to hunt the poor boy across the Empire. We can get around to taking care of him when other matters are settled, and the Romans can ignore the fact that we want to pardon a deserter as much as a mutineer. The matter with the Senator's daughter is the problem. The Romans are very prudish and self-confident. We have to allow the grass to grow densely over this issue."

"You talked quite differently some time ago, Mr. Engineer," Rheinberg replied. "Are you getting soft?"

"I'm getting older. And I see how hard everything is here. And how badly we were initially organized. Volkert shouldn't have to pay for this. I understand things better now. The only one I'd like to see hanging from a tree is von Klasewitz. And Tennberg, the weasel." Dahms raised his hands. "And before you ask: No, no one knows where they are. And that gives me much more headaches than young Volkert's whereabouts."

"I share the same concerns."

"Von Klasewitz really worries me. He hasn't failed forever just because his mutiny didn't work. And he didn't act alone. He had allies."

"We still know little about his backers."

"What about this Maximus – who was involved, in our history, in the downfall of Gratian?"

Rheinberg sighed. "This discussion about him evolves almost daily in Trier. He hasn't been guilty of anything in this course of time – or he is acting more cautiously than we would have liked. I cannot reproach him for his deeds in another timeline – in another world. This could trigger a witch hunt, because Maximus wouldn't be the only one to look out for."

"But we keep him in mind?"

"General Malobaudes has made this his personal task. If it were for him, we would dismiss the Comes from all responsibilities and kill him right away, only for the dear soul to find rest. I have opposed this notion, and so far Malobaudes has accepted. But he is the right man for the task of watching Maximus. He sent spies to Britain and reports to us regularly. Unfortunately, it always takes a long time for those reports to reach us."

Dahms smiled. "This can be remedied. My plans for a telegraph network are ready. As soon as we have enough electricity, it won't be a major technical problem to put at least a primitive, military facility into operation."

Rheinberg nodded. "Better today than tomorrow. We are barely able to cope with all the projects, and we are limited in our resources.

You have taken this long trip for this very reason. The coal we can mine, but men with the necessary technical knowledge and abilities can't be excavated with any shovel!"

Dahms nodded his head and continued to smile. He had hardly anything to say to counter this assertion. He looked into the fire the slaves had ignited in one of the mighty chimneys, which was both a source of warmth and of light. Then he sighed. "I'd really like to know what happened to Volkert," he murmured softly. "Damn, the boy makes me really feel sorry."

Rheinberg didn't reply.

22

"Bertius, stop whining."

The fat legionary grimaced as Volkert turned to him. He labored hard on his horse. The first twenty miles on the caterpillar of the expeditionary army, he'd tried to preserve some dignity. In the evening he'd gone to bed with loud complaints. Volkert had avoided divesting him for guard service, for that would have been a torture for his comrades. Now, two weeks after their departure from Noricum and with the instruction to increase the marching speed a little each day, the cavalry troops made a good four miles a day. Most of the foot soldiers, who had been selected because of their basic ability to hold on to a horse, now sat in the saddle like Alannian veterans. They rejoiced in the new invention of the stirrup and the fact that their back muscles were put to the test, but legs and feet stayed unmolested.

Except for Bertius.

This was by no means due to the fact that he couldn't ride. His heroic stories about the breathtaking escape from Germanic enemies were undoubtedly invented, but the basic prerequisite, namely the fact that the legionary knew perfectly well how to use a horse, was absolutely correct. Volkert had seen Bertius, when he thought being unobserved, cultivate his riding-animal with almost loving thoroughness. He tied it neatly, dried it, gave him food, and whispered encouraging and friendly words in his ear. The horse was obviously satisfied with the attention it received from his master, as it was never disobedient, willingly followed directions, and sometimes even looked around for his master when he was too distant.

But Bertius wouldn't be Bertius if he didn't find grounds for complaint. And he was grateful for any kind of audience: his comrades, his Decurion, his Centurion, and even the occasional senior officer, in whose ears he found attention. He had received two penalties, not from Volkert, but rather a highly annoyed tribune, who simply couldn't stand the chatter anymore.

Bertius, of course, didn't budge. Anyone who managed to doze off in the saddle during the day while his horse followed the line of the other horses with remarkable discipline, and without being asked to do so, was able to withstand minor infringements on his ability to complain.

Volkert didn't have any further idea how to deal with him. To shout at the man helped only for the moment. He reacted by sulking for a while, then quickly rejoiced, noticed his terrible hardships and the complainant began anew.

And he had an infallible sense of when Volkert appeared.

"Sir, I'm not complaining at all!" Bertius defended himself with a miserable voice. He had wrapped the cloak tightly around him, for it was chilly and became even colder as they advanced further east past Panonnia. Soon their marching column, now more like an army than an expedition, would be divided into ten squadrons of about a hundred men, and sweep like a fan in various directions from northeast to southeast. They would forward riders as scouts and send regular reports by courier to a prepared meeting place. And in each century, some German infantrymen would participate.

Volkert was afraid of that. So far, he'd managed to keep away from the other Germans. He'd watched them from afar, and had certainly been seen, but his altered appearance and the mere fact that he wouldn't be expected to be here, especially as a Roman NCO, had so far saved him from any discovery. He'd identified some men with whom he had had a somewhat closer contact on the *Saarbrücken*, and to whom he shouldn't come too close. They would, after a certain time, see through his weak masquerade.

Volkert didn't yet know to which of the ten groups he belonged to, nor any of the infantrymen. He knew that there were not enough German officers to be assigned to all ten groups, and the officers knew Volkert better than the lower ranks. Volkert had no choice but to hope for his luck.

"Bertius, you're unbearable, and if you're not carrying your load, somebody else will put another extra duty on you, and as badly as I am, I can see the Centurion working up a proper anger. I can't hear it anymore!"

Bertius looked at Volkert with a look that contained all the suffering of the Roman Empire, and of course a constant, silent reproach, indicating that it had been Volkert to whom he owed all this, a mistake which the young German had began to regret bitterly.

He hoped that Bertius wouldn't be in his unit, and that the Germans riding with him wouldn't recognize him. But he already knew that not all of his desires would be fulfilled. Bertius belonged to his century, and the probability was very high that the units wouldn't break up but would serve as the organizational basis for the division.

Perhaps the Huns were able to end Bertius' complaints their way.

In any case, the reprimand had helped, albeit for the moment. The legionary sulked, pressed his lips on each other like an unruly child, and stared at the military road, which the troops were still following. Volkert left it there. To continue the conversation contained the risk of getting Bertius out of his pout and encouraging him to talk again, and he had no real interest in that.

Volkert had his horse left the formation and trot ahead. When he reached the side of Centurion Levantus, he turned around in his saddle and nodded to Volkert.

"Are you all right?"

"I'm content."

"It gets dark soon. We'll make camp in about an hour, I've heard."

"Good."

Levantus looked searchingly at Volkert.

"Is there a problem?"

"No, everything is fine."

"You look thoughtful."

"I wonder where my trip will go once the troops will be divided."

"Ah. Well, we'll know soon enough. As I was told, this is to be decided tonight. All the officers and centurions are invited to the General, and I don't know what else could be the topic."

Volkert nodded to Levantus. That made sense.

"Is it also announced how the time travelers are divided up into units?"

"Maybe. Interesting people, right?"

"They're a bit strange," Volkert said cautiously.

"Yes, that's true. Their weapons fascinate me. If we'd had more of them, the barbarians wouldn't be a challenge for us. What happened at Thessaloniki could then be repeated, and they would immediately submit to our conditions."

"That was the one time. Don't you think the barbarians are also capable of learning? They will adjust their tactics to these new weapons. No more frontal attacks, more attempts to bypass our lines. New weapons of their own – sure, they will fight with losses, but will they always lose?" Volkert shook his head.

Levantus looked attentively at the young Decurion. "You've been thinking a lot about this," he said with a certain undertone in his voice.

Volkert hesitated. He walked on thin ice. If it became clear that he knew more about the possibilities and limits of the German arms than he was allowed to know, he would stir up suspicion. On the other hand, he was now fighting in an army that might react too euphorically to the new possibilities – and euphoria could claim the life of soldiers for whom he was responsible.

"I've been thinking about it," he said slowly, choosing his words carefully. "Of course, I could be mistaken, but I think we shouldn't forget some lessons despite all our enthusiasm."

"Tell me."

"The barbarians don't come to our borders because they are bloodthirsty savages who want to plunder us but because they have been expelled from their land by the Huns. They are refugees, traveling with their wives and children. They fight with the courage of despair, for they have no home, their life is all they cling to. And we mustn't make the mistake of regarding them as foolish. Valens, with all due respect, has proven the consequences of arrogance at Adrianople."

Levantus looked thoughtful. "I can't deny that."

"The superiority gained by the new weapons is only temporary. We must equip our legions on a large scale with them if they are to have a lasting effect. And how long will the principles of this technology remain hidden from the barbarians once we use them extensively? There are crafty men among them. They can build workshops, take prisoners and interrogate them, inspect loot. How long will it take for us to face the first barbarians with similar but perhaps not entirely equivalent weapons?"

Levantus nodded approvingly. "There's something to it."

"And now the Huns," Volkert continued, warming to the topic. "What do we know about them? Flexible attacks on horseback, strong archers with high shot frequency, extremely fast and agile. And the Hun leaders haven't proven to be idiots either. Yes, during the first attack against new weapons, they also will be surprised, perhaps flee, and their losses will be substantial. But what about the second? If they overcome their fear? A sea of arrows on our rifles, a few courageous attacks – and the matter will already be settled. And I'm sure they'll adjust fastly, Centurion. We mustn't be too confident. We must think about what we do, and carefully, otherwise our advantage will turn into a disadvantage because of our arrogance."

"You're right, Decurion," Levantus said softly. He looked sharply at Volkert.

The German instantly feared that he'd already said too much. He bit his lip and scolded himself a fool. Not to draw attention after his surprising promotion, that has been his motto. If only he'd kept his mouth shut!

"I'm impressed," Levantus finally said. "You have a head on your shoulders and know how to use it for more than just carrying a helmet. You can lead men and keep your counsel."

"I'm just a decurion," Volkert said.

"Diocletian, the great emperor, began as a simple legionary, and afterwards ruled the Empire."

"Not interested," Volkert grinned back.

Levantus smiled. "But officer ... that's a way for you, my friend. Anything else would be a waste of talent in the long run. And if the Roman army needs one thing, it is talent. Especially in these times."

Volkert remained silent.

Levantus looked at him searchingly. "If I had said this to another man, he would've been full of joy or at least grateful. Do you think I'm lying to you, that I'm making fun of your prospects?"

"No."

"But you look like you do."

"That's not it."

"So what?"

"Nothing. Nothing of importance. Your words honor me. But I'm not a volunteer in this army. I have been pressed into the service."

Levantus nodded. "I understand. You'd like to leave, rather than make a career."

"Yes. No. It is more difficult. There's a woman."

Levantus raised his eyebrows. "We don't have to talk about the relative seriousness of the marriage ban, or do we, Decurion?"

Volkert smiled weakly. "It's more difficult."

"Nothing is difficult if you put your mind to it," the Centurion replied. "I'm serious. There are officers who have an eye on you. Show them your abilities, and a promotion is almost certain. There is no limit in that direction. Perhaps this isn't the life that you have imagined, Decurion. But look at it from this perspective: Whatever is going to happen with you and your bride, how will the problem be solved better – with a gloriously returning legate or centurion, or a poor little decurion?"

Volkert had to laugh against his will. The practical intelligence of Levantus hadn't failed to impress him.

The Centurion hit Volkert with force on the shoulder, so that he almost lost his balance. "This pleases me better, Decurion. Head up and eyes open. These are special times with special opportunities. Things are happening that nobody would ever have thought possible. Why shouldn't you bask in these opportunities as well, my friend?"

Volkert could've told the man that he was correct, and to a far greater extent than he could imagine.

The conversation died until the evening when the camp was built.

It wasn't long before the officers were called to the commander's tent. It was therefore Volkert's job to help to ensure the proper construction of the camp and the necessary discipline. Before the men could wash themselves and prepare dinner, the first duty was to feed the horses. They were stripped off, rubbed dry, and fed. In groups, they were tied to suitable trees or pillars rammed into the ground. Horsewatches were set up. When Volkert and his comrades had convinced themselves that the animals were well taken care of, the soldiers were allowed to take care of themselves. Quickly there were fires everywhere, and the evening meal was prepared from the supplies. Volkert set up guards, for which the comrades would prepare the food. They were still within the confines of the Empire, but that didn't mean much in these troubled times, as he had had to experience at his own expense.

As he stretched out his tired bones at a bonfire and received a bowl of porridge and a wooden spoon, it was among the privileges of his rank that the food was prepared for him, even though he had nothing better to eat than anyone else. A few minutes later, Levantus came to him. Volkert nodded, his mouth already full of hot mash.

"As I said," the Centurion said, holding a cup of diluted wine in his hands. "The division of the ten squads. We ride under Tribune Marcus Lucius Sedacius in a contingent. Our time travelers will be under a decurion named Lehmann."

Volkert scratched his head. The transferability of the German ranks into the Roman nomenclature was extremely difficult. He didn't know Lehmann and suspected that he was an able NCO. Sedacius had previously been the leader of the entire unit, and had so far proven himself in this position.

"No German officer?" he asked.

"No, not for us. The division was adjusted anyway. Sedacius takes 520 of their infantry. He wants to visit the Quadi and find out what they know. They are very familiar with the East. We should visit them in strength."

Volkert nodded relieved. The probability that he would remain undetected had just increased significantly. "Which direction?"

"A northeastern route," Levantus replied, who had now also received bread. Both slid closer to the warming fire. It had grown dark and became somewhat chilly. It might be spring, but the nights were not yet warm.

Volkert said nothing. If he wasn't wrong, they would almost run into the arms of the Huns. Opportunity for probation, of which Levantus had spoken today.

He pushed a spoon of porridge into his mouth and chewed the tough mass patiently.

This opportunity would come, he was now sure of it. In the face of their opponents, however, it could also be an opportunity for an early death.

Volkert closed his eyes and tried to make Julia's image appear before his mind's eye. It warmed him for a moment, but then it faded.

He felt the fear creep up again.

An old and familiar enemy.

23

"Here it is."

Godegisel had to trust Valens in this case; what else could he do? The dilapidated walls didn't make a particularly stable impression, and if the former Emperor hadn't pointed him to the entrance, he would never have had the idea to enter. He looked around. The small village, not ten miles from Nemetacum, seemed as if its life had been drowned by the nearby city. Around twenty buildings had been placed at a crossroads, the most impressive of which was the hostel that in addition to a large barn offered accommodation for travelers and was at the same time a station of the *cursus publicus*, which was probably the main reason for the mere existence of this settlement. Here, however, and as Valens had pointed out, there were no walls and no guards to ask unpleasant questions. Godegisel had quickly realized that Valens didn't want to visit his "old acquaintance," as he called him, in the city, but rather looked for him here.

Valens struck a fist against the thick oak door, whose solidity was considerably diminished by the fact that it hung obliquely in its anchors. It was late afternoon, a cool day, and the travelers felt clammy and exhausted. The journey on the ox-cart had by no means been as difficult as a foot-march but had left a few bruises, especially on their hindquarters. Also, the nights that they had spent in the open air or in windy stables hadn't been very pleasant. The old ex-Emperor, however, had shown a remarkable degree of toughness. And the certainty with which he had steered toward this old house spoke of confidence. Godegisel looked at the roof of the building. At least a night in the dry for both of them would be a welcome change. The young nobleman was ready to show gratitude even for small graces.

Valens' hammering showed effect. The door opened squeakily, and a mountain of a man came to the fore. The massive body was as broad as long, and considerable amounts of bodily fat were visible under a patchy tunic. But Godegisel realized that this man had once been very strong, because on his naked arms was evidence of the muscles that were still hidden under the fat. His face was framed by a wild, unkempt beard, while on his head most of the hair had already disappeared. He blinked at the new arrivals. A sharp smell emanated from him. The usual Roman obsession with physical cleanliness didn't seem to take for this specimen.

Godegisel forced a smile.

Valens didn't hesitate. As soon as the man had appeared in the doorway, the former Emperor took a wide swing and struck the bearded man with great force.

The majestic fist sank in the tunic with a barely perceptible sound. The bearded man stared down at the hand, which had almost completely disappeared in his masses, and which seemed to give him no discomfort of any kind. Godegisel doubted that he had perceived the blow anyhow.

The man took hold of Valens' wrist, and pulled it out of the carnal recess. He looked at the imperial ring with great calm, then dropped it, scrutinized Valens' face, and shook his head.

"You have fallen deeply, my Emperor," he said, with a remarkably gentle, resonant voice. "Coming in rags to an old henchman who once betrayed you."

"Your betrayal is forgotten, Belucius. Your Emperor needs your help."

"How can I help anyone?" The question, with its plaintive, even miserable tone, was so starkly opposed to the man's massive appearance that Godegisel suddenly became very curious about the history of these two so unequal men.

"For a start, why don't you invite us inside?"

Belucius sighed, hesitated for a moment. Then he took a step back and made a welcoming gesture.

Godegisel followed Valens into the building. The house was made of stone and consisted of only one large room. To the great surprise of the Goth, it was tidy and, in contrast, to the owner of the property, even quite clean. Neatly folded blankets laid on a bed. A large, solidly built table dominated the center of the room. In a fire place, flames flickered under a kettle with water. Two walls were adorned with ancient, faded rugs that had once been very valuable. The pictures on it were no longer visible. In one corner were five large *amphorae*, four of them empty, as they lied on their side. The sour smell of bad wine filled the air. At the back wall was a second door that probably led to a stable. It was barely visible and could almost be mistaken for a wall.

"Sit down, gentlemen, be my guests," the landlord said, almost submissive, pointing to two uninviting looking chairs. He himself sat down unceremoniously on the only recliner, which groaned under the weight of his body. Apparently he had no intention of offering anything to the men.

Once Godegisel had sat and stretched his legs, his gaze fell on the opposite wall. There was a complete legionary's equipment, with a short sword, a shield, a metal breastplate, and a very detailed face mask, which probably depicted the face of the young Belucius, hanging neatly on the stone wall, fastened with iron hooks. Godegisel realized with an experienced glance that the owner of this equipment took it from the wall at regular intervals, cleaned and polished it, then hung it back. Although the equipment was surely very old, it could undoubtedly be used again any time. Godegisel was sure that the sword was sharpened and ready for battle.

"My friend Belucius," Valens told the bearded man. "This is Godegisel, a Goth. A fellow sufferer of my fate."

The old soldier growled. "We are all sufferers in this bad time, my Emperor, no matter on whose side we stand."

"Well put, old friend."

"How do you know each other?" Godegisel asked.

Valens didn't answer, but looked at the bearded man in silence. Belucius closed his eyes for a moment, as if to hide the presence of his guests from his perception, then a huge sigh escaped his gigantic chest before he began to speak.

"I once belonged to the personal guard of Valens," he said softly.

"He saved my life," Valens added.

"Then I displeased the Emperor when I told him my opinion."

"It was an insignificant affair, but I lost control," Valens said in a low voice.

"He banished me from his service and from the East," the bearded man continued his story. "I came here. I bought some land. I drink a lot."

He glanced at the big, empty amphorae. "Too much."

"I regretted it later," Valens said.

"Too late."

"I was too proud to take him back to my service."

"I was too proud to return to his services when my Emperor finally asked me to."

"How long has it been?"

"Three years, sir."

Valens just nodded. "I sent you gold."

"I've drunk it." The old soldier groaned. He hit the fat belly with his flat hand. "Now I'm no longer useful to you, my Emperor. No armor fits on this body anymore. It was pointless to go the long way to ask me personally." He blinked and looked at his visitors, as if he saw them for the first time. "On the other hand, I thought you were dead, sir. Fallen at Adrianople. Killed by the Goths."

"I caught him," Godegisel said. "And now we need help."

The bearded man nodded. "I'm no help to anyone."

"One last service," Valens said, in a pleading voice. "Then I will not bother you anymore. I can offer you neither gold nor position, old friend."

"No gold?"

"I don't have anything. Officially, I am dead."

"Ah, politics." The soldier spoke the word with an ardent disgust that seemed to shatter his massive body. "Then something else, Emperor."

"What?"

"An apology."

Valens was silent for a moment. "I have asked you to return to me."

"Yes. But without offering me an apology."

Valens pressed his lips on each other.

Belucius laughed. "It is hard even for a dead emperor to jump over his shadow."

Valens forced a smile. "I'm still a fool, am I not?"

"The gods or the emperor decide that, not me."

"As if you hadn't formed an opinion long time ago."

Now the bearded man had to laugh. He looked at Godegisel. "For you, it sounds like the bickering of an old couple, right?"

The Goth made a dismissing gesture. "Valens said you could help us. We need someone to go to Nemetacum and get someone for us."

"Who?"

"Septimus Tiberius Collatus," Valens said.

"He is no longer in town."

"You are well informed," the Emperor said, unmoved.

"One hears a lot. General Malobaudes himself has arrived in Belgica. One hears that he is not too well disposed toward the Comes of Britain. Rumors are making the round."

"Rumors?"

"Malobaudes seems to think that Maximus should be relieved of his post, and that the lions should be fed with him, and that only Gratian stands between the Comes and beasts."

"Is that so ..." Valens murmured to himself.

"That is the rumor."

"You have your sources."

"I go to many different tavernas – I have to, because I often have to drink without immediate payment. Really no gold in your pocket, my Emperor?"

Valens smiled. "So Malobaudes resides in Nemetacum?"

"They say that. But he doesn't govern anything. He is largely excluded from the administration. He only looks over the water and watches Maximus. No idea what that one is cooking up. I hear good news about him. He's very popular with his men."

"I heard that as well," Valens said neutrally. "Can you connect us to Malobaudes? We must speak to him. If we just ride into the city, it might happen that we aren't allowed to come close. It would be enough if we could talk to one of his staff officers."

The bearded man looked doubtfully at Valens. "Who will deny the Emperor of the East?"

"I'm considered dead."

"One more reason."

"Maybe I'm a fraud."

"No. You are not."

"How do you know?"

"You still haven't apologized to me."

Valens lowered his head. Against this form of argumentation, he evidently had nothing more to say.

"Will you help us, Belucius?"

"To Nemetacum, huh?"

"It's urgent."

The old soldier sighed and straightened. "Urgent. It's always urgent."

He rambled on his feet. "No horse is carrying me anymore, my Emperor."

"I see."

"I have a cart and two donkeys."

"That will help."

"I'll start right away. Shouldn't I bring Malobaudes? It will be difficult but I can try."

Valens exchanged a quick glance with Godegisel, who only lifted his shoulders. This was the expertise of the former Emperor, here the Goth couldn't help.

"Just get us a passport that instructs the guards not to stop the carrier of the paper. Then I'll come to the city myself."

Belucius nodded. "That's better. The General himself might not receive me. But I know others. I get the donkeys."

He walked over to a chest, rummaged around, then covered himself with a coat big enough to erect a two-man tent. He tied the gigantic fabric in front of his belly and now seemed to be all the more impressive. He scratched his chin.

"No gold, my Emperor?"

"No gold. Maybe later, but I can't promise."

The veteran nodded. He turned and trudged toward the door. Then he was stopped by the voice of his former master.

"Belucius?"

"Lord?"

Valens took a deep breath. "Please accept my apology."

The bearded man narrowed his eyes, nodded to himself, raised his hand and went without another word.

When he had closed the door behind him, Godegisel looked questioningly at Valens, who shrugged.

"I'm not used to that, Goth." Valens paused. "This is a very instructive episode for me."

Godegisel could only agree.

While the former legionary traveled to Nemetacum, Godegisel and Valens enjoyed the hospitality of the man. It was clear from the documents on his table that he possessed land, which he apparently farmed with slaves whose accommodation was outside the village. He seemed to care for his own domestic needs, there were no servants here at all. The two men quickly found to their relief that, in addition to the wine, some food was to be found in a small storage room so they didn't have to leave the house anymore. They didn't expect Belucius to return before the next day, so they found time to relax.

When Valens, after a brief investigation, discovered a small bathing-house on the property, with a stone tub and a large copper kettle under which to light a fire, the enthusiasm of the former Emperor was great. Godegisel wasn't too fond of the passionate enthusiasm of the Romans for baths, but he was at least as happy as his traveling companion, as the long trip had rarely given them the possibility of real hygiene. Once it became clear that Belucius also provided for good reserves in other matters, Valens could no longer be held. He lit a fire and poured abundant water, which the former soldier kept in two large barrels. It took some time until the large amount of water was hot enough to fill a decent bath, but as it was, both men settled down in the tub with a pleasant groan. It was just big enough to sit side by side, but that didn't stop their enthusiasm. With metal scrapers, they began to scratch the dirt from the skin, used coarse cloths to clean themselves thoroughly, and soon the skin of both men took a red color. Visibly relaxed, they left the bathroom and felt properly clean for the first time in many days. But as their clothes didn't deserve this attribute at all, they had no choice but to look for something suitable from the stores of the soldier. The oversized tunics were many times too big for them. Finally, they decided to wash their own clothes, and until they became dry again to tie their host's tunics around their bodies. The fact that a former Emperor had found himself in the situation of having to wash his own clothes had a certain irony, which escaped Valens in no way. He didn't complain, however, and was just as happy as the Goth when the work was completed and the clothes dried in the living room of their host.

Godegisel was astonished about the change visible in Valens. The man who had hardly been approachable, caught in madness and dreaming, whom he had met after the Battle of Adrianople, had given way to a completely different personality. Was it the martyrdom of his captivity that had changed him so much? Was it Maximus's betrayal that led him back to reason and shaped his own role in this game anew? Godegisel couldn't tell. But he sensed a special determination in Valens. Saving his nephew from betrayal was his way of repaying a debt. Godegisel didn't know what all this meant to him or to the future role of his people. Valens had been sent to Maximus to be a thorn in the flesh of his new masters, and now he helped the Emperor of the East to remove one. The Goth didn't know whether he was acting for the benefit of his people, but he was sure that all this could be for his personal advantage, and that wasn't a perspective he wanted to deny himself.

Yet ...

"What's going to happen to me?" he finally asked the question, as they sat together before two jugs from Belucius's wine store. Meanwhile, they wore their clothes again, although they were still a little stiff.

Valens raised his head tiredly, but his eyes seemed bright. He must have understood at once where the question of the young Goth was aiming at. He took his time with an answer. "What is your wish, my friend?"

"My desire is to live in prosperity and perhaps a bit more securely than in the past. I don't ask for anything excessive or for power. I get the impression that politics is not for me."

Valens smiled. "So young and so much wisdom! That would be a waste for the Empire! A *dux* you should make of yourself, my friend!"

Godegisel raised his hands. "No *dux*, no general, no agent. I was a soldier, I am of nobility, and my conspiratorial work has brought me here, into a situation I don't feel too comfortable with. No, noble Emperor, no such honors for me. I feel like your old henchman when I concentrate my interest on the sound of coins and the seclusion of my own house. I'm much better off with that."

Valens shook his head. "Do you really want to say that you would reject the offer of honors and position? Now you can easily make assertions, but if my nephew offers you a high-income office, a large villa with many slaves, a prestigious function of high responsibility – would you turn away and refuse?"

Godegisel thought for a moment before he answered. "I can't foresee how I will behave in the future." When he saw the triumphant smile on the face of the former Emperor, he quickly added, "I'm not yet as old as you, and perhaps I don't know myself good enough for a final judgment. But although I'm still young in years, I've already experienced a lot. We left our territory when I was hardly a boy, and all my life so far consisted of an endless journey and many struggles. I've fought against Huns and with them, and it seems as if the same fate awaits the Romans. Yes, I'm now nominally a Roman citizen, and perhaps that means that I'm now at rest. But my life experience has made me smart. I understand that I can rely on only a few things. On my brothers, on my immediate family, yes. But which office is so constituted that one could build his life on it? I mean, noble Valens, look at yourself. A few months ago an emperor, now a refugee in his own country!"

Valens nodded thoughtfully. "You have a point, my friend," he said with a lowered voice. "And yet what alternative remains to the man who has been pushed into this life? Should he let himself be moved by fate or should he try to take things into his own hands? When I am offered a title I have a chance to make something out of it. If the Lord has anything else in mind, it shall be so. But to crawl into a corner and try to escape all of this ... Did you hear about the hermits? Priests who retreat to the desert, in caves or elsewhere in the wilderness? They hope for what you are thirsting for – Peace."

Again Godegisel considered the right answer for a moment. "I don't believe, Valens, that you understood me," he said, without reproach in the voice. "I'm not concerned with shedding responsibility that is placed on my shoulders. Ultimately, it's about making decisions where I have the freedom to do so. If circumstances require it, I'll do all that is necessary. But if there is an alternative, I prefer to step into the second line and give myself some more rest."

Valens smiled knowingly. "That's all well said. For what the circumstances require that is ultimately determined by everyone for himself. So we wait until the day has come when you might be offered offices and honors, and whether you will, at that point, then define the circumstances either way. At the very latest, when your knighthood comes up and the Emperor pushes it into your hand, you might consider that the circumstances aren't that terrible. You should leave. Take your things. If Belucius brings someone from Malobaudes' retinue, I don't want you to be there. Stay outside, hide in the barn or near another building in the vicinity. You aren't concerned with imperial politics, and I feel that it might even be disgusting for you. I don't want you to go further into all this. If you're not looking for any reward, it's time for you to leave me alone with my dealings. I've been doing this business since my youth. But you can indeed take another path."

Godegisel couldn't help himself laughing. Valens had indeed become a different person. Instead of imposing honor and office on him, and, as far as possible, enticing him with the lure of a career, he had accepted the views of the young man, even respected them. And the Emperor's proposal was indeed wise. The Goth had done his work. It might be time for him to take care of himself. "I'll be close," he promised. "But shouldn't I stay?"

Valens raised his hands. "You are a Goth. The time travelers know you, as you told me. You are close to the Judge. Do you want to endanger your own people? What will happen if the Goths are linked to the betrayal of Maximus, no matter how honorably you acted? You risk the peace that your people have just gained. Remember this: As soon as Belucius approaches, disappear from here. After all, I'll have my bodyguard back."

Godegisel didn't reply. The last argument hadn't yet occurred to him. One more reason not to dive deeper into the snake-pit of Roman politics.

So they sat silently side by side, looking into the flames of the fire place that produced heat for their tired bones, waiting for something to happen. Both of them were exhausted, but both of them were also disturbed by an inner unrest. None of them wanted to sleep. Still, their bodies took their toll, and as the hours passed, they fell into a doze, only occasionally frightened by cracking firewood, or the rustle of a rat. Half-stretched out on their chairs, their eyes were closed.

Then the door opened, a cold gust of wind came in, and the two men jumped up from their seats, suddenly awake.

Belucius's massive body stood in the doorway. Outside, one could already discern the first hint of dawn. The veteran smiled, closed the door behind him, looked around as if to make sure that his guests hadn't done any harm. Then he lifted a bag from his back and dropped it onto the table. While Belucius gazed quietly at the extinct fire, Godegisel, somewhat relaxed, peered into the bag. Cheese, sausage, bread, as well as grain for the porridge of the Romans, which once being served in the legions, seemed to be a delicacy for the rest of their lives. Nevertheless, the Goth was grateful for the breakfast, because he felt hungry. Valens' appreciative smile indicated that the former Emperor felt the same.

Belucius re-ignited the fire then sank to a chair. He nodded gently at Godegisel, and he took out the food. The old legionary seized a piece of cheese, broke off a proper chunk, and put it in his mouth. It was obvious that the man wouldn't report until he had satisfied certain basic needs. When Valens broke open the remaining amphora and began to warm wine over the fire, the massive man grunted in agreement. His eyes twinkled. Godegisel got the impression that he wasn't a bearer of bad news and that his mission went well. Likewise, he decided to exercise patience and to strengthen himself.

Finally, Belucius wiped his mouth, glanced at Valens, and had a relaxing burp before he spoke. "I was able to talk to someone in the military administration. An old acquaintance. Drinks too much."

"And?"

"He was surprised, almost enthusiastic. At first, he didn't want to believe me, but I told him your story. He has agreed to meet you and understands the needs for your safety. Tonight he's coming."

"He's coming?"

"He said the city was full of people close to Maximus. He himself wouldn't know whom to trust and whom not. He will be on his way with some reliable men, and he hopes that no one will follow him. But he wants this encounter to remain secret, unlike what would happen if you were going to town."

Valens nodded. "He has a point. I wasn't aware that Maximus' reach is so visible here." He looked at the young Goth, who had nothing to complain about the plan either.

"So we're waiting," Belucius finally said. "It's better if you stay in the house and don't run around in the village. We shouldn't take any unnecessary risk."

The former Emperor agreed. Godegisel yawned. Hearing the good news, the tension had fallen from him. He felt leaden fatigue in his limbs. The breakfast also helped make him feel lazy. He grunted, got up, and spread his blanket in a corner of the living room. The two other men wished him a pleasant rest, but then they continued their conversation softly.

"What will happen to you when all this is over?" he heard Valens ask the old legionary.

"What will become of me, sir? I'm an old man, and although grateful to have done you a last service, I know that I'm not more than a wreck. Don't take it as an accusation, sir, but when you banished me, my life ended in many ways. I still exist, but I'm no longer alive."

Valens nodded thoughtfully. “If you rule and have power, but at the same time lose your right mind and neglect human reason, these things happen.”

“You sound like you’ve been cleansed of many misperceptions. Has a priest opened your eyes?” Belucius didn’t sound sarcastic, but honestly interested in the question.

“A priest? No. It all came by itself. A grace of life, if you will. I’m glad life led me back to you. I owe you a lot, Belucius, and I can never get rid of my feeling of guilt. Ultimately …” Valens hesitated as though he didn’t know whether he was really going to say what was on his mind. “… it’s like this, my old friend: You have decided to be thrown from your path by my wrong decision. I was unjust to you. But after that, when you left, there was only one person who mistreated you. And that was you yourself.”

Belucius said nothing and stared into the fire. Godegisel, however, was again astonished about the new Valens. And he was glad that he had been able to witness this transformation. She showed him that no one was ever lost. As soon as one saw the past as what it was – simply past –, one had the chance to change oneself and his life. So what did that mean to a young Gothic nobleman?

He would think about it in due course.

But now he was too tired.

Godegisel wanted to listen to some more, but as soon as he had settled down comfortably, his eyes closed.

24

Despite all the fearful events of the past, their journey continued smoothly. The meeting with Rome's governor in the Egyptian province had taken place early in the morning; afterwards came the farewell dinner for the expedition. The meeting had been very fruitful, with great enthusiasm for the idea of building ships like the *Valentinian* in Alexandria. Köhler and Africanus had officially given the Prefect the detailed plans for the steam engine, as well as the construction of ships like the *Valentinian*, with the request to copy and pass them on to the scholars in the Museion, as well as to every shipowner and shipbuilder who wanted them. The interest was lively, as they had already noticed. And Alexandria was the ideal place where this knowledge could fall on fertile soil. Africanus had been very confident.

The Governor had also supplied them with the latest information from Aksum, as far as things were known in Egypt. Accordingly, the political and economic situation in the neighboring Empire could be assessed as quiet. The old Emperor or "Negusa Nagast", King of Kings, as the Aksumites named his position, despite being quite old, enjoyed great health, and had even regulated his succession to the general satisfaction of his subjects. They didn't expect any difficulties, as the Romans were generally held in high regard.

And so they left. At almost the same time, the *Valentinian*, under the command of Sepidus, began its journey back to Ravenna, on board the captured Tennberg and the wounded but by now quite happy Marcellus. The parting had been quite difficult for them. Neumann had written a detailed report, and Marcellus promised to hand it over to Dahms. The fact that a second copy lay in the ship's main cabin in the possession of Sepidus hadn't been mentioned. Marcellus' disappointment that his journey was already coming to an end had been reduced somewhat by assigning this important task to him.

The fact that an Alexandrian street boy named Josaphat had been hired into the *Valentinian*'s crew also might have contributed to this. The two of them were big friends, welded together by their shared experiences. Neumann, however, feared that the predatory appetite of the new crew-member would diminish the supplies of the steamer for the return journey considerably.

The sailing ship, on which they'd continue along the canal on this sunny day, accompanied by a river galley of the Roman navy, which had been forced upon them, seemed to be a solid ship with a solid and loyal crew. For Köhler, Neumann and Africanus, the period of relaxation lasted a few days until they became nervous again and especially weary of doing nothing. It was as if the events in Alexandria had only been a temporary nightmare, fading into nothingness the farther and farther they sailed away from the port city. The pleasantly warm weather, the bright sunshine, the rippling of the Nile, the delicious dishes that the chef was able to conjure up – all this enticed a happy holiday mood. The German expedition members had initially reacted with great enthusiasm. They had spread canvas on the deck of the ship and placed themselves in the sun, drinking wine from sweat-*amphorae*, eating occasionally. But the leisure of the day had also led to a general downturn in their level of attention, and Africanus was convinced that at least the soldiers on board shouldn't let their guard down like that.

Anyway, they were all getting restless after few days. The entertainment program on board left much to be desired, despite the efforts of some crew members to delight the guests with all kinds of musical instruments. Also, the lessons intended to dispense further knowledge in Latin or Greek didn't work too well, not least because those with sufficient language skills were not necessarily the best teachers. It also turned out that the Germans had a lot more to gain in practical vocabulary if they simply dared to look for conversation. Since their Roman friends showed a great deal of tolerance when it came to the correct grammar or the choice of words, this kind of learning worked much better than formal lessons. It was a pleasant side effect that the teachers also caught up with a few chunks of German.

Köhler observed with particular interest that the sailing master of the ship was looking for a conversation with the Germans. He seemed to be very interested in the principle of the steam engine and squeezed out anyone who had something to say about it. Obviously, it was quite possible to find adequate Latin or Greek words, despite the fact that German concepts dominated for technical descriptions and German seemed to become something like the engineering language of the Roman Empire. The master, who, as Köhler was informed, owned a quarter of the freighter, wrote the German words carefully and fought for every emphasis. He seemed to perceive this knowledge as a potential competitive advantage in the future, a development that Köhler was a bit surprised about. They had only been in this time for a good half year, but the upheavals which they had caused were evident both on higher and lower levels. The fact alone that some of the sailors nodding knowingly, when Behrens told them of the merits of brandy, was enough to point out that some news spread at an astonishing pace even in Late Antiquity.

Although the wind was quite favorable, the journey drew. The realization that this pleasant canal trip was only another stretch, and that at the end they still had to endure a coastal journey to Adulis, didn't help to alleviate the impatience of the travelers. Köhler had to breathe deeply, as the captain wanted to explain to him the sights of the Nile. These were certainly not uninteresting, but the German was simply not able to muster the necessary patience.

"There!" Africanus suddenly said. He had been standing next to Köhler, a hand shadowing his eyes. "The jetty!"

"What about it?"

"When we get there, there are no more than two miles left to the village of my grandfather."

Köhler looked down at the inconspicuous spot, barely more than a fortified bank on which river ships could be moored. Agriculture was nurtured directly at the Nile to benefit from the regular floods that spread fertile mud across the fields. Here ships took over the harvested crops, brought them to Alexandria, where they were transferred onto bigger vessels and brought to Italy via the Mediterranean. Egypt was the granary of the Empire.

"We can take a break," Köhler offered.

"No. I was there when my grandfather had died, to set a memorial. I don't know if the stone is still standing, but I suspect my relatives have cared well for it. The rest of the family will still live in our old house, though I haven't seen it for many years."

"So you could return here once you have finished your service?"

"Sure, why not? Even my father could have done that, but he didn't. I won't be a peasant anymore, at least not a fellahin like my ancestors. When I collect my land, somewhere in Gaul or another patch of the Empire, I think I'll sell it and sign on. There is nothing to come back to here."

Köhler nodded, though he felt he could only understand half of what Africanus was telling him. The Trierarch seemed to notice this, for he regarded Köhler for a long time, then sighed, as if he had to choose the following words wisely.

"It's like this," he began slowly. "For an Egyptian farmer, joining the Navy is one of the few ways to get release from the bond to his land and the duty to endure as a farmer. The laws are strict, it has always been like that. Whoever is tired of working on his soil and of the suffering once the Nile doesn't come in time, went to the fleet. My grandfather did this, although he was the eldest son of his father and would've had inherited everything. But he decided otherwise. If he hadn't, I wouldn't be here with you. I might be over there on one of the fields and would look at the prospects of my seed."

Köhler said nothing. Africanus' gaze was lost in the palms and streaks of the shore, as though he was expecting to see himself there.

"I don't want to come back here, not even to be reminded of this place, because it has nothing to do with who I am."

"Apart from your name."

The Trierarch smiled. "Apart from that, yes. And I'm not even a famous man like Scipio, who has gotten the surname for good reason."

"That can still happen," Köhler replied.

"For sure. In any case, I'm no longer the son of a farmer; I never was, as already my father had arranged his life quite differently. I'm now a Roman officer, and as much as this province belongs to the areas I vowed to defend, this is not my homeland. I'm really at home on the *mare nostrum* and, if at all, in the little house where my father and my mother are still living, and that is a good hundred miles north of Ravenna. This one ..." He made a sweeping movement with his right hand. "... this is the past – and not even mine. It is that of my ancestors. And they played a real role for me only after the decision of my grandfather to depart from here. So I don't want to go back, not even in my mind. Do you understand that, Köhler?"

The German understood it, albeit on a purely intellectual level. But his own past had been quite different. No one had forced him to take up a certain profession or to do what his ancestors had done. But he had to admit that joining the Navy had been an escape from an otherwise very dull life. In this way, he felt akin to Africanus's grandfather, and so he understood why his grandson wouldn't return here or be too clearly reminded of his origin. "So we don't take a break," he said, half jokingly.

"Anything but that," Africanus confirmed. "Our aim is the Empire of Aksum, not a village, in which, with some luck, only an old memorial stone is of any remaining importance."

With this he turned away without appreciating the slow aft landing with another glance.

Köhler, too, didn't look back.

25

And so they were resting one last time on Roman soil. The place was called Brigetio and was not too far from Aquincum, the city that Thomas Volkert knew in his time as Budapest. From there, his column would advance northeasterly, into the land of the Quadi, with which the Roman Empire had an unpleasant altercation a few years ago. A unified attack of Quadi and Sarmatians had been repulsed, and here, in Brigetio, Valentinian I, father of Gratian, had died from a heart attack, caused by anger about the unruly demands of Germanic tribes. That had been a good four years ago, and the situation hadn't improved considerably. Since the end of the war and Valentinian's victory, no one knew who was currently governing the Quadi. King Gabinius, whose violent death in the year 373 had triggered the war during a banquet of the Roman governor Celestius, had died without any direct descendants. The leaders of the border troops in Pannonia had reported that a new Quadian king named Erminius had taken power. He, however, limited his contacts with his Roman enemies only to the essentials, as the bitter defeat which his people had received from the hands of Valentinian surely remained in vivid memory. It was relatively peaceful since then, after all, but this couldn't be interpreted as a sign of normalization. The history of relations with the barbarians was always characterized by a constant change between peaceful and warlike phases, and the Barbarian, who now sold his sword for a few coins to a Roman, would sink his blade with equal fervor into his former customer the next day – so at least went the stories.

Further northeast, it was said that the people of the Cottines and the Oser would live, the Markomans also settled there, the Racer, the Campi, and many other tribes, whose names passed to Thomas Volkert when he heard the more experienced subordinates tell their stories. At the latest in twenty years, Volkert knew from the historical lessons he had received from Rheinberg, the Quadi would fall under the rule of the Huns, and only shortly afterwards the attacks and extortion of the Empire by the Huns would begin, culminating in the victorious Attila's campaign, which would take him to Upper Italy – a campaign that would never take place if things went differently and according to Rheinberg's plans.

From there, they were ready to leave the fortified paths and fight through the barbarian wilderness. Because of all the contempt that was heard in the words of some men, Volkert had now learned enough about the representations to know that the image of this "wilderness" was drawn very one-sidedly. There were villages, even quite large, and some were linked by streets. Many barbarians had taken very Roman habits from their neighbors across the border. They built fortified settlements, no longer dressed in skins, and so the rumor went on, even went to bathe and shave regularly. Volkert knew that many an officer told particularly bloodthirsty stories to mentally arm the men who hadn't yet fought in this area. Volkert had often talked to veterans of the wars conducted by Gratian's father to understand that if Gabinius wouldn't have been murdered they would still live in peace with the Quadi. Valentinian had seen himself as a conqueror, and like many other emperors, he had wasted the military power of the Empire. Volkert was reminded of the way the Romans had treated the fleeing Goths in the East instead of taking them seriously, helping them, and assuring them of their good intentions. Had they done it right, Adrianople wouldn't have happened.

Afterwards everyone knew better. Volkert was in a good position to evaluate the truth of this statement.

The final deliberations were done fast and without ceremony. Soon Volkert's column, about 500 strong, left Brigetio. Embassies had informed the new Quadian King that this wasn't an attempt to conquer his land, and that peace would be maintained if he'd leave the legionaries undisturbed. Of course, there was no guarantee that Erminius would take these messages seriously. On the other hand, the memory of the Roman victory was still fresh enough to call into question a too premature action, Volkert hoped. A small Varus-like slaughter in the forests of the Carpathians was not one of the things he wanted to experience. Once shortly after the crossing of the imperial frontier, a small group of Quadi-cavalry joined to guide them – they were more likely observers of the Quadian King, who had an eye on the Romans – everyone relaxed. At least the chances of crossing the area undisturbed had increased significantly. The riders showed no hostility, were even courteous according to circumstances.

On the evening of the third day, when the troop had just begun to establish a night camp, the King wanted more than just keeping his eyes open. The sun was still just above the horizon, so the guard posts were able to have a good impression of the advancing riders, who were deliberately slow and moved unhindered toward the camp. Twenty men were, according to clothing and attitude, Quadian nobles joined by some guards. Everyone wore weapons, but none had pulled them, and just before the camp they got off the horses and led them slowly in. They wanted to talk, not to fight, there was no doubt.

Tribune Sedacius received the delegation and both Centurion Levantus and Volkert were summoned to the reception committee. When, from the middle of the newcomers, a tall man dressed in comparatively gorgeous clothing emerged, it was immediately apparent to everyone that after the murder of his predecessor, a Quadian King was again in the hands of the Romans: It could only be Erminius.

He looked like a king, straightened himself, struggled visibly for a majestic appearance, but Volkert saw in his eyes also fear and caution. Since his predecessor had been murdered by a Roman general, he couldn't blame him. It spoke for the man's courage to take this risk again.

"Noble King," said Sedacius, making a bow. "I'm pleased with your visit."

"I'm glad you received me, Tribune," the Quadian returned in a somewhat stumbling Greek. Wherever he ultimately came from, he had enjoyed education, and it wasn't even improbable that he had lived in the Empire for some time.

"What is the reason for your visit? Surely you will want to make sure that we have no evil intentions," the Tribune continued. "We obviously are not a conquering army."

"That's what we've heard." The King looked around, nodding. "It's true."

"We're not a threat."

"Sure," the man admitted. "You are looking for the Huns, how far they are already. Your messages have reached me. Many strange things seem to have taken place in Rome. One hears a lot. Your expedition is unusual."

The tribune nodded. "We protect ourselves as well as you."

Erminius looked at him for a moment. Then he caught sight of Lehmann, the commander of the German infantry, who had also joined them. Volkert found himself hiding behind the broad shoulders of Levantus, although he couldn't remember ever talking to Lehmann. He would certainly not even recognize him when he was standing in front of him.

And yet ...

"You have a time wanderer with you," the King observed.

Volkert concealed his surprise. Although this time neither knew the telegraph nor a modern postal system, had no trains and no cars, some news clearly spread.

The Tribune couldn't hide that he was impressed that Erminius seemed to be so well informed. "You've heard of the events."

"We've heard stories about what's going to happen."

Whoever was responsible for secrecy in the Empire had obviously failed in important points – if the version of the future, which the *Saarbrücken* crew knew, had already spread so widely, then ... Volkert felt a thought hitting him like a lightning bolt. Huns, apostates, but nevertheless Huns, had fought before Adrianople and had fallen before Thessaloniki.

If the main host of these people knew as well, was aware about what could happen in the not too distant future ...

Volkert got headaches at the thought of the possible consequences.

Sedacius remained calm. For him, the matter was clear – if the Quadians knew that within a few decades their territory would be under the Huns' supremacy and the independence of their kings would be swept away, then that was ultimately an advantage for him. He waved and a legionary brought cups and wine. "Shall we not sit in my tent, King?"

"With pleasure."

Erminius stepped forward then stopped for a moment. "Tribune."

"Noble King?"

"In what direction do you wish to go once you have crossed my territory?"

"To the northeast."

Erminius shook his head. "The Huns are in the East."

"We can't count on that."

"You don't understand, Tribune. The Huns are only a good 200 Roman miles away. They have already sent an ambassador."

Sedacius stared at the man. "An ..."

"I brought him with me."

The king made a commanding movement toward his retinue. Someone handed him a large cloth bag, saturated with blood. Erminius threw it to the ground, it opened and the severed head of a Hun rolled out. He had a wide-eyed stare, but his features didn't show any fear.

Just anger.

Great rage.

Erminius looked at the Tribune.

"They are near, Romans. Closer than you thought?"

"Much closer." Sedacius was very pale.

"Now we're drinking wine," Erminius said, taking a big step over the head.

The Tribune followed.

Volkert couldn't help but stare at the face of the dead, the angry expression of a man who knew that he was going to die, but with a vow of revenge written in his deadly features.

All this developed definitely too fast, he decided. That mustn't be. That couldn't be true. And in the eyes of Centurion Levantus, he saw the same astonishment and disbelief.

They turned away in silence.

26

They came in the night.

They knew their way.

Thus, they had two essential advantages on Rheinberg and Dahms, who had finally gone to bed after a long evening. Hours they had talked about plans and scrawled drawings of how they were to produce the iron from the primitive iron smelters and coal mines in this area, which was to become the Saarland. With a steam engine, they could achieve a lot, such as a professional underground construction, but also on the surface. Energy was the magic word and the prerequisite for a comprehensive production process. The potential was considerable because there were enough local workers who had shown themselves open to the ideas of the visitors. It would be necessary to plan more precisely and establish a permanent representation, but these weren't insurmountable difficulties. On the contrary; Dahms had pointed out that three crew members of the *Saarbrücken* had already worked as miners before their enlistment. They had begun to think about the logistics of such a company, the necessary workforce, the transport routes, but also the transfer of necessary technology. Dahms's progress in the construction of a puddle furnace for steel production might not be impressive yet, but it was less due to his lack of skill, but rather to the fact that he had too many things to do at the same time.

Then they were tired, and yet satisfied with the day's work, and went to bed. A small wing of the Summer Palace had been set up for them, torches and lamps burned, the servants hustled until late. The rest of the large facility was covered in complete darkness.

There was nothing here, and no adversary was to be expected. A sleepy, quiet corner of the Empire. Sure, the appearance of the strange Magister Militium had caused some excitement. But that was it.

No reason to worry.

What a fatal error.

It was a good dozen, dressed in black cloth, light-footed on wrapped sandals. They knew the palace – its official as well as its unofficial approaches. The guard posts at the main gate didn't notice anything, nor did the two soldiers on patrol through the empty halls of the estate. A slave, who watched the high guests' lodgings, to be ready should one of the honorable gentlemen need something, raised his head briefly, frowned.

Wasn't there a sound?

The last question of his life. A thin rope slung around his neck, was tightened forcefully. The slave's hands went up, but any energy left him quickly. A powerless rattle, barely audible, escaped his tormented throat, then he lost consciousness, died, strangled by an experienced hand. The carelessness with which the assassin dropped the dead body to the ground, without giving a last look to the swollen face, already showed clearly that there was someone at work for whom killing represented a nothing more than a trade.

And one that he mastered well.

They stopped in front of the large entrance doors leading to the bedrooms. Listened for a moment, gave themselves signs. No one had noticed the death of the lonely slave. No sound to hear, no commotion, no steps, nothing. Everything went according to plan.

They had been prepared for everything, like for suddenly appearing guards, even the possibility that someone would beat an alarm prematurely. What they hadn't expected was the chronic insomnia of two men who knew they were going to change world history – and couldn't take that lightly.

Rheinberg had thrown himself left and right on the bed. He heard his friend moving in the next room, maybe feeling thirsty, pouring himself water from a carafe. Problems and questions whirled in his head.

Rheinberg sat up with a sigh. He rubbed his eyes. All would've been easier if there would still be coffee available. He thought of the expedition to Aksum and wished Köhler and his comrades all the best. As a high official of the Empire, he was not lacking in quality of life, but there were certain things that were simply irreplaceable. Gratefully, the Captain remembered the fact that he wasn't smoking.

No coffee and no tobacco.

Many on the *Saarbrücken* had to endure a lot. And to try, like many Romans, to smoke dried cow shit instead, hadn't been too popular.

What did Dahms do there?

He seemed not to feel well, maybe something from dinner. He gasped as if he was fighting with his stomach. Rheinberg paused, rubbing his own. No, he was tolerating Roman food quite well, and he had only eaten lightly tonight in order not to get too tired too quickly.

An animal maybe?

Rheinberg decided to look for his friend. He swung himself out of the bed, automatically took his trousers, and put them equally fast on. Just as automatically, without thinking about it, he pushed the pistol into the belt holster. Movements that he unconsciously performed every time he got up and dressed. It was part of him ...

The door. Somebody was at the door.

Rheinberg was awake now. He scurried to the wall, which separated him from Dahms' room and knocked a short staccato with his knuckles. Morse code. DANGER. He didn't know whether he was exaggerating or whether his nervous mind was playing a trick on him – or whether a slave was about to see if the pisspot needed to be replaced. In any case, it was good ...

Somebody opened the door. Now Rheinberg's heart beat hard. A servant would never enter without knocking. This was absolutely unthinkable. And the sounds – hadn't they come from the area outside the door, by no means from the direction of the connecting door to Dahms's quarters?

Rheinberg slid behind the massive bench that dominated the room together with the bed. A strong jolt would suffice to overthrow it, a good defense against everything that would be directed at him from a distance. Rheinberg almost felt the approaching danger physically.

The connecting door opened, Dahms's head looked through, along with the barrel of his weapon. He saw Rheinberg behind the desk, nodded, and then saw the other door open.

A shadow slid in. He could hardly be seen in the pale twilight of the two small oil lamps, which illuminated the room only inadequately. And then, with a slight squeal, the door to Dahms'a room opened from the hallway as well. The engineer's face disappeared from the doorway. Everyone obviously had to deal with his own visitor first.

Rheinberg's weapon aimed, the safety released. A second shadow came in, but both seemed uncertain.

They had certainly expected the occupants of the room somewhere else.

And they were unclear as to what the metal thing in his hand meant.

"Who are you?" Rheinberg barked loudly. "What do you want, and who sent you?"

Three questions.

The answer consisted of a jump.

As if shot by a cannon, the first shadow rushed forward. Rheinberg had the fraction of a second to admire the acrobatic act and the underlying strength, then he lifted the barrel and pulled the trigger. The pistol barked, a sound that finally tore the stillness of the night. The attacker, still in the air, was hit, whipped to the side, lost his balance. He fell flat on the ground. Something slipped over the polished marble. A kind of garrote, as Rheinberg immediately noticed. *Assassins*, shot through his head.

He hadn't hit the attacker mortally. But blood flowed to the ground, discolored the white marble red. A gasp came out of his throat, but he straightened himself, a blade flashing weakly in the light of the lamps.

A shot, a falling body, this time from next door. Dahms had acted.

Rheinberg couldn't care for it. These men were not easy to impress. Despite the clear language his weapon had just spoken, the second attacker jumped forward. A third pushed through the door. Rheinberg began to worry. His 08 loaded eight 8 mm cartridges –

and now only seven were left. Rheinberg had two spare magazines, but these were foolishly left with his other items in the big chest at the other end of the room, near the door. Seven targeted hits were not to be expected, and when several attackers came at the same time ...

He had to be fast, to hope for the demoralizing power of his weapon, and to make sure that the shots quickly attracted the soldiers of their retinue.

A second shot broke from Dahms's room, almost at the same time as Rheinberg himself fired again. This time the bullet sat, hit directly into the chest of the mute, hurled him back. He fell to the ground, motionless, not even shrugging. Rheinberg had immediately killed him.

The first assassin had stood up, the blade of a short sword glittered in his hand. Rheinberg's weapon turned to the new old threat, as two more black dresses jumped through the door. Rheinberg moved his hand back to the right, the two men were already on the go.

From outside, shrieks, frantic steps, the clanging of swords. The bodyguard had awakened, at last.

Again the 08 barked. A body fell. The second was on Rheinberg. He didn't have time to shoot again when a practiced hand struck the gun away, and then Rheinberg stumbled back, struggling for balance. The shadow in front of him stood broad-legged, then a blade flashed in his hand, and he took a short, powerful stroke. Rheinberg sensed the direction of the sword more than he saw it, instinctively twitching, feeling the hot cold pain as the iron penetrated through his skin and descended deeply into his side.

Rheinberg screamed. His opponent gave a triumphant grunt, pulled the blade from the deep wound. Blood splashed on the black robe, leaving shining spots. Rheinberg looked down at himself. The sword had not hit him in the stomach, so he could survive this if he got help in time. He staggered back, felt his strength linger, pressed both hands on the wound to stop the flow of blood. Pain and weakness threatened to overcome him.

Again the blade ready, the assassin continued. Then a barking sound, the attacker was whirled around, fell, the blade slipped out of his hand and dropped toward Rheinberg. He let himself fall, grabbed the sword, got it right, drew it to himself, gasped, when his sight grew black. He saw legionaries of his bodyguard stream into the room, heard screams, pangs of pain, dying men, saw Dahms standing with his raised weapon in the connecting door. Another shot, another one. With mechanical precision, the engineer sought out his goals, shot, didn't pay any attention to the victims, sought the next, shot, shot again. The determination of the assassins faded, one tried to escape, ran right into the sword of a soldier.

Rheinberg closed his eyes.

Just a little rest, a little moment.

Then in front of him a sound. He tore open his eyelids, saw the assassin, his hood removed, sweating. He had lost his weapon, half a dozen blades were aimed at him.

"Do not ... kill ..." Rheinberg said. Dahms had heard him, gave the order, but when the man noticed that the soldiers were restrained, he cried aloud and threw himself into one of the opposing blades, clutching it with both profusely bleeding hands and driving it with force into his own chest.

The helpless soldier let go.

The assassin fell to the ground with a gurgling sound.

Then an almost unnatural silence fell over the room.

That was the last.

Rheinberg saw Dahms crouching next to him, the first-aid kit he had taken with him from the *Saarbrücken* beside him, slowly loosening the cramped hand from the wound.

"Clean cut, Jan," he muttered. "Clean cut. We'll get you back on your feet."

Rheinberg tried to smile.

Then everything went dark.

27

"It is time."

Valens rose and nodded to Godegisel. The idle wait had an end. Belucius opened a shutter and peered into the darkness. The sounds of arriving riders had awakened them from their lethargy.

"Men," the former legionary observed. "Maybe five or six, not more."

"Good, no unnecessary commotion," Valens said. "Godegisel, the back door. Go."

The young Goth left the room. He carefully closed the door behind him, but remained close, observing through a gap as agreed. Valens waited a moment, then instructed Belucius to open the front door and let the visitors in.

The bullish man nodded and moved surprisingly light-footed to the door, pulled the latch aside, and opened it a little. Someone stood outside, and spoke, quietly, hastily, but not urgently. Valens saw Belucius nod, then open the door further, and five men in wide dark coats came slowly inside.

Valens' face lit up recognition. He smiled and walked toward one of the new arrivals.

"Malobaudes," he exclaimed, handing an arm to one of the arrivals, an older man of squat stature. This one replied the smile.

"Valens! My Emperor! Who would have thought! We were all firmly convinced that you were killed at Adrianople!"

"I thought so for a while," Valens replied, and laughed. "Let's sit down. How is my nephew?"

Malobaudes followed the invitation. The remaining four men, now visibly relaxed, stood attentively and said nothing. It was, in Valens' assessment, the general's bodyguard. It was only natural that they didn't lose their attention. Belucius had assumed a similar attitude.

He was now, indeed, something like the bodyguard of Valens, as in the old days.

“Gratian is doing well,” Malobaudes answered the question, stretching his legs. “He grows in his office, more than we ever thought possible.”

“Great challenges sometimes wake unimagined abilities,” Valens agreed, pouring wine for his guest. “I’ve been very stupid, and I didn’t want to understand Gratian’s good intentions. There should never have been such a catastrophe as before Adrianople.”

Malobaudes winked his hand. He took the offered chalice, raised it toward Valens, and took a sip before he spoke again.

“That’s the past, Emperor!”

“Don’t call me so, my friend,” said Valens. “I may now be the Emperor’s uncle, but I won’t demand the office back from him.”

“He’ll give it back to you!”

“I wouldn’t expect that. In the present situation, it may seem advisable not to divide the Empire. I’ve heard that strange things happened.”

Malobaudes nodded and took another sip of wine.

“Yes that’s true. The arrival of the time wanderers has changed a lot.”

They were silent for a moment.

“How come you are still alive, Emperor?”

Valens accepted the title without further fuss and began to tell his story in concise terms. He didn’t mention either Godegisel or his role in his liberation. He described it in a way that he had received help but left the details behind. Belucius had vowed not to mention the existence of the Goth. Thus, the role of the young man was to be hidden, and thus any suspicion of a possible deceit by his people should be avoided.

Valens found a very attentive listener in Malobaudes who didn’t interrupt him even once. After about a quarter of an hour, he had given him a rough summary and looked at him expectantly.

“So you don’t want your title back?” the General made sure. He didn’t seem to believe it.

Valens leaned forward. “I know that you serve Gratian faithfully, and my sudden resurgence is a matter of great concern to you. No, I won't harm my nephew and give him no trouble. I've already caused more than enough problems with my stubbornness. If he thinks I can best serve the Empire by retiring, perhaps to a nice estate somewhere in the country, I will do so. He won't hear a word from me."

Malobaudes didn't show whether these words convinced him or made him feel easy. He barely nodded.

"But before that happens," Valens continued, "I must warn him and all who are with him. The fact that I'm still alive depends not least on a conspiracy that builds up against Gratian. I had the role of giving legitimacy to a usurper! I was supposed to make Maximus the emperor, and thereby to justify a revolt." Valens's voice sounded haunting. "The preparations of the enemy have gone a long way, my friend. And the Comes has help from an unexpected side: A high-ranking time-traveler is on his side. I could discern this from a conversation in my presence. Near London, they run a large manufactory and workshop, where they experiment with firearms. They want to build something they call a cannon. In any case, Gratian must be prepared for a potentially large-scale and well-organized uprising. He must be warned, Malobaudes! Immediately Maximus must be deposed of, the conspiracy has to be crushed! Every day that is lost increases the danger!"

In the end, Valens's voice had almost begging. Malobaudes had listened to the lecture with a stony face. He shook his head as Valens had finished, as if a heavy grief or disappointment were oppressing him. "You really want to help Gratian," he said in a low voice. "You want your nephew to succeed with what he's doing and you don't want to be a burden for him. I understand that now. He can be lucky to have an uncle like you, Valens."

Valens raised his hands. "My time is over, Malobaudes, whether I appreciate it or not. My last service after the disaster of Adrianople can only be to remedy some of the damage. To stop the conspiracy of Maximus would perhaps rekindle the gaze of history on my life's work. Let me go to Treveri, or wherever Gratian may be staying. I will prostrate myself before him, give him all the information, reveal every detail that has come to my attention." Valens glanced at Belucius. "My old friend here, of course, is included. He helped me a lot and served me better than I deserved."

The old legionary nodded, but said nothing.

"Who else is with Maximus?"

Valens shrug. "I have no detailed information. I only know what has been expressed in my presence, probably in the opinion that I'm not fully in command of my senses, and wouldn't even understand what was said." He paused and smiled. "Of course this was not even a completely false assessment. But I don't know much more. I think Maximus has allies on the mainland, some Germanic tribes. And there is Ambrosius, the Bishop of Milan."

The General looked at Belucius for a moment, as if to measure the magnitude of his service by mere gazing, then he nodded heavily. "An important piece of information, indeed. Gratian has allies in a completely unpredictable position. I'm amazed of what has become of the boy. He manages to miraculously create loyalty among the strangest men. Even in you, his unruly uncle." With the last sentence he had turned to Valens again.

"As I said, General, that's the past. How can you take me to Treveri without the conspirators getting any notion of it? I can leave tonight if it has to be I will not stay longer than necessary."

Malobaudes looked for a moment as if to think about a suitable answer, but then he sighed deeply. "It won't be possible."

Valens suddenly had an uncomfortable feeling. He looked at Malobaudes without understanding. "What does that mean? Is the situation too dangerous? Do we still have to wait?"

Malobaudes looked at him sadly, then rose slowly. There was a sword in his hand. "No, Valens, it's not."

The former Emperor stared at the blade. When the other four men who had dispersed in the room were also pulling their weapons, understanding grew in the face of Valens, and he suddenly looked very, very old. "Ah ... ah ... Malobaudes ... the faithful general," he murmured softly to himself.

"Yes, I am," the man replied. "I am faithful. But not to an emperor who wants to open a new era for the Empire that challenges our values and traditions, but to the idea that the Empire has grown so great for good reason, and that any shock to its foundation is much more likely to cause its downfall than any barbarians."

"So you're on the side of Maximus," Valens said silently. He sat, squeezed together, had apparently lost all hope. And yet his hand had been placed round the sword, a weapon which he had received from Belucius. At least two of the men watched him suspiciously.

"I'm on the side of the Empire," Malobaudes corrected. "And I had expected exactly the same from the Emperor of the East."

"Ex-Emperor," Valens insisted. "And I didn't get the impression that it was Maximus's intention to put me back in office. It seemed to me that he had taken the plan of becoming emperor of all of Rome. Or am I wrong?"

Malobaudes pressed his lips on each other for a moment. Then he made a wiping hand movement. "This is no longer worth discussing. You've definitely decided for yourself. You have also become a traitor to the ideals of Rome, just like your nephew. If Valentinian had learned of all this ..."

"My brother would have cut your throat," Valens growled. An astonishing transformation took place with the collapsed figure. One moment crouched on the chair, hopeless, surrendered, the body of Valens suddenly rose. In the right hand of the former emperor the blade flashed openly, and he pushed it toward the General's belly.

The man staggered back, repulsed the blow with the movement of an experienced warrior. The blade drove into his raised forearm, blood shot out as it opened the skin. There was no grief passing the General's lips, and with deadly calm he lowered his sword into Valens' chest. He made a gurgle, sagged as sudden as he had jumped up. Belucius, as if struck by thunder, saw how life had left him, now finally and forever.

And so it ended.

The old legionary, who saw his master die, uttered an unarticulated cry. With an agility that wouldn't have been expected of the fat colossus, he tore his sword from the wall and attacked Malobaudes. Two of his guards stood in the way of the angry man.

Belucius fought like a bull. One of his opponents sank to the ground. The former bodyguard of Valens also suffered deep wounds. He bled, his mighty torso dipped in shining red. But to reach the vital organs through the fat masses was a difficult task for a short sword, and the old legionary fought with the power of a wounded beast of prey. Again and again he struck the remaining guard, while Malobaudes exited through the door.

"Die!" Belucius shouted, as he stabbed his second opponent like a pig. One of the other men, who had bent over the corpse of the Valens to convince himself of his death, turned around in alarm and stared at Belucius, who approached like a berserker. The fourth guard finally entered the battle.

The fat man bled, had bled just too much. No part of his body seemed to be dry, and he had wiped his bloody hands over his sweaty face, so that he looked like a monster.

His opponent found the old legionary's gaze, saw the tiredness, much pain, the dwindling energy, and the barely visible nod, as if the man knew that his end was now near.

There was a cry, a heavy impact, a triumphant exclamation of the victor. Then sudden, deafening silence.

The old legionary had followed his master.

Outside, hidden by the darkness, a young Goth, escaping the turmoil, heard more than he saw. He listened to screams and the noise of the battle, involuntarily clutching the handle of his sword. He didn't know what was going on there since he left the premises, but it smelled of betrayal and it smelled of futility. Even if he were to turn back now and take up the fight, the enemy was too strong. Men left the building as silence returned, visible only as shadows. Whoever Belucius had contacted in the city – it must have been a traitor, a man of Maximus. The infection of usurpation had advanced further than he and Valens had suspected, and there was no doubt that the former Emperor of the East had lost his life.

Then two torches flew to the roof of the house. It immediately caught fire. In the adjoining homesteads, there were shouts. Torches and lamps were ignited. But then the assassins had already swung themselves on the backs of their horses and had ridden away.

Godegisel didn't want to be suspected of being the arsonist. He retreated across the fields, hid behind bushes, and waded through the muck until he had gained enough distance between himself and the house, which caught fire with a vengeance. Then he paused, staring at the flickering flames and realized that he was mourning for Valens.

And he mourned because his work had not yet been done.

With a last glance at the crackling fire, Godegisel turned away and set off.

– To be continued –

Register of persons

Aurelius Africanus	Roman Trierarch
Ambrose of Milan	Roman Bishop
Andragathius	Roman General
Arbogast	Roman General
Aurelia	a slave girl
Peter Behrens	Infantryman
Belucius	former Roman legionary
Bertius	Roman legionary
Claudia	a slave girl
Johann Dahms	Chief Engineer of the *Saarbrücken*
Dionos	Alexandrian scholar
Erminius	King of the Quadi
Karl Forstmann	Engineer of the *Valentinian*
Fritigern	leader of the Goths
Godegisel	Gothic nobleman
Flavius Gratianus	Roman Emperor
Dietrich Joergensen	Officer of the *Saarbrücken*
Josaphat	Alexandrian street boy
Jovius	Roman Decurion
Julia	Daughter of Marcus Gaius Michellus
Harald Köhler	NCO of the *Saarbrücken*
Klaus Langenhagen	Officer of the *Saarbrücken*
Levantus	Roman Centurion
Lucia	Wife of Marcus Gaius Michellus
Malobaudes	Roman General

Marcellus	Crew member of the *Saarbrücken*
Caius Martinus	son of a Roman businessman
Magnus Maximus	Governor of Britain
Marcus Gaius Michellus	Roman senator
Marcus Necius	Roman fisherman
Dr. Hans Neumann	Physician of the *Saarbrücken*
Marcus Flovius Renna	Roman military prefect
Jan Rheinberg	Captain of the *Saarbrücken*
Richomer	Roman officer
Septimus Secundus	Roman NCO
Sepidus	Crewman of the *Valentinian*
Lucius Tellus Severus	Roman General in Retirement
Quintus Aurelius Symmachus	Roman senator
Markus Tennberg	Ensign of the *Saarbrücken*
Theodosius	Roman aristocrat
Valens	Roman Emperor
Thomas Volkert	Ensign of the *Saarbrücken*
Klaus von Geeren	infantry officer and deputy company commander
Johann Freiherr von Klasewitz	First Officer of the *Saarbrücken*
Hannes Weinkamp	crewman of the *Valentinian*